"The Cliff Climbers"

by

Captain Mayne Reid

Double 9
BOOKS

"The Cliff Climbers"
by Captain Mayne Reid

ISBN: 978-93-59393-13-1

Published by

DOUBLE 9 BOOKS

2/13-B, Ansari Road
Daryaganj, New Delhi – 110002
info@double9books.com
www.double9books.com
Tel. 011-40042856

ABOUT THE AUTHOR

Thomas Mayne Reid (Captain Mayne Reid)(4 April 1818 - 22 October 1883) was an Irish-American author who battled in the Mexican-American Conflict (1846-1848). His many deals with American life depict a provincial approach in the American states, the horror of slave work, and the lives of American Indians "Captain," Reid composed adventure books likened to those by Frederick Marryat and Robert Louis Stevenson and set in the American West, Mexico, South Africa, the Himalayas, and Jamaica. He was a fan of Master Byron. His novels contain action that takes place primarily in untamed locations. He was a truly prolific author, with over 60 titles published in his lifetime, including both fiction and non-fiction.

CONTENTS

Chapter One.
The Himalayas.

Who has not heard of the Himalayas—those Titanic masses of mountains that interpose themselves between the hot plains of India and the cold table-lands of Thibet—a worthy barrier between the two greatest empires in the world, the Mogul and the Celestial? The veriest tyro in geography can tell you that they are the tallest mountains on the surface of the earth; that their summits—a half-dozen of them at least—surmount the sea-level by more than five miles of perpendicular height; that more than thirty of them rise above twenty thousand feet, and carry upon their tops the eternal snow!

The more skilled geographer, or *geognosist,* could communicate hundreds of other interesting facts in relation to these majestic mountains; vast volumes might be filled with most attractive details of them—their *fauna,* their *sylva,* and their *flora.* But here, my reader, we have only space to speak of a few of the more salient points, that may enable you to form some idea of the Titanic grandeur of these mighty masses of snow-crowned rock, which, towering aloft, frown or smile, as the case may be, on our grand empire of Ind.

It is the language of writers to call the Himalayas a "chain of mountains." Spanish geographers would call them a "sierra" (saw)—a phrase which they have applied to the Andes of America. Either term is inappropriate, when speaking of the Himalayas: for the vast tract occupied by these mountains—over 200,000 square miles, or three times the size of Great Britain—in shape bears no resemblance to a chain. Its length is only six or seven times greater than its breadth—the former being about a thousand miles, while the latter in many places extends through two degrees of the earth's latitude.

Moreover, from the western termination of the Himalayas, in the country of Cabul, to their eastern declension near the banks of the Burrampooter, there is no continuity that would entitle them to the appellation of a "chain of mountains." Between these two points they are cut transversely—and in many places—by stupendous valleys, that form the channels of great rivers, which, instead of running east and west, as the mountains themselves were supposed to trend, have their courses in the transverse direction—often flowing due north or south.

It is true that, to a traveller approaching the Himalayas from any part of the great plain of India, these mountains present the appearance of a single range, stretching continuously along the horizon from east to west. This, however, is a mere optical illusion; and, instead of one range, the Himalayas may be regarded as a *congeries* of mountain ridges, covering a superficies of 200,000 square miles, and running in as many different directions as there are points in the compass.

Within the circumference of this vast mountain tract there is great variety of climate, soil, and productions. Among the lower hills—those contiguous to the plains of India—as well as in some of the more profound valleys of the interior—the flora is of a tropical or subtropical character. The palm, the tree fern, and bamboo here flourish in free luxuriance. Higher up appears the vegetation of the temperate zone, represented by forests of gigantic oaks of various species, by sycamores, pines, walnut, and chestnut trees. Still higher are the rhododendrons, the birches, and heaths; succeeded by a region of herbaceous vegetation—by slopes, and even table-plains, covered with rich grasses. Stretching onward and upward to the line of the eternal snow, there are encountered the *Cryptogamia*—the lichens and mosses of Alpine growth—just as they are found within the limits of the polar circle; so that the traveller, who passes from the plains of India towards the high ridges of the Himalayas, or who climbs out of one of the deeper valleys up to some snow-clad summit that surmounts it, may experience within a journey of a few hours' duration every degree of climate, and observe a representative of every species of vegetation known upon the face of the earth!

The Himalayas are not uninhabited. On the contrary, one considerable kingdom (Nepaul), with many petty states and communities (as Bhotan, Sikhim, Gurwhal, Kumaon, and the famed Cashmere), are found within their boundaries—some enjoying a sort of political independence, but most of them living under the protection either of the Anglo-Indian empire, on the one side, or that of China upon the other. The inhabitants of these several states are of mixed races, and very different from the people of Hindostan. Towards the east—in Bhotan and Sikhim—they are chiefly of the Mongolian stock, in customs and manners resembling the people of Thibet, and, like them, practising the religion of the Lamas. In the western Himalayas there is an admixture of Ghoorka mountaineers, Hindoos from the south, Sikhs from Lahore, and Mahometans from the old empire of the Moguls; and here, also, are to be found, in full profession, the three great representative religions of Asia—Mahometan, Buddhist, and Brahmin.

The population, however, is exceedingly small compared with the surface over which it is distributed; and there are many tracts in the Himalayan hills, thousands of square miles in extent, where no human being dwells—where no chimney sends up its smoke. Indeed, there are vast tracts, especially among the high snow-covered summits, that have either never been explored, or only very rarely, by the adventurous hunter. Others there are quite inaccessible; and it is needless to say, that the highest peaks—such as Chumulari, Kinchinjunga, Donkia, Dawalghisi, and the like—are far beyond the reach of even the most daring climber. Perhaps no one has ever ascended to the height of five miles above the level of the sea; and it is a question whether at that elevation a human being could exist. At such a height it is probable that animal life would become extinct, by reason either of the extreme cold or the rarity of the atmosphere.

Though the Himalaya mountains have been known from the earliest historic times—for they are the *Imaus* and *Emodus* of the ancient writers—it is only within the present century that we in Europe have obtained any definite knowledge of them. The Portuguese and Dutch—the first European colonists of India—have told us very little about them; and even our own Anglo-Indian writers were long silent upon this interesting theme. Exaggerated accounts of the hostility and cruelty of the Himalayan highlanders—more especially the Ghoorkas—prevented private explorations; and with the exception of some half-dozen books, most of them referring to the western section of the Himalayas, and comparatively valueless, from the want of scientific knowledge on the part of their authors, this vast tract has remained almost a *terra incognita* up to the present time.

Of late, however, we have obtained a better acquaintance with this interesting portion of the earth's surface. The botanist, lured thither by its magnificent *flora*, has opened to us a new world of vegetation. Royle and Hooker have ably achieved this task. The zoologist, equally attracted by its varied *fauna*, has made us acquainted with new forms of animal life. Hodgson and Wallich are the historians in this department. Scarcely less are we indebted to the sportsman and hunter—to Markham, Dunlop, and Wilson the "mountaineer."

But in addition to these names, that have become famous through the published reports of their explorations, there are others that still remain unrecorded. The *plant-hunter*—the humble but useful commissioner of the enterprising nurseryman—has found his way into the Himalayas; has penetrated their most remote gorges; has climbed their steepest declivities; and wandered along the limit of their eternal snow. In search of new forms of leaf and flower, he has forded the turbid stream, braved the roaring torrent, dared the dangerous avalanche, and crossed the dread crevasse of the glistening glacier; and though no printed book may record his adventurous experience, not the less has he contributed to our knowledge of this great mountain world. His lessons may be read on the parterre, in the flowers of the purple magnolia, the deodar, the rhododendron. They may be found in the greenhouse, in the eccentric blossoms of the orchis, and curious form of the screw-pine—in the garden, in many a valuable root and fruit, destined ere long to become favourites of the dessert-table. It is ours to chronicle the story of an humble expedition of this kind—the adventures of a young plant-hunter, the *employé* of an enterprising "seedsman" well-known in the world's metropolis.

Chapter Two.
A view from Chumulari.

Our scene lies in the very heart of the Himalayas—in that district of them least explored by English travellers, though not the most distant from the Anglo-Indian capital, Calcutta. Almost due north of this city, and in that portion of the Himalayan ranges embraced by the great bend of the Burrampooter, may be found the spot upon which our interest is to be fixed. Literally may it be termed a spot, when compared in superficies with the vast extent of wilderness that surrounds it—a wilderness of bleak, barren ridges, of glistening glaciers, of snow-clad summits, soaring one above another, or piled incongruously together like cumuli in the sky.

In the midst of this chaos of rock, ice, and snow, Chumulari raises his majestic summit, crowned and robed in white, as becomes his sacred character. Around are other forms, his acolytes and attendants, less in stature, but mighty mountains nevertheless, and, like him, wearing the vestment of everlasting purity.

Could you stand upon the top of Chumulari, you would have under your eye, and thousands of feet below your feet, the scene of our narrative—the arena in which its various incidents were enacted. Not so unlike an amphitheatre would that scene appear—only differing from one, in the small number of the *dramatis persona,* and the entire absence of spectators.

From the top of Chumulari, looking down among the foot hills of this majestic mountain, you might behold a valley of a singular character—so singular as at once to fix your attention. You would note that it is of a regular oval shape; and that instead of being bounded by sloping declivities, it is girt by an almost vertical cliff that appears to be continuous all around it. This cliff of dark granitic rock you might guess with your eye to rise several hundred feet sheer from the bottom of the valley. If it were in the season of summer, you might further observe, that receding from its brow a dark-coloured declivity of the mountain rises still higher, terminating all around in peaks and ridges—which, being above the snow-line are continually covered with the pale white mantle that has fallen upon them from the heavens.

These details would be taken in at the first glance; and then your eye would wander into the valley below, and rest there—fixed by the singularity of the scene, and charmed by its soft loveliness—so strongly contrasting with the rude surroundings on which you had been hitherto gazing.

The form of the valley would suggest the existence of the grand elliptical crater of some extinct volcano. But instead of the black sulphuric *scoria*, that you might expect to see strewed over its base, you behold a verdant landscape of smiling loveliness, park-like plains interposed with groves and copses, here and there a mound of rock-work, as if piled artificially and for ornament. Around the cliffs appears a belt of forest of darker green; and occupying the centre a limpid lake, on whose silver surface at a certain hour of the day you might see reflected part of the snow-crowned summit on which you are standing—the cone of Chumulari itself.

With a good glass you might distinguish quadrupeds of several *species* straying over the verdant pastures; birds of many kinds upon the wing, and others disporting themselves upon the surface of the lake.

You would be tempted to look for a grand mansion. You would send your glance in every direction, expecting to see chimneys and turrets overtopping the trees; but in this you would be disappointed.

On one side of the valley, near to the base of its bounding cliff, you might see a white vapour ascending from the surface of the earth. It would be an error to believe it smoke. It is not that—only the *rime* rising over a hot-spring bubbling out from the rocks and forming the little rivulet, that, like a silver string, connects it with the lake.

Charmed with the view of this lovely valley, you would desire to visit it. You would descend the long slope of Chumulari, and straggling through the labyrinth of rugged foot hills that surround it, you would reach the brow of the bounding precipice; but there you must come to a halt. No path leads downward; and if you are still determined to set foot on the shores of that smiling lake, you will have to make the descent of the cliffs by means of a rope or rope-ladder several hundred feet in length.

With comrades to help you, you may accomplish this; but once in the valley, you can only get out of it by remounting your rope-ladder: for you will find no other means of exit.

At one end of the valley you may perceive a gap in the cliffs; and fancy that through this you may make your way out to the side of the mountain. The gap may be easily reached, by going up a gentle acclivity; but having passed through it, you will discover that it only guides you into a gorge, like the valley itself, bounded on both sides by precipitous cliff's. This gorge is half filled by a glacier; on the surface of which you may pass for a certain distance downward. At the end of that descent you will find the glacier cut by a deep crevasse, a hundred feet in depth and a hundred in width. Without bridging the crevasse, you can go no further; and if you did succeed in bridging it, further down you would find others deeper and wider, over which it would be impossible for you to pass.

Return then, and examine the singular valley into which you have made your way. You will find there trees of many kinds, quadrupeds of many kinds, birds of many kinds, and insects of many kinds—you will find every form of animal life, except that of the human being. If you find not man, however, you may discover traces of him. Close to the hot-spring, and forming a sort of "lean-to" against the cliff, you may observe a rude hut built with blocks of stone, and plastered with mud from the bed of the rivulet. Enter it. You will find it empty, cold, untenanted by living thing. No furniture. Stone couches covered with sedge and grass, upon which men may have slept or lain; and two or three blocks of granite upon which they may have sat. That is all. Some pieces of skin hanging around the walls, and the bones of animals strewed over the ground outside, give a clue to the kind of food upon which the inhabitants of the hut may have subsisted. Hunters they must have been. That will be your natural conjecture.

But how did they get into this valley, and how got they out of it? Of course, like yourself, they descended into it, and then ascended out again, by means of a rope-ladder.

That would be the explanation at which you would arrive; and it would be a satisfactory one, but for a circumstance that just now comes under your observation.

Scanning the *façade* of the cliff, your eye is arrested by a singular appearance. You perceive a serried line, or rather a series of serried lines, running from the base in a vertical direction. On drawing nearer to these curious objects, you discover them to be ladders—the lowest set upon the earth, and reaching to a ledge, upon which the second is rested; this one extending to a second ledge, on which the third ladder finds support; and so on throughout a whole series of six.

At first sight, it would appear to you as if the *ci-devant* denizens of the hut had made their exodus from the valley by means of these ladders; and such would be the natural conviction, but for a circumstance that forbids belief in this mode of exit: *the ladders do not continue to the top of the cliff!* A long space, which would require two or three more such ladders to span it, still intervenes between the top of the highest and the brow of the precipice; and this could not have been scaled without additional ladders. Where are they? It is scarcely probable they had been drawn up; and had they fallen back into the valley, they would still be there. There are none upon the ground.

But these conjectures do not require to be continued. A short examination of the cliff suffices to convince you that the design of scaling it by ladders could not have succeeded. The ledge against which rests the top of the highest must have been found too narrow to support another; or rather, the rocks above and projecting over would render it impossible to place a ladder upon this ledge. It is evident that the scheme had been tried and abandoned.

The very character of the attempt proves that they who had made it must have been placed in a desperate situation—imprisoned within that cliff-girt valley, with no means of escaping from it, except such as they themselves might devise.

Moreover, after a complete exploration of the place, you can find no evidence that they ever did escape from their strange prison; and your thoughts can only shape themselves into conjectures, as to who they were that had wandered into this out-of-the-way corner of the world; how they got into, and how out of it; and, finally, whether they ever succeeded in getting out at all. Your conjectures will come to an end, when you have read the history of the *Cliff-climbers*.

Chapter Three.
The Plant-Hunter and his companions.

Karl Linden, a young German student, who had taken part in the revolutionary struggles of 1848, had by the act of banishment sought an asylum in London. Like most refugees, he was without means; but, instead of giving himself up to idle habits, he had sought and obtained employment in one of those magnificent "nurseries" which are to be met with in the suburbs of the world's metropolis. His botanical knowledge soon attracted the attention of his employer, the proprietor of the nursery—one of those enterprising and spirited men who, instead of contenting themselves with merely cultivating the trees and flowering-plants already introduced into our gardens and greenhouses, expend large sums of money in sending emissaries to all parts of the earth, to discover and bring home other rare and beautiful kinds.

These emissaries—botanical collectors, or "plant-hunters," as they may be called—in the pursuit of their calling, have explored, and are still engaged in exploring, the wildest and most remote countries of the globe—such as the deep, dark forests upon the Amazon, the Orinoco, and the Oregon in America; the hot equatorial regions of Africa; the tropical jungles of India; the rich woods of the Oriental islands; and, in short, wherever there is a prospect of discovering and obtaining new floral or sylvan beauties.

The exploration of the Sikhim Himalaya by the accomplished botanist, Hooker—recorded in a book of travels not inferior to that of the great Humboldt—had drawn attention to the rich and varied *flora* of these mountains; and in consequence of this, the enterprising "seedsman" who had given Karl Linden temporary employment in his garden, promoted him to a higher and more agreeable field of labour, by sending him as a "plant-hunter" to the Thibetan Himalayas.

Accompanied by his brother, Caspar, the young botanist proceeded to Calcutta; and, after a short residence there, he set out for the Himalayas—taking a direction almost due north from the city of the Ganges.

He had provided himself with a guide, in the person of a celebrated Hindoo hunter or "shikaree," called Ossaroo; and this individual was the sole attendant and companion of the two brothers—with the exception of a large dog, of the boar-hound species, which had been brought with them from Europe, and that answered to the name of Fritz.

The young botanist had come to India furnished with a letter of introduction to the manager of the Botanical Garden of Calcutta—an establishment of world-wide renown. There he had been hospitably received on his arrival in the Oriental city; and during his sojourn he had spent much of his time within its boundaries. Moreover, the authorities of the place, interested in his expedition, had given him all the information in their power as to the route he intended pursuing—though that was not much: for the portion of the Himalayas he was about to explore was at that time a *terra incognita* to Englishmen—even in the city of Calcutta!

It is not necessary here to detail the many adventures that befel our plant-hunter and his party, during the progress of their journey towards the Himalayas, and after they had entered within the grand gorges of these mountains. Suffice it to say, that in pursuit of a beautiful little animal—a "musk-deer"—they had gone up a gully filled by one of those grand glaciers so common in the higher Himalayas; that the pursuit had led them far up the ravine, and afterwards conducted them into a singular crater-like valley—the one already described; that once in this valley, they could find no way out of it, but by the ravine through which they had entered; and that on returning to make their exit, they discovered to their great consternation that a crevasse in the glacier, over which they had passed, had opened during their absence, and to such an extent as to render their exit impossible!

They had endeavoured to span this crevasse; and had spent much time in making a bridge of pine-trees for the purpose. They had succeeded at length in getting across the chasm—but only to find others in the glacier below, which no ingenuity could enable them to get over.

They were compelled to abandon the idea, and return again to the valley; which, though lovely to the eye, had now become hateful to their thoughts: since they knew it to be their *prison*.

During their residence in the place, many adventures befel them with wild animals of various kinds. There chanced to be a small herd of "yâks," or grunting oxen, in the valley; and these formed for a time the staple article of their food. Caspar, who, though younger than Karl, was the more skilled hunter of the two, had a very narrow escape from the old yâk bull; though he succeeded at length in killing the dangerous animal. Ossaroo was very near being eaten up by a pack of wild dogs—every one of which he afterwards succeeded in killing; and Ossaroo was also in danger of being swallowed up by an enemy of a very different kind—that is by a *quicksand,* into which he had got his legs while engaged in taking fish out of a net!

Karl was not without *his* hair-breadth "'scape"—having been chased by a bear along a ledge of the cliff, from which he was compelled to make a most perilous descent. The bear itself took refuge in a cave, where it was afterwards pursued and killed, by all three acting in concert, materially assisted by the dog Fritz. They had incurred great risk in this chase of the bear: for although they had succeeded in destroying the formidable animal they lost themselves in the great labyrinthine cavern, and were only able to find their way out by making a fire with the stocks of their guns, and rendering the bear's-grease available for candles—which fortunately enabled them to extricate themselves.

During the pursuit of the bear, and their subsequent endeavours to find their way out, our adventurers had been struck by the enormous dimensions of the cavern in which the animal had taken refuge; and in the hope that some of its great galleries might lead out through the mountain, and offer them a way of escape from the valley, they had made torches, and explored it from end to end. It was all to no purpose; and becoming satisfied that there was no exit by way of the cavern, they had at length desisted from the search.

From this point shall we continue, in more circumstantial detail, the history of their attempts to escape from their mountain prison; which they were now convinced could only be done by *climbing the cliff* that encircled it.

Chapter Four.
Home to the hut.

Emerging from the cave after their fruitless exploration, all three—Karl, Caspar, and Ossaroo—sat down upon the rocks in front of the cliff, and for some time remained silent. The looks of all betokened a deep and hopeless despair. The same thought was passing in their minds. A painful thought it was—that they were completely cut off from all communication with the world, and might never again look on human faces, save their own!

Caspar was the first to give expression to this gloomy foreboding.

"Oh, brother!" groaned he, addressing himself to Karl, who sat nearest to him, "oh! it is an awful fate! Here must we live, here must we die, far away from home, far away from the world—alone—alone!"

"No," replied Karl, deeply moved by the distress of his brother, "no, Caspar, not alone—God is with us. Let Him be our world."

However Caspar in his conscience might have acknowledged the justice of the admonition, it failed to cheer him. Indeed, he could not help perceiving, that Karl had uttered the speech half doubtingly, and with the design of affording consolation. Moreover, the effort which Karl was making to look hopeful and cheerful was evidently constrained; and only the more convinced his companions that neither hope nor joy was in his breast.

To Karl's consolatory words his brother made no rejoinder. Ossaroo, however, gave vent to his thoughts by an ambiguous shake of the head, and a brief speech characteristic of that belief in fatalism peculiar to that race.

"Ah, sahibs," said he, addressing himself to both, "if the Great Sahib in the sky will we go out from here, we go—if He no will, we no go—nivvamore."

Ossaroo's speech, however compatible with a true faith, did not contribute much towards cheering the spirits of the party; and for another long interval all remained silent.

Caspar and Ossaroo appeared completely prostrated by the new disappointment. Karl, on the other hand, seemed less disposed to view things despairingly; and as he sate, was evidently engaged in active thought.

After awhile his companions observed this; though neither made any attempt to rouse him from his reverie. They guessed, that, whatever was passing in his mind would soon be communicated to them.

They were right in this conjecture: for in a few minutes Karl terminated the silence by addressing them.

"Come!" said he, speaking in a tone of encouragement, "we are wrong in so soon yielding to despair. Let us not give up, till we are beaten at all points. I have told you what my object was, when I first mounted upon that ledge, and discovered the cave and its surly occupant, the bear. I thought then, that, if we could find a series of ledges one above another, and sufficiently near each other, we might plant ladders upon them, and so reach the top. You see that there is such a succession of ledges—just before your faces there. Unfortunately there is one of the spaces high up yonder—where the cliff is darkest—that cannot be less than sixty or seventy feet in width. I have ascertained that by comparing it with the height from the ground to the cave—which I had just finished measuring when I met the bear. It would be impossible for us to make a ladder that length—or even to hoist it up there if made—so that all thought of scaling the cliff at this point must be given up."

"Perhaps," interposed Caspar, catching at Karl's idea, "there may be some other part of the precipice where the ledges are nearer to each other? Did you examine it all around?"

"No. I had got no further than this place, when I met Master Bruin; and, as you know, our adventures with him and our exploration of the cave have taken up our time ever since, and, indeed, driven the design of the ladders quite out of my head. Now, however, we may return to it; and our next move will be to go all round, and see whether a better place may not be discovered. To-night it is too late. It already begins to darken; and we must have clear daylight for such a purpose. Let us home to our hut, and have some supper and then go to rest—having first prayed to Him for success. We may rise in better spirits, and continue our examination in the morning."

To this proposal there was no objection on the part of either Caspar or Ossaroo. On the contrary, the mention of supper—both being very hungry—had caused them to start to their feet with remarkable alacrity; and Karl, taking the lead, they followed him, Fritz in turn following them.

On arriving at their hut, supper was cooked and eaten, with that zest which hunger always gives, even to the coarsest viands; and, having carried out the remaining part of the programme which Karl had suggested—that is, the offering up a prayer for success on the morrow—the trio sought their grass-covered couches with a feeling of renewed hopefulness.

Chapter Five.
A midnight intruder.

They had been asleep several hours, when all three were suddenly awakened by the barking of Fritz. During night hours the faithful creature stayed habitually within the hut—where he also had his bed of dry grass. On hearing any unusual noise without, he would rush forth and prowl about for awhile; and, after satisfying himself that there was no enemy in the neighbourhood, would return quietly to his lair.

Fritz was far from being a noisy dog. He had seen too much service, and gathered too much wisdom, to waste his breath in idle barking; and it was only upon grand and important occasions that he condescended to give tongue. Then, however, his bark—or bay, it should rather be termed—was terrific.

On the occasion in question—which happened just about the hour of midnight—the three sleepers were suddenly awakened by his expansive "yowl," that filled the whole valley, and reverberating from the cliffs, appeared continuous. The dog, after uttering this warning note, had rushed out of the hut—which had no door to it—and it was from some place down near the lake that his barking appeared to proceed.

"What can it be?" was the prompt and *very* natural inquiry of the three individuals, whom Fritz had so abruptly awakened from their slumbers.

"Something Fritz is frightened at," said Caspar, who knew the dog's nature better than either of the others. "He don't bark that way at any sort of game that he knows he can conquer. It's some animal that's a match for him, I warrant. If the old yâk bull were still alive, I should say it was he."

"There may be tigers in this valley; I never thought of that," rejoined Karl. "Now that I do think of it," continued he, drawing upon the reminiscences of his zoological reading, "it is quite probable. People believe the tiger to be exclusively an inhabitant of tropical or subtropical regions. That is an error. On this continent (the speaker was in Asia) the royal Bengal tiger ranges at least as far north as the latitude of London. I know he is found on the Amoor as high as the fiftieth degree."

"Mercy on us!" broke in Caspar; "it may be a tiger, and we have never thought of having a door to our hut! If it should be one—"

Here the hypothetic speech of Caspar was abruptly brought to a conclusion, by a singular noise from without—which was heard mingling in chorus with the baying of Fritz.

The noise in question bore some resemblance to the sound of a trumpet, only sharper and more treble in its character. It was in effect more like the squeak of a *penny trumpet* than the real article; and yet, withal, there was something terrifying in the sound.

It must have terrified Fritz: for the moment after it was heard, the dog came rushing back into the hut, as if pursued by a legion of horned bulls; and, though he kept up his angry baying, he appeared altogether disinclined to venture out again.

Just then, the singular noise was heard outside the door—something between a shriek and a whistle—and this time with a far more terrifying effect: since, whatever produced it—bird, beast, or man—was evidently near, and still approaching nearer.

Of the three individuals within the hut, only one had ever before heard a sound exactly similar to that. Ossaroo was the one. The old shikaree recognised the noise the moment it reached his ears, and knew perfectly well the sort of instrument that must have been producing it; but he was hindered for a time from proclaiming his knowledge, by surprise, as well as a strong feeling of terror at hearing such a sound in such a place.

"By de wheels ob Juggernaut car!" he gasped out. "Can't be—can't be; no possible him be here."

"Who? What?" demanded Karl and Caspar, in a breath.

"See, sahibs! it him—it him!" hurriedly rejoined the Hindoo, in a sort of shrieking whisper. "We all perish—it him—it him—de god—de mighty— de terrible—"

There was no light within the hovel, except a faint glimmer from the moon shining brightly enough outside; but it did not require any light to tell that the shikaree was frightened pretty nearly out of his senses. His companions could discover by his voice that he had suddenly changed position, and was retreating backward to that corner of the hut furthest from the doorway. At the same time his words reached them in whispers, cautioning them to lie close and keep silent.

Both, without knowing what the danger was, of course obeyed injunctions thus emphatically delivered; and remained sitting up on their couches without uttering a word. Ossaroo, after having delivered his cautioning speeches, kept equally silent.

Once more the strange sound fell upon their ears—this time as if the instrument that produced it had been thrust into the doorway of the hovel. At the same instant the turf outside, hitherto glistening under a bright moonlight, became darkened by the shadow of an enormous creature—as if the queen of night had suddenly disappeared behind the blackest of clouds! Still the light could be seen beyond, and the moon was shining. It was no cloud that had obscured her; but some vast body moving over the earth, and which, having come up to the front of the hovel, was there halting.

Karl and Caspar fancied they could see a gigantic living form, with huge thick limbs, standing outside; but, indeed, both were as much terrified by the apparition as Ossaroo himself, though perhaps for a different reason.

Fritz must have been as much frightened as any of the four; and fear had produced upon him an effect exactly similar to that it had produced upon Ossaroo. It kept him silent. Cowering in a corner, Fritz was now as quiet as if he had been born a voiceless *dingo*.

This speechless trance seemed to have its influence upon the awe-inspiring shadow outside the door: for, after giving utterance to another specimen of shrill piping, it withdrew with as much silence as if it had been but the shadow it appeared!

Caspar's curiosity had become too strong to be kept any longer under the control of his fears. As soon as the strange intruder was seen moving away from the hut, he stole forward to the entrance, and looked out. Karl was not slow in following him; and Ossaroo also ventured from his hiding-place.

A dark mass—in form like a quadruped, but one of gigantic size—could be seen going off in the direction of the lake. It moved in majestic silence; but it could have been no shadow, for on crossing the stream—near the point where the latter debouched into the lake—the plashing of its feet could be heard as it waded through the water, and eddies could be seen upon the calm surface. A simple shadow would not have made such a commotion as that?

"Sahibs!" said Ossaroo, in a tone of mysterious gravity, "he be one ob two ting. He eider be de god Brahma, or—"

"Or what?" demanded Caspar.

"An ole rogue."

Chapter Six.
A talk about elephants.

"An old rogue?" said Caspar, repeating the words of the shikaree. "What do you mean by that, Ossy?"

"What you Feringhee, sahib, call *rogue* elephant."

"Oh! an elephant!" echoed Karl and Caspar—both considerably relieved at this natural explanation of what had appeared so like a supernatural apparition.

"Certainly the thing looked like one," continued Caspar.

"But how could an elephant enter this valley?"

Ossaroo could not answer this question. He was himself equally puzzled by the appearance of the huge quadruped; and still rather inclined to the belief that it was some of his trinity of Brahminee gods, that had for the nonce assumed the elephantine form. For that reason he made no attempt to explain the presence of such an animal in the valley.

"It is possible for one to have come up here from the lower country," remarked Karl, reflectively.

"But how could he get into the valley?" again inquired Caspar.

"In the same way as we got in ourselves," was Karl's reply; "up the glacier and through the gorge."

"But the crevasse that hinders us from getting out? You forget that, brother? An elephant could no more cross it than he could fly; surely not?"

"Surely not," rejoined Karl. "I did not say that he could have crossed the crevasse."

"Oh! you mean that he may have come up here before we did?"

"Exactly so. If it be an elephant we have seen—and what else can it be?" pursued Karl, no longer yielding to a belief in the supernatural character of their nocturnal visitant—"it must of course have got into the valley before us. The wonder is our having seen no signs of such an animal before.

You, Caspar, have been about more than any of us. Did you never, in your rambles, observe anything like an elephant's track?"

"Never. It never occurred to me to look for such a thing. Who would have thought of a great elephant having climbed up here? One would fancy such unwieldy creatures quite incapable of ascending a mountain."

"Ah! there you would be in error: for, singular as it may appear, the elephant is a wonderful climber, and can make his way almost anywhere that a man can go. It is a fact, that in the island of Ceylon the wild elephants are often found upon the top of Adam's Peak—to scale which is trying to the nerves of the stoutest travellers. It would not be surprising to find one here. Rather, I may say, it *is* not: for now I feel certain what we have just seen is an elephant, since it can be nothing else. He may have entered this valley before us—by straying up the glacier as we did, and crossing the chasm by the rock bridge—which I know he could have done as well as we. Or else," continued Karl, in his endeavour to account for the presence of the huge creature, "he may have come here long ago, even before there was any crevasse. What is there improbable in his having been here many years—perhaps all his life, and that may be a hundred years or more?"

"I thought," said Caspar, "that elephants were only found on the plains, where the vegetation is tropical and luxuriant."

"That is another popular error," replied Karl. "So far from affecting tropical plains, the elephant prefers to dwell high up on the mountains; and whenever he has the opportunity, he climbs thither. He likes a moderately cool atmosphere—where he may be less persecuted by flies and other troublesome insects: since, notwithstanding his great strength and the thickness of his hide, so small a creature as a fly can give him the greatest annoyance. Like the tiger, he is by no means exclusively a tropical animal; but can live, and thrive too, in a cool, elevated region, or in a high latitude of the temperate zone."

Karl again expressed surprise that none of them had before that time observed any traces of this gigantic quadruped, that must have been their neighbour ever since the commencement of their involuntary residence in the valley. Of course this surprise was fully shared by Caspar. Ossaroo participated in it, but only to a very slight degree. The shikaree was still inclined towards indulging in his superstitious belief that the creature they had seen was not of the earth, but some apparition of Brahma or Vishnu.

Without attempting to combat this absurd fancy, his companions continued to search for an explanation of the strange circumstance of their not having sooner encountered the elephant.

"After all," suggested Caspar, "there is nothing so strange about it. There are many large tracts of the valley we have not explored; for instance, that wide stretch of black forest that lies at its upper end. Neither of us has ever been through there since the first two days, when we followed the deer all round, and went afterwards to examine the cliff. For myself, I never strayed that way while hunting—because I always found the game in the open grounds near the lake. Now the elephant may have his lair in that piece of forest, and only come out at night. As for tracks, no doubt there are plenty, but I never thought of looking for them. You know, brother, we have been too busy in making our tree-bridge, and afterwards exploring the cavern, to think of much else."

Karl admitted the truth of these observations; for it was as Caspar had alleged. During the whole time of their residence in the valley, the minds of all three, filled with anxiety about the future, had been keenly bent upon devising some means of escape; and on this account they had given very little attention to anything that did not in some way contribute to that end. Even Caspar, in his hunting excursions, had not gone over one-half of the valley; nor had these excursions been very numerous. In three or four days he had procured as much *meat* as was necessary. This had been carefully cured by Ossaroo, and formed the staple of their daily food. Only upon rare occasions were the guns afterwards used to procure a little fresh provision—such as a brace of wild duets from the lake, or one of the smaller game animals which could be found almost any morning within gunshot distance of the hut. For these reasons many parts of the valley had been left unvisited; and it was deemed possible enough for even a great elephant to have been all the time dwelling within its boundaries, unseen by any of the party. Indulging in these conjectures, all three remained awake for more than an hour; but as the subject of their speculations appeared to have gone altogether away, they gradually came to the conclusion that he was not going to return at least for that night—and their confidence being thus restored, they once more betook themselves to sleep—resolved in future to keep a sharp lookout for the dangerous neighbour that had so unexpectedly presented himself to their view.

Chapter Seven.
Re-stocking the guns.

Next morning all three were astir betimes, and out of the hut by the earliest light of day. Karl and Caspar were anxious to obtain more definite information about the elephant, whose existence Ossaroo was still inclined to doubt. Indeed, with the exception of the three or four shrieking whistles to which the animal had given utterance, so silently and mysteriously had he come and departed, that they might almost have fancied the whole thing a dream.

But such an immense creature could not move about, without leaving some traces of his presence; and as he had crossed the stream, or rather a little embayment of the lake into which the stream emptied itself, no doubt his tracks would be found on the sandy shore.

As soon, therefore, as the day broke, all three started for the spot where the creature had been seen to cross.

On reaching it, they could no longer doubt that an elephant had paid them a visit. Huge footprints—nearly as big as the bottom of a bushel measure—were deeply indented in the soft sand; and looking across the "straits" (for so they were in the habit of calling the narrow mouth of the bay), they could see other similar tracks on the opposite shore, where the animal had waded out.

Ossaroo was no longer doubtful as to the character of the creature that had made those tracks. He had hunted elephants in the jungles of Bengal, and knew all the peculiarities of the grand quadruped. Such footmarks as were now under his eyes could not have been made by a mere visionary animal, but only by a real elephant in the flesh.

"And one of the biggest kind," asserted the shikaree, now speaking in full confidence, and declaring, at the same time, that he could tell its height to an inch.

"How can you do that?" asked Caspar, in some surprise.

"Me berra easy tell, young sahib," replied Ossaroo; "only need takee size ob de rogue's foot. Dis way, sahibs."

Saying this, the shikaree drew forth from one of his pockets a piece of string; and, choosing one of the tracks which had made the clearest impression, he carefully applied the string around its outer edge. In this way the circumference of the elephant's foot was obtained.

"Now, sahibs," said Ossaroo, holding the string between his fingers—that portion of it which had been applied around the footprint—"*twice* the length of dis reachee to the top of he shoulder; that how Ossaroo know he biggee elephant."

The circumference of the foot thus measured being nearly six feet, it would follow, from the rule laid down by the shikaree, that the elephant in question was nearly twelve feet high; and this Karl knew to be one of the largest. Nor did Karl question the correctness of the deduction: for he had often heard, from hunters whose word was not to be doubted, that the height of an elephant is exactly twice the circumference of his foot.

Ossaroo, having now yielded up his belief—that the elephant was one of his gods in disguise—declared with full confidence that the animal was a *rogue*. Karl needed no explanation of what was meant by this. He knew that the rogue elephant is an old male, who, for some reason or other—perhaps for bad behaviour—has had the cold shoulder given him by the rest of the herd, and from whose association he has been driven away. Thus *cut* by his former acquaintances, he is compelled to lead a solitary life—the consequence of which is, that he becomes exceedingly spiteful and morose in his disposition, and will not only attack any other animal that may chance to cross his path, but will even seek them out, as if for the mere purpose of indulging in a spirit of revenge! There are many such in the jungles of India, as well as in Africa; and, since man himself is not excepted from this universal hostility, a rogue elephant is regarded as an exceedingly dangerous creature in the neighbourhood where he takes up his abode. There are many instances recorded—and well authenticated too—where human beings have been sacrificed to the fury of these gigantic monsters: and cases are known where a rogue elephant has purposely placed himself in waiting by the side of a frequented path, with the object of destroying the unwary traveller! In the valley of the Dheira Doon an elephant of this class—one, too, that had once been tamed, but had escaped from his servitude—is known to have taken the lives of nearly twenty unfortunate people before his destruction could be effected.

Well knowing these proclivities on the part of the *rogue*, Ossaroo at once counselled caution in the future movements of all—a counsel which Karl was too prudent to reject; and even the bold, rash Caspar did not think it proper to dissent from.

It was resolved, therefore, before continuing their projected exploration of the cliffs, to set their weapons once more in proper order—against any chance of an encounter with the elephant.

Their guns had to be re-stocked, and a new handle put into the axe—as well as a shaft into the boar-spear of Ossaroo—for all the woodwork of these weapons had been broken up and burnt into ashes in the manufacture of the candles of bear's-grease that had lighted them out of the cave.

The search after the ledges must necessarily be postponed; until they could go upon that errand properly armed and equipped, against any enemy that might oppose their progress.

Having come to this wise determination, they returned to their hut; kindled a fire; cooked breakfast; and having despatched the meal, at once set about selecting pieces of wood for the various purposes for which they were required.

They had no difficulty in procuring just what was wanted: for the valley contained many valuable sorts of timber; and several kinds that had been already cut for other purposes, now well seasoned and ready to hand, were found lying about the hut.

Setting about their work in earnest, and labouring diligently from morning to night—and even into the night hours—they knew they would not be long in accomplishing a task so trifling as the stocking of a gun, or putting the handle to a boar-spear.

Chapter Eight.
Inspecting the cliffs.

Working diligently with their knives two days sufficed to make guns, axe, and spear as good as ever. Ossaroo also made himself a new bow and a full quiver of arrows.

On the third morning, after breakfasting, all three set out with the determination not to leave any portion of the cliff unexamined.

The part which lay between their hut and the cave, Karl had already scrutinised with great care; so they went direct to the point where he had left off, and there commenced their new survey.

It is true they had already examined the cliffs all around; but this was just after they arrived in the valley, and the purpose of that exploration was very different from that of the present one.

Then they were only looking for a place by which they might climb out; and the idea of making ladders had not occurred to them.

Now that this scheme had suggested itself, they entered upon their second survey with the view of ascertaining whether it was practicable or possible. Consequently, they went in search of facts of a different nature— viz., to see if there existed a series of ledges, one above another, that could be spanned by an equal number of such ladders as they might be able to construct.

That they could make ladders of a prodigious length—allowing sufficient time for the execution of the work—all felt confident. They knew that the Thibet pine-trees—the same sort as they had used in making the bridge for the glacier crevasse—grew in great numbers not far from their hut; and by selecting some of the slenderest trunks of these, they would have the sides of as many ladders as they might want, almost ready made, and each forty or fifty feet in length.

If there should only be discovered a series of ledges, with not more than forty feet space between each two, there would be a fair hope of their being able to escalade the cliff, and escape from a place which, although one of the pleasantest-looking spots in the world, had now become to them loathsome as the interior of a dungeon.

Sure enough, and to the great joy of all, such a set of shelves was soon after presented to their eyes—having, at least in appearance, all the requirements of which they were in search. The spaces between no two of them appeared to be greater than thirty feet, some were much nearer to each other.

The part of the cliff where these terraces were found was not quite so low, as that where Karl had made his measurement. It did not appear, however, to be more than three hundred and fifty feet—a fearful height, it is true—but nothing when compared with other sections of the same precipice. To reach to its top, more than a dozen ladders would be required—each between twenty and thirty feet in length. The labour of making these ladders, with such tools as they had, might be looked upon as something stupendous—sufficient, you might suppose, to deter them from the task. But you must endeavour to realise the situation in which they were placed—with no other hope of being delivered from their mountain prison—and with this idea in your mind, you will comprehend why they should have been willing to undertake even a far greater labour. Of course, they did not expect to complete it in a day, neither in a week, nor in a month: for they well knew that it would take several months to make the number of ladders that would be required. And then there would be the additional labour of getting each into its place: as all, after the first one, would have to be carried up the cliff to the ledge for which it should be constructed. Indeed, to raise ladders of thirty feet in the manner contemplated, would seem an impossibility—that is, for such strength or mechanism as they could command.

And so it might have proved, had they intended to make these ladders of the ordinary weight. But they foresaw this difficulty, and hoped to get over it by making them of the very lightest kind—something that would just carry the weight of a man.

Becoming more than half satisfied that at this point the precipice might be scaled in the manner contemplated, they remained upon the ground in order to give it a thorough examination. That done, they intended to make the complete circuit of the valley, and ascertain whether there might not be some other place still easier of ascent.

The point where they had halted was behind the tract of heavily-timbered forest—of which Caspar had spoken, and which up to this time none of them had entered. Between the trees and the cliff they were now contemplating, there was a narrow strip of ground destitute of timber; and covered with a shingle of loose stones which had fallen from the mountain above. Several boulders of large dimensions rested upon the ground, at short distances apart; and there was one of a pillar-shape that stood some twenty-feet high, while it was only about five or six in diameter. It bore a sort of rude resemblance to an obelisk; and one might easily have fancied that the hand of man had accomplished its erection. For all that, it was a mere freak of Nature, and had probably been set up by ancient glacier ice. Up one of its sides there was a series of projections, by which an active man might climb to the top; and Ossaroo *did* climb it, partly out of playfulness, and partly, as he said, to get a better view of the cliff. The shikaree stayed only a few minutes on its top; and his curiosity having been satisfied, he had let himself down again.

Chapter Nine.
A reconnoissance interrupted.

Though the three had set out that morning with a wholesome dread of the elephant, and a determination to go about their reconnoissance with caution, their joy at the discovery of the ledges, and the eagerness with which they were scanning them, had for the moment banished from their minds all thoughts of the great quadruped. They were thinking only of ledges and ladders, and talking loudly of how the latter might best be made and placed upon the former.

Just then, and just at the moment Ossaroo descended from the obelisk rock, Fritz, who had been prowling about among the trees, set up a fearful baying—such another as that to which he had given utterance on the night when the elephant had paid its visit to the hut.

There was a certain intonation of terror in the dog's voice—as if whatever called it forth was something that inspired him with fear. The apprehension that it was the elephant occurred to all three at once; and with a simultaneous impulse they faced towards the spot whence the baying of the dog appeared to proceed. Simultaneously, too, they clutched more firmly their respective weapons—Karl his rifle, Caspar his double-barrel, and Ossaroo his bow, with an arrow at the string.

It is superfluous to say, that there was a certain amount of consternation visible in the countenances of all three; which was rather increased than diminished by the sight of Fritz dashing suddenly out of the underwood, and running towards them at full speed, with his tail considerably below the horizontal. Fritz, moreover, was giving utterance to something that very closely resembled a howl. The dog had evidently been attacked by some animal that had put him to flight; and his masters knew that it must be a formidable creature that was causing the variant Fritz to behave in such an ignominious manner.

They were not kept long in doubt as to the character of Fritz's conqueror and pursuer: for close behind his hips, almost touching them, appeared a long, cylindrical, or trumpet-shaped object, of a bluish-grey colour, protruding between two yellowish crescents, like a pair of huge ivory horns. Behind those appeared a pair of large ears, like flaps of sole leather; and in the rear of these last appendages came the round, massive form of an enormous elephant!

Crashing through the underwood, the monstrous creature soon cleared his body from the timber, and rushed straight across the open ground—winding his terrible trumpet as he went. He was following Fritz as straight as he could go, and evidently enraged at the dog.

The latter, on escaping from the tangle of the thicket, made direct for the spot occupied by his masters—thus directing the elephant upon them.

It was no longer a question of protecting Fritz from his formidable pursuer; for the elephant, on seeing three adversaries more worthy of his tusks, seemed to forget all about the puny four-footed creature who had provoked him; and at once directed his attack upon the upright bipeds—as if resolved to punish them for the misbehaviour of their subordinate.

The three, standing close together, saw at a glance that Fritz was no longer the object of the elephant's animosity: for the massive monster was now charging directly down upon them.

There was no time for concerted counsel—neither to take nor to give it. Each had to act upon his own instinct; and following this each acted. Karl sent the bullet from his rifle right between the tusks of the advancing foe; while Caspar fired both barrels of his piece "bang" into the forehead of the monster. Ossaroo's arrow was seen sticking through the elephant's trunk; and the moment after Ossaroo's heels were presented to the enemy.

Karl and Caspar also ran: for it would have been sheer madness to have remained a moment longer in that perilous proximity. Indeed, it is but justice to the shikaree to say, that Karl and Caspar ran first: for they had been the first to deliver their fire; and as soon as they had done so, each scampered as he best could. They ran together; and fortunately for both a large tree was near, with low horizontal limbs, which favoured a rapid ascent towards its top.

There was only a second of time between the commencement of their flight and that of Ossaroo; but short as it was, it decided the preference of the pursuer, and Ossaroo became the sole object of pursuit.

The shikaree would fain have made for the tree, to which the others were retreating; but the proboscis of the elephant was already so far advanced in that direction, that there was every probability it might get lapped upon him before he could climb beyond reach. For a moment he was in a dilemma, and his customary coolness seemed to have forsaken him.

The elephant was advancing upon him, its little switch of a tail oscillating rapidly in the air, and its trunk stretched horizontally towards him, with Ossaroo's own arrow still sticking in it. It seemed to know that it was he who had sent that skewer through its gristly snout—perhaps giving it far more pain than the leaden missiles that had flattened against its thick skull; and for this reason it had chosen him as the first victim of its vengeance.

In truth, Ossaroo's position was one of extreme peril—so much so that Karl and Caspar—now perceiving themselves comparatively safe from the pursuit—uttered a simultaneous cry: both believing that their faithful guide and follower was on the point of "coming to grief."

Ossaroo seemed bewildered at the very imminence of the danger. But it was only for a moment—only while he hesitated as to whether he should try to reach the tree. On perceiving that he could not do this with a fair chance of safety, he turned and ran in an opposite direction.

Whither? To the obelisk. Yes, by good fortune, the pillar from which he had just descended was only ten paces distant; and Ossaroo, in returning towards it, measured the ground with less than five. Flinging away his now useless weapons, he clutched hold of the prominent points of the rock, and "swarmed" up it like a squirrel.

He had good occasion to employ all his powers of agility. A second— half a second more—and he would have been too late: for ere he had reached the summit of the pillar, the digit point of the elephant's trunk was inserted under the skirt of his tunic; and had the garment been of tougher material; Ossaroo would have been jerked back to the ground more rapidly than he had ascended.

As it was, the cotton fabric—frail from long wear and exposure—gave way with a loud "screed;" and although the shikaree was stripped of his coat-tail, and suffered a rather ignominious exposure, still he had the satisfaction of knowing that to this circumstance he was indebted for the safety of his skin.

Chapter Ten.
Ossaroo on the obelisk.

The moment after, Ossaroo stood upon the summit of the obelisk. But even there he was far from being confident of security: for the pursuer had not abandoned the hope of being able to reach him. On the contrary, the infuriated animal, on finding itself baulked by the worthlessness of the fabric composing the skirt of the shikaree, spitefully tossed the piece of cloth from its trunk; and, rearing itself on its hind-legs, threw its body into an erect attitude, with its fore-feet resting high up against the rock.

One might have fancied that it was about to climb the obelisk; and this it would certainly have done had the thing been possible. As it was, however, Ossaroo was not out of danger: for as the elephant stood on its hind-legs, with its prehensile proboscis extended to the full length, the tip of the latter was not more than six inches from the soles of his feet.

The shikaree stood upright like a statue on its pedestal—though unlike to a statue in his features, which were anything but unmoved. On the contrary, his countenance exhibited the utmost consternation. And no wonder: for he could plainly perceive that should the elephant succeed in lengthening its carcase only another twelve inches, he himself would be brushed from the summit like a fly.

In fearful suspense, therefore, did he stand, contemplating the monster which was making every effort to reach him.

These efforts were made with as much sagacity as energy. Not only did the quadruped erect itself to its greatest height—standing, as one might say, upon its toes—but on finding that it was not tall enough, it fell back upon all fours, and then reared up afresh in an endeavour to stretch still higher.

Several times did it repeat the attempt—on each occasion trying a different side of the rock—as if in hopes that a greater elevation of the ground around the base might give it that advantage of twelve inches which it required for seizing its victim.

Fortunately for Ossaroo, the elephant had reached its very highest on first rearing up; and though it kept going round and round the rock, from no side could it do more than just touch with the top of its trunk the edge of the little flat space, upon which the feet of the shikaree were resting.

Ossaroo was beginning to be satisfied with this fact; and probably might have come to believe himself secure in his position, but for a circumstance that was making him uneasy. It was, that, standing upon such a limited surface—a pedestal whose diameter was but little over the length of his own feet—he found it exceedingly difficult to keep his balance. Had he been on the ground, there would have been no difficulty about it; but, perched as he was full twenty-feet aloft, the thing was quite different; and, with nerves unstrung by the fearful danger that threatened him below, it was just as much as he could do to keep his equilibrium.

Though only a "mild Hindoo," Ossaroo was possessed of a high degree of courage; and, most of his life having been spent as a shikaree, he had become well inured to the risk of losing it. Had he been a coward, or unused to such perils as at that moment surrounded him, he would in all likelihood have succumbed through fear; and toppled helplessly over upon the shoulders of the merciless monster that was threatening to destroy him. With all his bravery, however, it was just as much as he could do to keep his balance. Unfortunately, in climbing up the rock, he had been compelled to abandon his boar-spear: else with that he might have supported himself. His long knife was still in his belt; and this he drew forth—not with the design of using it upon his antagonist, but only the better to balance himself. It is true he would have been fain to take a chop or two at the gristly proboscis of the elephant; but he dared not bend his body into a stooping attitude, lest his centre of gravity might get beyond the supporting base, and thus bring about the result he dreaded.

No other course remained for him, than to preserve his body in an upright attitude; and, conscious of this fact, he braced his nerves to the utmost, and maintained himself erect and rigid as a statue of bronze.

Chapter Eleven.
A wholesale tumble.

In this attitude he remained for several minutes—the elephant all the while continuing its efforts to reach him Karl and Caspar, seated upon the branches of the tree, to which they had retreated, were witnesses of the whole scene from beginning to end. The situation of Ossaroo would have bean sufficiently ludicrous for Caspar to have laughed at it, but for the danger in which the shikaree was placed. This was so evident, that instead of indulging in anything akin to levity, Caspar looked on with feelings of deep anxiety, Karl being equally apprehensive about the result. Neither could do anything to aid or rescue him, as they were unarmed—both having dropped their pieces when ascending the tree.

I have said that Karl was as uneasy about the result as his brother. He was even more so. It was not that he liked Ossaroo better, or would have more bitterly lamented his fate, had the latter perished by the proboscis of the elephant. No, that was not the reason; but simply that Karl more clearly comprehended the danger in which the shikaree was placed.

After watching the efforts of the elephant for a short time, Caspar had become convinced that the animal could not reach Ossaroo—so long as the latter preserved his balance upon the summit of the rock. Karl was equally satisfied of this; and both by their shouts kept encouraging the shikaree to stand firm. But Karl soon noted another circumstance, which was as yet unperceived by Caspar, and it was this that was inspiring him with keener apprehension than that felt by his brother. He had noticed that, each time as the elephant erected himself against the obelisk, the rock seemed slightly to shake. Ossaroo was himself well aware of the circumstance—and more troubled at it than any of them—for it rendered it more difficult for him to preserve his equilibrium. Caspar at length also observed the trembling of the rock, but it gave him no particular uneasiness: as, after what had passed, he felt confident that Ossaroo would be able to keep his place. Nor was it the fear of his falling in that way that was distressing the young botanist; but rather a deduction which he drew from the circumstance, not apparent to the less philosophic mind of his brother.

The shaking of the rock had suggested to Karl a dangerous contingency. What was it? The speech addressed by him at that moment to Caspar will explain.

"Oh, brother!" he exclaimed, on perceiving the danger, "if the rock should fall—"

"No danger of that," said Caspar, interrupting him; "it stands firm enough. True, I see it shake a little, but only a very little; and that only when the brute springs up against it. No danger, I should think!"

"But I fear there is clanger," rejoined Karl, in a tone of undiminished anxiety. "Not," added he, "so long as the elephant acts as he is doing; but he may not continue thus. These creatures are wonderfully sagacious; and if he only perceives that the pillar moves under his weight, a new idea may get into his brain, and then it will be all up with Ossaroo."

"Ha! I begin to comprehend you," said Caspar, beginning to share the alarm of his brother. "There is danger in that. What is to be done? If we only had our guns up here, we might open fire on the brute. Whether we succeeded in killing him or not, we might at all events divert his attention from Ossaroo, and perhaps hinder him from thinking of the plan you speak of. We might go down and get our guns. What is to hinder us?—the elephant is too busy to notice us."

"True—an excellent idea of yours, brother Caspar."

"Well, then, to put it in execution. I shall slip down to the ground; you follow to the lowest branch, and I can hand the guns up to you. Keep steady, and don't you fear, Ossy!" added the young hunter in a louder voice, addressing himself to the shikaree. "We'll fetch him away from you directly—we'll tickle him with an ounce or two of lead through that thick hide of his."

So saying, Caspar commenced letting himself rapidly down from branch to branch, Karl following more leisurely.

Caspar had got upon the lowest limb of the tree, and Karl on that immediately above it, when a loud crash, accompanied by a piercing shriek, arrested the progress of both, causing them suddenly to turn their faces towards the obelisk. During the short time that their eyes had been averted from it, a complete change had taken place in that curious tableau. Instead of a tall column of stone, standing twenty-feet perpendicular, the same column was now seen lying along the earth in a nearly horizontal position, with a huge mass of broken boughs and branches of trees crushed under its top. Near its base, now upturned and standing almost vertically, was the elephant, no longer on its hind feet, nor yet on all fours, but down upon its back, kicking its huge hoofs in the air, and making the most stupendous efforts to recover its legs. Ossaroo was nowhere to be seen!

The contingency dreaded by Karl had come to pass. The elephant, finding it impossible to reach the shikaree with its trunk—and no doubt judging by the "feel" that the rock was not immobile—had at length dropped down on all fours and, placing its broad shoulder against it, backed by the enormous weight of its bulky body, had sent the column crashing among the tops of a chestnut tree growing near—the trunk of which, yielding to the weight, gave way with a crash, and trunk, limbs, and branches were all borne downward to the earth!

The elephant itself, not calculating that it should find the task so easy of performance, had fallen at the same time—its cumbrous body losing balance by the impetus which it had thrown into the effort. In short, of the four objects that formed the tableau—rock and tree, quadruped and man—not one was standing any longer in its place—for it is superfluous to say that Ossaroo had gone down with the obelisk.

But where was Ossaroo? That was the question that occurred to both Karl and Caspar.

"Oh! brother!" groaned Caspar, "I fear he is killed!"

Karl made no reply; but for all that, Caspar's reflection, delivered in a loud tone, was not left without rejoinder. Directly after the phrase had issued from his lips, an answer was heard proceeding from among the branches of the fallen chestnut tree, in a voice and with words that caused the hearts of the brothers to beat with joy.

"No, young sahibs," replied the unseen Ossaroo; "me no killee, me no bit damage. If I only can get pass de old rogue, I safe and sound as ibber. Here go for run!"

At the same moment the shikaree was seen shooting out from among the branches under which he had been for the time buried; and, then running with all his might towards the tree upon which the brothers had found refuge.

Long before the elephant could regain its feet, Ossaroo had reached a position of perfect security among the upper branches of the great tree; which Karl and Caspar, no longer thinking of their guns, had also re-ascended.

Chapter Twelve.
A ring performance.

As the tree into which they had retreated was a very large one, there was no longer any present fear of danger from the elephant, however furious the latter might be; and they could look down upon it and watch its movements with a feeling of perfect security. The only one of the party that was in dangerous proximity to that dreaded proboscis was Fritz; but Fritz had already been well warned of the wicked designs of the great brute, and was sufficiently swift-footed and sage enough to give the animal a wide berth.

As for the elephant itself, having recovered its feet, it stood for some seconds flapping its huge ears, and apparently in a kind of quandary—as if taken aback by the unexpected accident that had befallen it. Not for long, however, did it continue in this tranquil attitude. The arrow still sticking in its trunk reminded it of its purposes of vengeance. Once more angrily elevating its tail, and sounding its shrill trumpet, it rushed towards the fallen tree, and buried its long proboscis among the branches. One by one it turned them over, as if in search of some object. It was searching for the shikaree.

After a time it desisted from this manoeuvre, and looked around—evidently with a puzzled air, and wondering what had become of the man. It had not seen him as he rushed towards the great tree: for his retreat had been made while the creature was sprawling upon its back. Just then Fritz chanced to show himself—crouching under the branches upon which his masters had taken refuge, and evidently envying them their secure situation.

The sight of Fritz was enough. It was he who had first challenged the elephant on its approach through the woods, and had conducted it under that terrible battery of bullets and arrows. As soon, therefore, as the latter set eyes upon the dog, its fury not only became rekindled, but apparently redoubled; and, hoisting its tail on high, it charged full tilt upon its original adversary.

Had the assailant been a boar, or even a bull, no doubt Fritz would have stood his ground, or only swerved to one side, the better to elude the onset, and make an attack in turn. But with a quadruped as big as a house—and of which Fritz, not being of Oriental origin, knew so little; and of that little nothing that was good—one, too, evidently provided with most formidable weapons, a tongue several feet long, and tusks in proportion—it is not to be wondered at, nor is it any great blot upon his escutcheon, that Fritz turned tail and fled. So fast fled he, that in less than a score of seconds he was out of sight—not only of his masters in the tree, but of his pursuer, the elephant. The latter only followed him for some half-dozen lengths of its own carcase; and seeing that the pursuit was likely to be a wild-goose chase, declined following Fritz any farther.

They in the tree, as the elephant started after the dog, were in hopes that the pursuit might carry the dangerous animal to some distance, and thus give them time to get back to the ground, and make their escape from the spot.

In this, however, they were doomed to disappointment; for having desisted from the chase of the dog, the great pachyderm returned to the point from whence it had started; and, after once more tossing the broken branches of the fallen chestnut tree upon the point of its proboscis, it commenced pacing round and round the fallen obelisk, keeping in regular circles, as if it were training itself for some performance in an amphitheatre.

For more than an hour did the brute continue this circular promenade, at intervals stopping to give utterance to its shrieking note; but most of the time moving on in sullen silence. Now and then it directed its eyes, and once or twice its trunk, towards the branches of the prostrate tree as if it had still some suspicion that he who sent that stinging arrow was there concealed. Indeed, it appeared by its movements to be keeping guard over that particular spot, lest its enemy should escape. It had long since extracted the arrow, by placing its great foot upon the shaft, and drawing it forth.

Fritz had stolen back to the edge of the thicket, but kept cowering so close that the elephant could not see him.

The parties perched above were more than annoyed by their imprisonment thus procrastinated, and began to think of how they might set themselves free. They talked of making a rush to possess themselves of their guns; but to Karl this appeared too perilous to be attempted. It was not twenty yards from the tree to the spot where rested the dismounted monolith; and the elephant, whose eye was in a state of continual activity, could not fail to see them descending from the branches. The massive creature, though it moved about with apparently a gentle griding step, could go almost as fast as a galloping horse; and should it espy them in time, there would be but slight chance of eluding its prehensile trunk.

Moreover, the sight of them—even should they succeed in regaining the tree—would rekindle its rage, and cause it to prolong its stay upon the ground.

There was yet another consideration that influenced them to remain patiently on their perch. They knew that they had provided themselves with only a very limited quantity of ammunition. That article had become scarce with them; and they had prudently determined to economise it. Karl had only two bullets left, with just powder enough to make two charges; while Caspar's horn and pouch were not better filled. They might fire their whole stock of lead into the elephant, and still not succeed in killing a creature that sometimes walks off triumphantly with a score of bullets "under his belt." These shots might only have the effect of incensing it still more, and causing it to stay upon the ground to an indefinite period.

It was a true *rogue*—Ossaroo had long since pronounced it one—and an "old tusker" at that. It was therefore a most dangerous creature; and though they knew they would never be safe in that valley until it should be destroyed, it was agreed by all that it would be more prudent to leave it undisturbed until some more favourable opportunity occurred for effecting its destruction.

For these various reasons they resolved to remain quiet in the tree, and patiently await the termination of that curious "ring performance," which the old tusker still continued to keep up.

Chapter Thirteen.
An odd appearance.

For the full length of another hour did the trio in the tree have their patience tested. During all that time the "rogue" remained upon the ground, continuing his perambulations around the rock—until he had trodden out a path that resembled the arena of a circus at the close of a night's performance.

It is not necessary to say that the time hung heavily upon the hands of the spectators—to say nothing of Fritz, who would no doubt have been satisfied with a much shorter programme.

As regards the former, the hour might have been spent less pleasantly than it was; for it so chanced that an *interlude* was introduced, of so interesting a character to all, but more especially to the naturalist Karl, that for a while the proximity of their savage besieger was forgotten, and they scarcely remembered that they were besieged.

Favoured by the accident of their situation, they became spectators of a scene—one of those scenes only to be viewed amid the wild solitudes of Nature.

Not far from the tree on which they had found shelter, stood another of equal dimensions, but of an entirely different species. It was a sycamore, as even Caspar, without any botanical skill, could testify. Its smooth bark, piebald with white and green spots, its widely-straggling limbs and leaves, left no doubt about its being one. It was the sycamore, identical with its European congener, the *Platanus orientalis*.

It is the habit of this fine tree to become hollow. Not only does the lower part of its trunk exhibit the phenomenon of great cavities, but holes are found high up in its main shaft or in the larger limbs.

The tree in question stood within a few yards of that on which Karl, Caspar, and Ossaroo were perched. It was just before their eyes, whenever they looked in a horizontal direction; and occasionally, when tired with watching the monotonous movements of the elephant, one or other of them *did* look horizontally. The scanty foliage upon the sycamore enabled them to see its trunk and most of its larger limbs, without any obstruction of leaves or branches.

Caspar had not cast his eyes more than twice in the direction of this tree, when he saw there was something peculiar about it. Caspar was a youth of quick sight and equally quick perception. In the main stem of the tree, and about six feet above its first forking, he perceived an object that at once fixed his attention. It looked like a goat's horn, only that it was more like the curving tusk of a rhinoceros or a very young elephant. It was sticking out from the tree, with the curve directed downwards. Altogether, it looked quite different from a branch of the sycamore, or anything belonging to the tree.

Once or twice, while Caspar had his eyes upon it, he thought or fancied that it moved; but not being sure of this, he said nothing, lest the others might laugh at him. It would not have been the first time that Karl, from his superior knowledge, had indulged in a laugh at his brother's expense.

Caspar's attention being now engrossed by the peculiar appearance he had noted, he continued to scrutinise it; and soon perceived that around the curved excrescence there was a circular disc some eight or ten inches in diameter, and differing in colour from the bark of the sycamore—by being many shades darker. This disc appeared composed of some substance that was not ligneous: for it no more resembled wood than the curved ivory-like object that protruded from its centre. Had Caspar been asked what it did look like, he would have answered that it resembled the agglutinated mud used by swallows in building their nests—so like it, that it might have been the same substance.

Caspar continued to scrutinise these two curious objects—the tusk-like excrescence, and the dark disc from which it protruded; and not until he became fully aware that the former had life in it, did he communicate his discovery to his companions. Of this fact he was convinced by seeing the crescent suddenly disappear—as if drawn within the tree, while in its place a dark round hole was alone visible. Presently the yellowish horn reappeared through the hole, and protruded outside, filling it up as before!

Caspar was too much astonished by this exhibition to remain any longer the sole proprietor of such a mysterious secret, and without more delay he communicated his discovery to Karl, and indirectly to Ossaroo.

Both at the same time turned their eyes towards the tree, and bent them upon the indicated spot. Karl was as much mystified by the strange appearance as had been Caspar himself.

Not so Ossaroo. The moment he saw the carving ivory and the dark-coloured disc, he pronounced, in a tone of careless indifference, the simple phrase,—

"Hornbill—de bird on him nest."

Chapter Fourteen.
A curious nest.

Just then the curved projection was observed to recede within the tree; and in its place appeared a small dark hole, apparently the entrance to a larger cavity. Karl, as Caspar had done the moment before, saw this with surprise.

"Nest?" repeated Caspar, astonished at the shikaree's statement. "A bird's nest? Is that what you mean, Ossy?"

"That just it, sahib. Nest of great biggee bird. Feringhees him call *horneebill*."

"Well," rejoined Caspar, not greatly enlightened by Ossaroo's explanation, "that's very curious. We have seen something like a horn sticking out of the tree, though it looks more like ivory than horn. It may be the bill of a bird; but as to a bird itself, or the nest of one, where is that, pray?"

Ossaroo intimated that the nest was inside the tree; and that the bird was on the nest just behind its beak, where it ought to be.

"What! the bird is in that hole where we saw the white thing sticking out? Why, it quite filled the hole, and if there's a bird there, and what we saw be its bill, I have only to say that its bill must be as big as its body—else how can it get out and in through so small an aperture? Certainly I see no hole but the one. Oh! perhaps the bird is a *toucan*. I have heard there are some of that sort that can go through any place where they can pass their beaks. Is it a toucan, Ossaroo?"

Ossaroo could not tell what a toucan was, never having heard of such a bird. His ornithological knowledge went no further than to the birds of Bengal; and the toucan is found only in America. He stated that the bird in the tree was called by the Feringhees a "hornbill," but it was also known to some as the "rhinoceros bird." Ossaroo added that it was as large as a goose; and that its body was many times thicker than its bill, thick as the latter appeared to be.

"And you say it has its nest inside that hole?" interrogated Caspar, pointing to the little round aperture, which did not appear to be over three inches in diameter.

"Sure of it, young sahib," was Ossaroo's reply.

"Well, certainly there is some living creature in there, since we have seen it move; and if it be a bird as large as a goose, will you explain to me how it got in, and how it means to get out? There must be a larger entrance on the other side of the tree."

"No, sahib," confidently asserted Ossaroo; "that you see before your eye—that the only way to de horneebill nest."

"Hurrah for you, Ossy! So you mean to say that a bird as large as a goose can go in and out by that hole? Why, a sparrow could scarcely squeeze itself through there!"

"Horneebill he no goee in, he no goee out. He stay inside till him little chickees ready for leavee nest."

"Come, Ossy!" said Caspar, in a bantering way; "that story is too good to be true. You don't expect us to believe all that? What, stay in the nest till the young are ready to leave it! And how then? How will the young ones help their mother out of the scrape? How will they get out themselves: for I suppose they don't leave the nest till they are pretty well grown? Come! good shikaree; let us have no more circumlocution about the matter, but explain all these apparently inexplicable circumstances."

The shikaree, thus appealed to, proceeded to give the explanation demanded.

The hornbill, he said, when about to bring forth its young, selects a hollow in some tree, just large enough conveniently to hold the nest which it builds, and also its own body. As soon as the nest is constructed and the eggs all laid, the female bird takes her seat upon them, and there remains; not only until the eggs are hatched, but for a long time afterwards—in fact, until the young are nearly fledged and able to take care of themselves. In order that she may be protected during the period of her incubation against weasels, polecats, ichneumons, and all such vermin, a design exhibiting either wonderful instinct or sagacity, is carried into execution by the male. As soon as his mate has squatted upon her eggs, he goes to work at the masonic art; and using his great horned mandibles, first as a hod, and afterwards as a trowel, he walls up the entrance to the nest—leaving an aperture just large enough to be filled up by the beak of the female. The material employed by him for this purpose is a kind of agglutinated mud, which he procures from the neighbouring watercourse or quagmire, and somewhat similar to that used by the common house-swallow for constructing *its* peculiar nest. When dried, this mud becomes exceedingly hard—bidding defiance to the teeth and claws of all would-be intruders, whether bird or quadruped; and with the horny beak of the old hen projected outward, and quite filling up the aperture, even the slippery tree-snake cannot find room enough to squeeze his body through. The female, thus free from all fear of being molested, quietly continues her incubation!

When Ossaroo had got thus far with his explanation, Caspar interrupted him with a query.

"What!" said he, "sit all the time—for weeks, I suppose—without ever coming out—without taking an airing? And how does she get her food?"

As Caspar put this question, and before Ossaroo had time to answer, a noise reached their ears which appeared to proceed from the sky above them. It was a noise well calculated to inspire terror in those who had never before heard it, or did not know what was causing it. It was a sort of fluttering, clattering sound, or rather a series of sounds, resembling the quickly repeated gusts of a violent storm.

The moment Ossaroo heard it, he knew what it was; and instead of giving a direct answer to Caspar's question, he simply said—

"Wait a bit, sahib. Here come old cockee horneebill; he show you how de hen getee her food."

The words had scarcely passed from the lips of the shikaree, when the cause of that singular noise became known to his companions. The maker of it appeared before them in the form of a great bird, that with a strong flapping of its wings flew past the tree in which they were seated, towards that which contained the nest.

In an instant afterwards, it was seen resting on a spur-like projection of the trunk, just below the aperture; and it needed not Ossaroo to tell them that it was the cock hornbill that had there alighted. The large beak—the tip of it resembling that which they had already seen sticking out of the hole, and which was once more visible and in motion—surmounted by an immense helmet-like protuberance, rising upon the crown, and running several inches along the top of the upper mandible, which might have been taken for a second beak—this singular appendage could belong to no other bird than the *hornbill*.

Chapter Fifteen.
The hornbill.

Karl, although he had never seen one of these birds alive, had yet examined stuffed specimens of them in museums, and he had no difficulty in recognising the bird. He was able even to identify the species, for there are many species of hornbill, known under the generic name, *Bucerus*. That before their eyes was the *Bucerus rhinoceros*, or "rhinoceros hornbill," called also the "topau," and sometimes the "horned Indian raven," from a sort of resemblance which it bears both in shape and habits to the well-known bird of this name.

Ossaroo had not exaggerated the size of these birds when he compared it to that of a goose. On the contrary, he had rather moderated the dimensions: for the one in question looked much larger than either goose or gander. It was rather more than three feet in length—reckoning from the tip of its tail to the point of its curving beak, which of itself was nearly a foot long! Its colour was black above, and yellowish-white underneath, the tail feathers being a clear white, with a broad black band crossing them near the middle. Its bill, like that of its mate already observed, was of a yellowish-white, the upper mandible being reddish around the base, while the casque-like protuberance exhibited a mottled surface of white and black.

Ossaroo had to tell them pretty nearly all he knew in relation to this curious bird; for although there are several species of hornbills natives of India, it is by no means a common creature, even at home in its own country.

Karl could have told them much more about its species and habits, and no doubt he would have done so had they been otherwise engaged. But situated as they were, with an angry elephant besieging them in the tree, and now for a while interested in observing the movements of the bird itself, Karl was in no humour to deliver an ornithological lecture. He might have told them that ornithologists have differed much about the classification of the hornbill—some of them placing it among the toucans, while others assert that it belongs to the crow family. Its immense beak—out of all proportion to its body—is not the only point of resemblance it bears to the toucans. Like them, it flings its food into the air, catching and swallowing it as it comes down. Unlike the toucans, however, it cannot climb trees, and is therefore not of the Scansorial order. It is said to be omnivorous in its food; and in this it resembles the crows and ravens: but, indeed, as already stated, there are many species of hornbills, and the habits of the different kinds, by no means uniform or alike, have been confounded by most writers. There are species in Africa, others in India and the Indian islands, and New Guinea is known to have one or two distinct species of its own. All these differ not only in size, colour, shape of their beak, and the protuberance that surmounts it; but also in the kind of food which they live upon. For instance, the African hornbills, and one or more of the Asiatic species, are carnivorous, and some even carrion-eaters. These are filthy birds, their flesh and feathers smelling rank as those of vultures. On the other hand, there is a species in the Indian islands—the Moluccas more particularly—whose sole food is the nutmeg, which gives to its flesh an exquisite aromatic flavour, causing it to be much relished at the tables of Oriental epicures. The bill of this species after a certain time appears with a number of grooves or furrows in it. As these furrows are observed only on the beaks of the old birds, the Dutch colonists established in the Moluccas believe them to indicate their age, each wrinkle standing for a year. Hence the hornbill has obtained among the colonists the name of *Yerrvogel* (year bird).

Karl, as I have said, was acquainted with all these facts in the natural history of the hornbill; but just then he did not think of making them known to his companions—all three being too much occupied in watching the movements of the male bird. It was evident that he was not one of the vegetable feeders: for on his alighting they could see hanging from his beak a long cylindrical object, which they were able to identify as a portion— the head and part of the body—of a dead snake. It was equally evident that his mate was not accustomed to a vegetable diet: for from the way in which he was manoeuvring, the spectators saw that the mutilated reptile was intended for her. No doubt it was her dinner, for it had now got to that hour of the day.

She was not to be kept waiting any longer. Almost on the instant her provider alighted on the projecting spur, with a toss of his head he jerked the piece of snake up into the air, and then caught it as it came down again—not with the intention to swallow it, but only to get a better grip, in order that he might deliver it the more adroitly into the mandibles of his mate—now protruding through the aperture, and opened to receive it.

In another instant the savoury morsel was transferred from the beak of the male to that of the female; and then the ivory forceps of the latter, with the snake held tightly between them, disappeared within the cavity.

The old cock stayed not a moment longer upon the tree. He had served his mate with her dinner, and perhaps he had yet to bring on the dessert. Whether or not, he rose immediately afterwards into the air, with the same clangorous clapping of his wings; but this time the noise was accompanied by the clattering of his horny mandibles, like a pair of castanets, causing a sound not only singular, but, if heard by strangers, calculated to beget within them a considerable feeling of alarm.

Chapter Sixteen.
A four-footed burglar.

After the departure of the bird, that had taught our young adventurers so interesting a chapter of natural history, the elephant once more engrossed their attention. Not that there was anything new in the movements of the latter—for it was acting just as before—but simply because they knew that, so long as it remained upon the ground, they would have to stay in the tree; and they naturally bent their eyes upon it, to see if it was showing any signs of moving off. They could perceive none. Not the slightest appearance to indicate its intention of departing from the spot.

While engaged in regarding the besieger, their eyes were of course removed from the sycamore; nor might they have been again turned towards that tree—at least, not for a good while—but for a sound that reached their ears, and which appeared to proceed from the direction of the hornbill's nest. It was a soft and rather plaintive sound—unlike any that had been made by the rhinoceros bird; nor was it at all like the voice of a bird, of any kind. It was more like the utterance of some four-footed creature; or it might even have been a human voice pronouncing the syllable "wha," several times repeated.

That it was neither bird nor human being, Ossaroo could tell the moment he heard the first "wha." Almost as soon were the others convinced that it was neither: for on turning their eyes to the sycamore, they saw upon the projecting spur that had been so lately occupied by the hornbill, a creature of a very different kind—in short, a quadruped.

Had it been in an American forest, they might have taken the creature for a racoon though a very large one. On closer scrutiny, many points of resemblance, and also of difference, would have become apparent. Like the racoon, it had plantigrade feet, a burly, rounded body, and a very thick hairy tail—ringed also like that of the American animal—but unlike the latter, its muzzle, instead of being long and slender, was short, round, and somewhat cat-like; while its hair, or more properly its fur, formed a thick even coat all over its body, limbs, and tail, and presented a smooth and shining surface. Its general colour was a very dark brown, streaked and mottled with golden yellow; and Caspar remarked, upon the moment of seeing it, that it was one of the handsomest creatures he had ever beheld.

The naturalist Cuvier had made the same remark long before Caspar's time. So said Karl, on hearing the observation escape from the lips of his brother.

Ossaroo knew that the animal was the "wha," a name derived from its ordinary call; and that it was sometimes known as the "chetwa," and also the "panda."

Karl, on hearing Ossaroo's name for it, and indeed, on hearing it pronounced by the creature itself, was able to identify the animal, and to give it still another name—that which has been bestowed upon it by Frederick Cuvier—*ailurus*. This is the generic name, of which, up to the present time, it has been left in undisturbed possession. Since only one species has been discovered, it has the name all to itself; and therefore would not require any specific appellation. But for all that, one has been given to it. On account of its shining coat, it has been called the *ailurus fulgens*.

Though the closet naturalists, in following out their pedantic propensities, have created a genus expressly for this animal, there is nothing either in its appearance or habits to separate it from the badgers, the racoons, the coatimondis, and such other predatory creatures. Like them it preys upon birds and their eggs, as also on the smaller kinds of quadrupeds, and like the racoon, it is a nimble tree-climber.

The situation in which the particular panda, of which we are writing, first appeared to the eyes of Karl and Caspar, proved this capacity, and its actions the moment after testified to its fondness for birds'-eggs. It had not been a minute under the eyes of the spectators, when they saw that it was after the eggs of the hornbill; perhaps, too, it might have had a design of tasting the flesh of their owner.

Resting its thick plantigrade hind feet upon the projection of the tree, it erected itself like a little bear; and with its fore-paws commenced scraping at the barrier wall which the male bird had spent so much time and taken so much pains in building. It is possible that if it had been left to itself, it might in time have succeeded in forcing an entrance into the nest, and highly probable too—or it would scarcely have entered upon the task. But it was not left to itself. Not that the sitter inside could have done much to hinder it: though it was evident from the way in which her beak was repeatedly projected and drawn back through the hole, and also from her angry hissing, that she knew there was danger without, and that an enemy was assailing her citadel.

Most likely after a time, and by constant scraping, the clay wall would eventually have been pulled down; but before that event came to pass, a loud flapping and fluttering, and cracking and clattering, was heard among the tops of the trees; and in an instant afterwards the broad, shadowy wings of the old male hornbill were swashing about the ears of the four-footed robber, where the long cutlass-like beak, armed at its edges, at once interrupted the intent.

The panda, taken by surprise, quailed at this first onset: for like any other *paterfamilias* who on returning home finds a burglar breaking into his house, the cock bird charged in the full tide of impetuous fury.

The robber, however, evidently used to this sort of thing, soon recovered his self-possession; and instead of retreating from the tree, he only planted himself more firmly upon the projection; and, facing towards his feathery assailant, prepared to show fight.

And fight was instantly shown on both sides—the bird swooping repeatedly at its adversary, striking with its strong wings and thrusting with its ensiform beak; while the quadruped played back both with teeth and claws—several times plucking a mouthful of feathers from the breast of its winged adversary.

Chapter Seventeen.
Fritz interferes.

How the affair might have ended had the panda and the hornbill been the only parties to the combat, can but be guessed at. In all likelihood the quadruped would have triumphed over the biped: the entrance would have been forced; the old hen dragged off her nest—perhaps killed and eaten—and the eggs after her.

But it was not written in the book of destiny that this should be the *dénouement* of that little drama: for at that moment an incident occurred which changed the whole character of the contest—followed by a series of other incidents which brought the affair to a termination unexpected by all parties engaged, as well as by those who witnessed it.

The first of these incidents—and that which formed the key to this change in the circumstances of the combat, was one of a very ludicrous character—so much so as to elicit laughter from the spectators in the tree.

It chanced that the eyes of the panda, as the animal stood erect on its hind quarters, were directly opposite the little aperture that represented the entrance to the nest. Not dreaming of any danger in that direction, the robber only thought of guarding his "daylights" against the hornbill upon the wing. But the hen bird inside the nest—who could see well enough what was passing outside—had no idea of remaining a passive spectator; and perceiving her opportunity—for she was within striking distance—she quietly drew back her long ivory beak, and, throwing all the strength of her neck into the effort—assisted by the weight of her heavy helmeted head—as if with the blow of a pick-axe, she struck the panda right in the eye—the sharp point penetrating almost to its skull.

Terror-stricken, partly by surprise at this unexpected stroke, and partly by the pain caused by it, the quadruped uttered a shrill cry; and at once scrambling down from the tree, seemed only anxious to make his escape. In this design he, no doubt, would have succeeded, with only the loss of an eye; but the eye of still another enemy had been upon him—one whom he had yet to encounter. Fritz, from his position near the bottom of the tree, attracted by the noise of the strife, had drawn nearer; and looking up, had been watching the combat throughout. It is scarcely probable that the sympathies of honest Fritz could have been otherwise than in favour of the innocent bird, and against the guilty beast; but whatever way they may have been inclined, certain it is that as the panda came to "grass," the dog "jumped" it upon the instant, and commenced worrying it, as if the creature had been the oldest and bitterest of his enemies!

Despite the suddenness of this new attack—equally unexpected as the peck in the eye—the fierce panda showed no signs of yielding without a struggle; and, although far overmatched by its canine antagonist, it was likely to give the latter a scratch or two, as souvenirs that he would carry to his grave.

But at this moment a much greater danger was threatening Fritz than any harm he might suffer from the claws of the panda; and had chance not favoured him, as he jumped about in the struggle, by turning his eyes in a particular direction, he would have found himself in the clutches of an antagonist, that would have shown him as little mercy as he was himself extending to the poor panda.

But he was favoured by chance: for it was nothing more that directed his glance towards his old pursuer, the elephant; and showed him the latter, at that moment advancing upon him at a charging pace, with eyes sparkling in silent vengeance, and trunk extended to seize him. Under the circumstances, it did not cost Fritz a moment's calculation as to what course he should pursue. Suddenly dropping the panda—as if he had discovered the quadruped to be a lump of poison—he bounded from the spot in a direction the very opposite to that by which the elephant was approaching; and in less than a score of seconds the only part of him to be seen was the tip of his tail just disappearing into the thicket.

Of all the creatures that had borne part in this curious affray, the poor panda was perhaps the most to be pitied. At all events he was the most unfortunate: for with the drama ended also his life. In every one encountered by him he had found an enemy; and in the last he met with a dread foe that soon made a finish of him. This last was the elephant. The great animal, rushing forward upon Fritz, seeing that the latter had escaped, was determined this time not to be baulked of a victim. Instead of carrying out the design it had only partially resolved upon—that of following Fritz into the forest—it suddenly altered its plan, and transferred its hostility to the panda. It saw that the latter was within reach: for half blinded by the beak of the bird, and half worried to death by the dog, the creature did not perceive, as Fritz had done, the approach of the elephant. It is possible it may have seen the danger, but not until the elephant had got in such dangerous proximity as left it no chance of escape.

Before the panda could make the slightest effort to get away from the ground, the elephant had lapped its prehensile proboscis around it, and lifted it into the air as if its body had been no heavier than a feather. Holding it aloft, the merciless monster took several long strides in the direction of the fallen obelisk; and then, as if choosing a spot suitable for its design, it placed the still struggling body of the panda upon the ground, set its huge fore-feet upon it, and using them alternately, continued to trample it until the only vestige left of the crushed creature was a shapeless mass of fur and flesh!

It was a painful spectacle to those in the tree; but it was succeeded by a sight that was pleasant to all three—the sight of the elephant's hind quarters as it walked off toward the woods, evidently with the intention of retiring from the ground.

Whether its vengeance had been satisfied by the destruction of the panda, or whether it had gone off in search of Fritz, none of the three could conjecture; but whatever may have been the motive, certain it is that it guided the rogue from the spot, and raised a siege that was on the point of becoming exceedingly irksome.

Chapter Eighteen.
"Death to the rogue."

As soon as the elephant was fairly out of sight, the besieged took counsel among themselves about descending to the earth. They were sorely tired of the positions which they had been so long constrained to keep; for, to tell the truth, sitting astride upon the hard branch of a tree, though easy enough for a short spell, becomes in time so painful as to be almost unendurable. Caspar especially had grown impatient of this irksome inaction; and highly exasperated at the *rogue* who was forcing it upon them. Several times had he been on the point of forsaking his perch, and stealing down for his gun; but Karl, each time perceiving his design, very prudently persuaded him to forego it.

All were anxious enough to get out of the tree; and they would have vacated their sents at once on the disappearance of their dreaded enemy, had they been certain that he was gone for good; but they were suspicious that it might be only a temporary absence—perhaps some *ruse* of the rogue to decoy them down: for elephants of this character have been known to practise tricks with almost as much cunning as rogues among men.

While holding counsel as to how they had best act, Ossaroo cut short their deliberations by volunteering to descend first; and by stealing a short way along the track which the elephant had taken, ascertain whether he was really gone from the ground, or only tying in ambush near the skirt of the forest.

As the shikaree could creep through underwood as silently as a snake, there could be no great danger in his doing this, provided he did not go too far. He could not fail to see the elephant before approaching too near to it; and in the event of its turning and pursuing him, he could once more flee to their tree-fortress.

He scarcely waited for the consent of his companions; but, immediately after conceiving the idea, he let himself down among the branches; and once on the ground, glided hurriedly, but cautiously, off in the direction taken by the elephant.

Karl and Caspar stayed some five minutes longer upon their perch; but the shikaree not returning as soon as they had expected, they became impatient, and also dropped down from the tree.

Their first act was to recover their guns, and reload them; and then, taking stand in a position from which, in case of being suddenly attacked, they could easily spring back among the branches, they awaited the return of Ossaroo.

A considerable time elapsed, without their either seeing or hearing aught of the shikaree. Indeed they heard nothing: for a complete silence reigned around them, broken only now and then by the fluttering of the wings of the old male hornbill—who was still keeping in the neighbourhood of the nest, apparently puzzled to make out by what mysterious combination of circumstances he had been so abruptly disembarrassed of his adversary, the panda.

The movements of the bird had no longer any interest for Karl and Caspar—who were beginning to grow uneasy at the prolonged absence of Ossaroo.

Soon after, however, they were relieved from their suspense, by seeing the shikaree emerging from the underwood, and advancing at a quick pace to the open ground. They had the additional pleasure of beholding Fritz following at his heels. The dog had joined Ossaroo near the edge of the timber—where he had been quietly secreting himself from the eyes of the dreaded elephant.

As Ossaroo drew near, both Karl and Caspar noticed an expression upon his countenance, which, combined with his hurried advance, told that he had something of an important nature to communicate.

"Well, Ossy," asked Caspar, who was the first to speak, "what news? Have you seen anything more of the rogue?"

"Ah, rogue indeed!" replied Ossaroo, in a tone expressive of some secret fear. "You speakee true, sahib; the rogue, if he no worse."

"Why, what now? Have you seen anything since you left us?"

"Seen, sahibs! Where you tinkee he now gone?"

"Where?"

"Hee go for de hut."

"For the hut?"

"Straight trackee. Ah, sahibs!" continued the shikaree, speaking in a low voice and with an air of superstitious terror; "dat animal too wise for dis world; he know too much. I fear him be no elephan' after all, but only de devil, who hab takee elephan' shape. Why he go back there?"

"Ah! why, I wonder," inquired Caspar. "Do you think," added he, "it is in the hope of finding us there? If that's his purpose," he continued, without waiting for a reply, "we shall have no peace so long as he remains alive. We must either kill him, or he will do as much for us."

"Sahibs," observed the Hindoo, with a significant shake of the head, "we no able killee him; that elephan' he nebba die."

"Oh, nonsense, Ossy! If that's what you mean," rejoined Caspar, disdainfully repudiating the superstitious belief of the shikaree; "there is not much doubt of our being able to kill him, if we once get a fair shot; and by my word, the sooner we set about it the better. It's evident, from his having gone back to our hut, that he has some wicked design. Very likely he remembers being first attacked there by Fritz; and as he may be under the belief that the dog has retreated there, he is gone in search of him. Ho, Fritz, old fellow! you needn't be afraid. You can easily get out of his way, whenever you like. Your masters are in more danger than you, my boy."

"You are sure, Ossaroo," said Karl, who had stood for some time silently reflecting, "you are sure he has gone to the hut?"

In reply to this interrogation, Ossaroo would not state positively that he had seen the elephant arrive on the very spot where the hovel stood; but he had followed his track through the belt of heavy timber; and then, having climbed a tree, had descried the great quadruped moving in the direction of the hut. He had no doubt it was for that point he was making, though with what design Ossaroo could not guess—his superstitious dread having hindered him from venturing upon any conjecture.

"One thing is clear," said Karl, after another interval spent in reflection: "it will be no list our attempting to continue the survey we have commenced, until the elephant be got out of the way. What you say, brother Caspar, is quite true. Now that he has become aware of our presence, and has, moreover, been roused to fury by the wounds we have given him, it is not likely he will forget what has passed; and we can hope for neither peace nor safety till we have succeeded in destroying him. There is no reason why we should not set about it at once, but every reason why we should. Our very lives depend upon his destruction; and they will not be safe till that has been accomplished."

"Let us after him at once, then," cried Caspar; "and be our motto, '*Death to the rogue*'!"

Chapter Nineteen.
A home in ruins.

Without further delay, our adventurers took the back track towards the hut, which was exactly that which the elephant had taken—as they could tell by traces of the animal all along the route, which the experienced eye of the shikaree had already discovered, and which he now pointed out to his companions as they passed on. Here and there its great footprints were visible in the turf, in places where the ground was soft; and at other places where no tracks appeared, leaves and twigs freshly strewn upon the earth, and also branches of considerable size broken off from the trees, and borne for some distance before being dropped, clearly indicated to Ossaroo the route which the rogue had taken.

The shikaree had often followed the spoor of wild elephants through the jungles of Bengal, and knew everything about their way of travelling. He was therefore able to tell the others that the rogue had not been browsing as he went—for the leaves and twigs showed no signs of his teeth—but on the contrary, he had moved forward rapidly, and as if with some special determination. The broken branches which they saw were more likely to have been torn off out of spite at the ill-usage he had received, and the disappointment at not having succeeded in his purposes of vengeance.

It did not need for Ossaroo to caution his companions to circumspection. They knew as well as he that an elephant enraged as this one was, whether a *rogue* elephant or an *honest* one, was anything but a safe customer to come in contact with; and that this particular rogue was most particularly angry they had just had both ocular and auricular evidence.

They went forward, therefore, with unusual caution, taking care to keep both their eyes and ears on the alert, and at the same time moving in perfect silence, or conversing only in whispers.

The path upon which they were returning was not that by which they had gone forth. The reconnoissance of the cliffs had carried them a good distance around the edge of the valley; but now they were following the track taken by the elephant, which, as already ascertained by Ossaroo, led almost in a direct line to the hut.

As they drew nearer to their rude habitation, they saw indications that the enemy was still before them. As they knew that in the immediate neighbourhood of the hot-spring, and consequently of the hut itself, there were no large trees or other place of safety to which they might retreat in case of being again attacked, they began to advance with increased caution. From the direction in which they were approaching, the hovel could not be seen until they should get within less than two hundred yards of it. There was a belt of rather tall jungle to be passed through, and then it would be in sight.

Through this jungle they commenced advancing; and there, to their no slight uneasiness, they also observed fresh traces of the elephant. They were now certain that he had passed through it before them, still going direct for the hut.

What on earth can he want there? was the query that once more suggested itself to the minds of all three. It certainly looked as if he had proceeded there in search of *them*! As if, missing them from the scene of the encounter, he believed they had returned home, and was following up their acquaintance.

From what they had observed, they could not help attributing to the great quadruped the possession of an intelligence something more than natural; and this, though it may have been only an absurd fancy on their part, had the effect of begetting within their minds a very painful feeling of apprehension. What they saw on coming out on the other side of the jungle not only strengthened this feeling of apprehension, but increased it all at once to a positive terror.

The hut, which should now have been before their eyes, and at a distance of not quite two hundred paces, *was no longer there*! The ruins of it alone were visible. The large boulders with which its walls had been built, the beams and thatch that had composed its roof, the grass couches upon which they had slept, the rude improvised utensils and other articles which had served them for furniture, were all strewed far and wide over the ground; and not the semblance of a house, or even hovel, remained to show that the spot had been occupied by a human habitation!

Yes—in what had been their rude dwelling our adventurers beheld only a ruder ruin—scarce one stone standing upon, another!

They beheld all this with feelings of fear—ay, something stronger—with awe. The Pagan worshipper of Brahma or Vishnu was no longer alone in his superstitious imaginings. His young Christian companions were almost equally victims to a belief in the supernatural. They comprehended well enough what had caused the destruction of the house. Though the author of that mischief was nowhere to be seen, they knew it was the elephant. There was no alternative but to accept that explanation; and it was not the act itself that was awing them, but the contemplation of the human-like, or rather demon-like, intelligence that had guided the animal thither, and instructed it to this act of retribution, perhaps only preliminary to a still greater one.

Though the work of devastation could not have been completed many minutes before their arrival, the elephant appeared to have gone away from the ground. At east, it was not to be seen anywhere near the spot; and it is needless to say that it was carefully looked for. Dreading its dangerous proximity, they had kept under cover of the bushes while contemplating the ruin from a distance; and it was not until after a considerable interval had elapsed that they ventured forward over the open space to ascertain the full extent of the damage.

This they at length did, and found that it was *total* destruction. So far as the hut was concerned, not a vestige of construction remained—walls and roof had been alike levelled with the ground. But what was a greater source of chagrin to the now homeless plant-hunters, was that their little store of ammunition—the gunpowder, which during all the period of their imprisonment they had been carefully hoarding—was spilled among the rubbish, and of course irrecoverable. It had been deposited in a large gourd-shell prepared for the purpose; and this, among other similar chattels, the enraged quadruped had crushed under its feet. Their cured provisions had also been turned out from their place of deposit, and trampled into the dust of the earth. But this, though also a chagrin, was one of less bitterness. Other provisions might be obtained—not now so easily, since the powder was destroyed—but the latter they could not replace.

Chapter Twenty.
Up a tree again!

They might have remained longer on the ground lamenting this irreparable loss, but that they were still apprehensive of the return of the elephant. Whither had it gone? That was the question which one was addressing to the other, while the eyes of all kept turning in different directions, and with glances that betrayed their uneasiness.

The rogue could not have been off the ground more than a very few minutes: the grass that he had trampled down was still wet with its own sap, crushed out by his ponderous weight. And yet he might have been seen all around for nearly a quarter of a mile's distance. There was no timber within that distance that could have given concealment to an animal so bulky as an elephant?

So thought Karl and Caspar; but Ossaroo was of a different opinion. The bit of jungle through which they had passed would suffice to screen the rogue, said he: adding at the same time a piece of intelligence derived from his shikaree experience: that an elephant, large as it is, can hide in a slight cover with wonderful cunning; that its sagacity enables it to select the best place for concealment; and that, although it neither crouches nor squats, it contrives, by keeping perfectly still—added to the circumstance of its being a shapeless sort of mass—ofttimes to elude the eye of the most vigilant hunter. Though Karl and Caspar could scarcely credit him, Ossaroo expressed his belief, not only that the elephant might be hid in the scant jungle they were talking about, but that it actually *was* there.

Unfortunately for them, Ossaroo's argument was too soon to be supported by facts which left no doubt of its accuracy. As they stood scanning the jungle with keen glances, and with ears acutely bent to catch every sound that might issue from it, a movement was perceptible among the tops of some tall saplings that grew near its centre. In the next moment a brace of the beautiful argus pheasants rose on whirring wing, at the same time giving forth their loud note of alarm.

The birds, forsaking the jungle, in their flight passed over the heads of our adventurers, and by their cries caused such a clangour as to set Fritz off into a prolonged fit of baying.

Whether it was that the enemy had been only lying in ambush, waiting for a good opportunity to charge, or whether the voice of the dog—already known and hated—had been just then heard by the elephant, stirring him to a fresh thirst for vengeance, certain it is, that before a sentence could be exchanged among the terrified trio, the long conical trunk and broad massive shoulders were visible through the scanty jungle; and it was plain to all that the monster was making towards them with that deceptive shamble which, though only a walk, carries the huge quadruped over the ground almost with the speed of a galloping horse.

For a moment our adventurers stood their ground—not, however, with any idea of awaiting the attack or attempting to repel it; but simply because they knew not in what direction to retreat.

So dismayed were they at the sight of the advancing enemy, that it was some seconds before any of the three could suggest a plan that offered a prospect of escape. Rather mechanically than otherwise did Karl and Caspar bring their pieces to the level, with the intention of firing in the face of the foe: for they had but little hope that the lead from their guns, both of light calibre, would stop his impetuous charge. Both fired at the same instant; and then Caspar delivered his second shot; but, just as they had expected, the elephant continued to charge onward.

Fortunately for them, the shikaree had not condescended to draw the string of his bow. Experience had taught him that under such circumstances an arrow was an useless weapon. He might as well have attempted to kick the elephant, or stick a pin into its trunk; either of which proceedings would have damaged the animal nearly as much, and perhaps irritated it a little less, than would one of Ossaroo's arrows. Knowing this, the shikaree, instead of bothering himself with his bow, or wasting time by any thoughts of resistance, had occupied the few seconds left for consideration in a rapid reconnoissance of the neighbourhood—to see if it offered any chance of escape.

To tell the truth, the vicinity appeared rather unpromising. The cliffs offered no ledge upon which they might have climbed out of reach of the rogue, the jungle might have afforded them a temporary shelter; but although it had concealed the elephant from their eyes, it could not long conceal them from the eyes of such a sagacious creature as their antagonist appeared to be. Besides, the elephant was between them and it, and to retreat in that direction would be to run point blank upon its proboscis!

Fortunately in this moment of uncertainty and irresolution a point of safety appeared to the eye of the shikaree, in the shape of a tree—the only one near the spot. It was a tree that had already been instrumental in saving his life: for it was the same that stood by the little straits where Ossaroo had set his nets, and by means of which Caspar had been enabled to hoist him up out of the quicksand.

This tree was a very large one; and standing alone, its branches, free to extend their growth, had spread far out in every direction, almost stretching across the straits.

Ossaroo wasted not the precious moments in idle reflection, but shouting to the young sahibs, and signalling them to follow his example, he struck off towards the tree with all the speed that lay in his legs; and not till he had got up to the third or fourth tier of branches did he look behind him, to see whether his advice had been taken.

The young sahibs had adopted his suggestion with alacrity, without staying a moment to question its propriety; and both were up the tree almost as soon as the shikaree himself.

Chapter Twenty One.
An implacable besieger.

Fritz had retreated with his masters as far as the bottom of the tree; but possessing only canine claws, he was not a climber; and of course could follow them no further. But if he could not ascend the tree, he had no intention of remaining under it—when he saw no chance of avoiding the vengeance of the elephant—and, without pausing for a moment, he plunged into the water, and swam across the straits. Then wading out on the the opposite bank, he scuttled off into a cover of reeds which grew along the shore of the lake, and there concealed himself.

This time the elephant paid no attention to the dog. It was upon the hunters alone that its eyes were fixed; and towards them its vindictive designs were now specially directed. It had been close upon their heels, as they ran over the open ground, and distinctly saw them ascending into the tree. Indeed, so near was it, that both Karl and Caspar were once more obliged to let go their guns, in order that they might have both hands free for climbing. Otherwise they might have been too late to get out of reach, and the least delay on their part might have been fatal to one or both.

Karl was the last to climb up; and just as he lifted his feet from a branch to set them on one higher up, the rogue twisted his trunk around the former, and snapped it in two, as if it had been only a slender reed.

But Karl, with the others, was now beyond his reach; and all three congratulated themselves on once more having escaped from a danger that was nothing short of death itself.

If possible, the elephant was now more enraged than ever. It had not only been a second time baulked in its vengeance, but had received three fresh bullet-wounds; which, though mere scratches upon the skin of its huge cranium, were sore enough to irritate it to an extreme degree. Uttering its shrill, trumpet-like screech, it flourished its proboscis high in the air; and seizing the branches that were within its reach, it snapped them off from the main stem as if they had been tiny twigs.

In a short time the tree, which had been furnished with low-spreading limbs, was completely stripped of these to a height of nearly twenty-feet from the ground; while the space underneath had become strewn with twigs, leaves, and broken branches, crushed into a litter under the broad, ponderous hooves of the mammoth as he kept moving incessantly over them.

Not content with stripping the tree of its branches, the old tusker seized hold of its trunk—lapping his own *trunk* as far as he could around it—and commenced tugging at it, as if he had hopes of being able to drag it up by the roots.

Perceiving after trial that this feat was beyond his power, he relaxed his hold, and then set about another experiment—that of pushing down the tree with his shoulder.

Although he succeeded in causing the tree to tremble, he soon became satisfied that it stood firm enough to resist all his strength, great as it was: and under this conviction he at length desisted from the attempt.

He showed no sign, however, of any intention to leave the ground; but, on the contrary, took his stand under the tree: since the very opposite was the determination which he had formed in his mind.

Although confident that they were in security, our adventurers were anything but exultant. They saw that they were only safe for the time; and, that although their dreaded adversary might after a while withdraw and leave them free to descend, still there could be no security for the future. They had now less hope of being able to destroy this powerful enemy: as they had only one charge left for their guns, and that might not be sufficient to take away his life. The spilling of their powder by the elephant itself seemed like a piece of strategy on his part, leaving them in a sad dilemma.

Inside any house they might build, they would be no better protected against him than on the open ground: for the rogue had proved himself capable of demolishing the strongest walls they might construct; and to be out of his reach, they would be obliged to keep eternally among the tops of the trees, and lead the life of monkeys or squirrels—which would be a very disagreeable kind of existence.

Just then an idea occurred to Caspar that offered them an alternative to this unpleasant prospect of an arboreal life. He bethought him of the cave in which they had killed the bear. It could only be reached by a ladder, and would of course be inaccessible to the elephant. Once out of their present dilemma, they might seek refuge there.

Chapter Twenty Two.
Drawing their drink.

The idea about the cave was a good one, and gave them some little comfort in the midst of their tribulation.

Still, it was not much; for although they would be safe enough while in the cavern, they could not accomplish anything there. The want of light would hinder them from working at the ladders; and while cutting the timber out of which to make them, and every hour that they might be engaged upon them, they would be exposed to the attacks of their implacable enemy.

The prospect was sufficiently discouraging—even with the knowledge that the cave would offer them a safe asylum to which they could retreat whenever pursued.

As the elephant remained comparatively tranquil for a length of time, these thoughts of future operations had engaged their attention. Confident in their present security, they were not troubled by the fear of any immediate danger.

Very soon, however, this confidence began to forsake them. How long were they going to be kept in the tree? That was a question that now presented itself; and as the time passed, became a source of uneasiness.

Though none of them could answer this question, yet all could understand that the siege promised to be a long one—perhaps much longer than that which had so lately been raised: for the rogue, inspired by a rage profound and implacable, exhibited in his sullen look a determination to stand his ground for an indefinite period of time. Seeing this, our adventurers once more became uneasy. Not only was their situation irksome—from the fact of their having to sit astride slender branches—but should the siege be continued, they would be subjected to that danger peculiar to all people besieged—the danger of starvation. Even at the outset all three were as hungry as wolves. They had eaten but a very light breakfast, and nothing since: for they had not found time to cook dinner. It was now late in the afternoon; and should the enemy continue there all night, they would have to go to bed supperless. Ah! to bed indeed. Perhaps there would be neither bed nor sleep that night: for how could they slumber upon those hard branches? Should they lose consciousness for a moment, they would drop off, and tumble down upon their sleepless besieger! Even should they tie themselves in the tree, to go to sleep upon such narrow couches would be out of the question.

Thus, then, they saw no prospect of either supper or sleep for that night. But there was another appetite now annoying them far worse than either hunger or longing for sleep. It was the desire to drink. The rough and varied exercise which they had been compelled to take since starting in the morning—climbing trees, and skulking through pathless jungles—combined with the varied emotions which their repeated perils had called up—all had a tendency to produce thirst; and thirst they now felt in an extreme degree. It was not lessened by the sight of the water shining beneath them. On the contrary, this only increased the craving to an extent that was almost unendurable.

For a considerable time they bore the pain, without any hope of being able to get relieved of it; and with the lake glistening before their eyes under the clear sunlight, and the current gently gliding through the straits underneath, they could realise, in something more than fancy, what must have been the terrible sufferings of poor Tantalus.

After submitting to this infliction for a considerable length of time, an exclamation escaping from Caspar drew upon him the attention of the others.

"Dunder und blitzen!" cried he; "what have we been thinking about all this time? The three of us sitting here choking with thirst, and a river of water within our reach!"

"Within our reach? I wish it were, Caspar," rejoined Karl, in rather a desponding tone.

"Certainly it is within our reach. Look here!"

As Caspar spoke, he held out his copper powder-flask, now nearly empty. Karl did not yet quite comprehend him.

"What is to hinder us from letting this down," he inquired, "and drawing it up again full of water? Nothing. Have you a piece of string about you, Ossy?"

"Yes, sahib, I have," briskly replied the shikaree, at the same time drawing a roll of hempen twist out of the breast of his cotton shirt, and holding it out towards the young hunter.

"Long enough, it is," said Caspar, taking the cord; which the next moment he attached around the neck of the flask. After pouring the powder into his bullet-pouch, he permitted the flask to drop down till it became immersed under the current. Allowing it to remain there, till it had become filled with water, he drew it up again; and with a congratulatory exclamation presented it to Karl, telling him to drink to his heart's content. This injunction Karl obeyed without the slightest reluctance.

The flask was soon emptied; and once more let down and re-filled, and again emptied; and this series of operations was continued, until all were satisfied, and there was no longer a thirsty individual in the top of that tree.

Chapter Twenty Three.
A gigantic syringe.

Having by Caspar's ingenious artifice obtained as much water as they wanted, the besieged felt better able to endure their irksome situation. They were resigning themselves with as much philosophy as they could command to bear it a little longer, when to their great astonishment they were treated to more water than they wanted, and from a source as curious as was unexpected.

Whether the elephant had taken a hint from seeing the flask plunged down into the water, or whether the idea had occurred to it without being suggested by anything in particular, it would be difficult to say. Certain it is, that just after the last flask-full had been pulled up, and before the eddying ripples had subsided from the surface, the rogue was seen to make a rush into the water, at the same time deeply submerging his proboscis, as if about to take a drink.

For some moments he remained in a stationary attitude, apparently filling his capacious stomach with the fluid.

There was no reason why he should not be as thirsty as themselves; and the spectators in the tree had no other thought, than that the great quadruped had waded into the pool simply for the purpose of quenching his thirst.

There was something about his movements, however, and the style in which he had set about sucking up the water, which betrayed a different determination; and it was not long before this was evinced by a performance which, under other circumstances, might have evoked laughter from those who witnessed it. In this instance, however, the spectators were themselves the victims of the joke—if joke it might be termed—and during its continuance, not one of the three felt the slightest inclination to indulge in mirth. It was thus that the elephant acted:—

Having filled its trunk with the water of the stream, it raised it aloft. Then pointing it towards the tree, and even directing it with as much coolness and precision as an astronomer would have used in adjusting his telescope, it sent the fluid in a drenching stream into the faces of the three individuals whom it was holding in siege. All three, who chanced to be sitting close together, were at the same instant, and alike, the victims of this unexpected deluge; and before any of them could have counted half a score, they were wet from head to foot, every rag upon their backs, and fronts too, becoming as thoroughly saturated as if they had been exposed for hours to a drenching rain storm!

But the elephant was not satisfied with giving them a single shower-bath. As soon as its first supply was exhausted, it once more immersed its pliant sucker, re-filled the reservoir, took a good aim, and ejected the fluid into their faces.

In this way the creature continued drawing up the water from the stream, and squirting it from its vast muscular syringe, until it had douched them nearly a dozen times.

Their situation was anything but enviable; for the watery stream, propelled against them with as much force as from the hose-pipe of a fire-engine, almost washed them from their unstable seats; to say nothing of the great discomfort which the douche occasioned them.

It would be difficult to guess what could be the object of the elephant in this curious performance. Perhaps it may have conceived a hope either of driving them out of the tree, or forcibly washing them from the branches; or perhaps it merely designed to make their situation as uncomfortable as possible, and thus to some extent satisfy its spite.

It would be equally difficult to tell how long the performance might have lasted. Perhaps for hours longer—since the supply of water was inexhaustible; but it was brought to a conclusion which neither the great pachyderm himself foresaw, nor they who were the subjects of his aqueous dispensation.

Chapter Twenty Four.
Swallowed wholesale.

Just while it was in the midst of its performance, keeping its *water-battery* in full play, and apparently with malicious enjoyment, it was seen all at once to desist; and then its huge body commenced rocking from side to side, one shoulder now upheaving, then the other, while the long trunk was swept in circles through the air, at the same time emitting, instead of water, shrill sounds that proclaimed either pain or terror.

What could it mean? The quadruped was evidently smitten with some sudden fear; but who and what was the enemy it dreaded? So mentally inquired Karl and Caspar; but before either had time to shape his thought into an interrogative speech, the shikaree had answered it.

"He-ho!" he exclaimed. "Goot! vair goot!—praise to the God of the Great Gangee! See, sahibs, the rogue he go down, down—he sinkee in de quicksand that near swalley Ossaroo; he-ho; sinkee! he sinkee!"

Karl and Caspar easily comprehended the meaning of Ossaroo's broken but exultant speeches. Bending their eyes on the brute below, and watching its movements, they at once perceived that the shikaree had spoken the truth. The elephant was evidently sinking in the quicksand!

They had noticed that when it first entered the bed of the stream, the water had not reached far above its knees. Now it was up to its sides, and slowly but gradually rising higher. Its violent struggles, moreover—the partial and alternate raising of its shoulders, its excited shrieks—and the proboscis, rapidly extended now to this side, now to that, as if searching to grasp some support—all proved the truth of Ossaroo's assertion—the rogue was sinking in the quicksand. And rapidly was the creature going down. Before the spectators had been watching it five minutes, the water lapped up nearly to the level of its back, and then inch by inch, and foot by foot, it rose higher, until the round shoulders were submerged, and only the head and its long trumpet-like extension appeared above the surface.

Soon the shoulders ceased to play; and the vast body exhibited no other motion, save that gentle descent by which it was being drawn down into the bowels of the earth!

The trunk still kept up its vibratory movement, now violently beating the water into foam, and now feebly oscillating, all the while breathing forth its accents of agony.

At length the upturned head and smooth protuberant jaws sank beneath the surface; and only the proboscis appeared, standing erect out of the water like a gigantic Bologna sausage. It had ceased to give out the shrill trumpet scream; but a loud breathing could still be heard, interrupted at intervals by a gurgling sound.

Karl and Caspar kept their seats upon the tree, looking down upon the strange scene with feelings of awe depicted in their faces. Not so the shikaree, who was no longer aloft. As soon as he had seen the elephant fairly locked in the deadly embrace of that quicksand that had so nearly engulfed his own precious person, he lowered himself nimbly down from the branches.

For some moments he stood upon the bank, watching the futile efforts which the animal was making to free itself, all the while talking to it, and taunting it with spiteful speeches—for Ossaroo had been particularly indignant at the loss of his skirt. When at length the last twelve inches of the elephant's trunk was all that remained above the surface, the shikaree could hold back no longer. Drawing his long knife, he rushed out into the water; and, with one clean cut, severed the muscular mass from its supporting stem, as a sickle would have levelled some soft succulent weed.

The parted tube sank instantly to the bottom; a few red bubbles rose to the surface; and these were the last tokens that proclaimed the exit of that great elephant from the surface of the earth. It had gone down into the deep sands, there to become fossilised—perhaps after the lapse of many ages to be turned up again by the spade and pick-axe of some wondering quarry-man.

Thus by a singular accident were our adventurers disembarrassed of a disagreeable neighbour—or rather, a dangerous enemy—so dangerous, indeed, that had not some chance of the kind turned up in their favour, it is difficult to conjecture how they would have got rid of it. It was no longer a question of pouring bullets into its body, and killing it in that way. The spilling of their powder had spoiled that project; and the three charges that still remained to them might not have been sufficient with guns of so small a calibre as theirs.

No doubt in time such gallant hunters as Caspar and Ossaroo, and so ingenious a contriver as Karl, would have devised some way to circumvent the rogue, and make an end of him; but for all that they were very well pleased at the strange circumstance that had relieved them of the necessity, and they congratulated themselves on such a fortunate result.

On hearing them talking together, and perceiving that they were no longer in the tree, Fritz, who had all this while been skulking only a few paces from the spot, now emerged from his hiding-place, and came running up. Little did Fritz suspect, while swimming across the straits to rejoin his masters, that the huge quadruped which had so frequently given him chase was at that moment so very near him; and that his own claws, while cutting the water, came within an inch of scratching that terrible trunk, now *truncated* to a *frustrum* of its former self!

But although Fritz had no knowledge of strange incident that had occurred during his absence—and may have been wondering in what direction the enemy had gone off—while swimming across the straits, the red colour of the water at a particular place, or more likely the scent of blood upon it, admonished him that some sanguinary scene had transpired; and drew from him a series of excited yelps as he buoyantly breasted the wave.

Fritz came in for a share of the congratulations. Although the faithful creature had retreated on each occasion of his being attacked, no one thought of casting a slur upon his canine courage. He had only exhibited a wise discretion: for what chance would he have stood against such a formidable adversary? He had done better, therefore, by taking to his heels; for had he foolishly stood his ground, and got killed in the first encounter by the obelisk, the elephant might still have been alive, and besieging them in the tree. Besides, it was Fritz who had sounded the first note of warning, and thus given time to prepare for the reception of the assailant.

All of the party regarded Fritz as worthy of reward; and Ossaroo had made up his mind that he should have it, in the shape of a dinner upon elephant's trunk. But in wading back into the stream, the shikaree perceived to his chagrin that the brave dog must be disappointed: since the piece which he had so skilfully lopped off, had followed the fortunes of the part from which it had been severed, and was now far below the surface of the sand!

Ossaroo made no attempt to dig it up again. He had a wholesome dread of that treacherous footing; and treading it gingerly, he lost no time in returning to the bank, and following the sahibs—who had already taken their departure from the water's edge, and were proceeding in the direction of the ruined hut.

Chapter Twenty Five.
The deodar.

The idea that had occurred to them—of making the cave their home—was no longer deemed worthy of being entertained. The dangerous proximity of the elephant had alone suggested it; and this no longer existed. It was not likely that there was another *rogue* in the valley. Indeed, Ossaroo was able to set their minds at rest on this point—assuring them that two animals of the kind are never found occupying the same district: since two creatures of such malignant dispositions would certainly enact the tragedy of the Kilkenny cats—though Ossaroo did not illustrate his meaning by quoting this celebrated expression.

Possibly there might be other animals in the neighbourhood as much to be dreaded as the elephant had been. There might be panthers, or leopards, or tigers, or even another bear; but against any of these the cave would be no safe asylum—not safer than their old hut. They could reconstruct it more strongly than ever; and put a stout door upon it to keep out any midnight intruder; and to this work did they apply themselves as soon as they had eaten dinner, and dried their garments—so thoroughly saturated by the colossal syringe of the defunct elephant.

Several days were spent in restoring the hovel—this time with considerable improvements. The winter weather had now fairly set in; and household warmth had become an important object: so that not only did they fill up the chinks with a thick coating of clay, but a fireplace and chimney were constructed, and a strong door was added.

They knew that it would take them a long time to make the ladders—more than a dozen long ladders—each of which must be light as a reed and straight as an arrow.

During the milder days of winter they might work in the open air; indeed, the greater part of their work they must needs do outside the hut. Still it would be necessary to have shelter not only during the nights, but in times of storm and severe weather.

Prudence therefore counselled them to providence; and before proceeding farther with their design of scaling the cliff, they made all snug within doors.

They had no fear of suffering from the winter's cold—either for want of clothing by day, or covering by night. Some of the yâk-skins were still in good preservation—with the pelts of several other animals that had fallen before the double-barrel of Caspar—and these would suffice for warm clothing by day and bed-covering by night.

About their winter's food they were a little more anxious. The elephant had succeeded not only in destroying their means of obtaining provisions, but had also damaged the stock which was on hand, by trampling it in the mud. Those portions of the dried venison and yâk-beef that the brute had not succeeded in completely spoiling, were once more collected, and stored in a safe place; while it was resolved, in the event of their not being able to procure more, that they should go on rations proportioned to the time which they might have to continue in their rock-bound prison. Of course, though their ammunition was exhausted, they were not without hopes of being able to add to their store of provisions. The arrows of Ossaroo still existed, independent of either powder or lead. Snares and traps would enable them to capture many of the wild creatures that, like themselves, appeared to have found a prison in that secluded and singular valley.

When all the arrangements regarding their winter residence were completed, they returned once more to the survey of the cliffs, which had been interrupted by the elephant.

After a prolonged examination of the ledges, that had been discovered on that eventful day, they continued on until they had made the circuit of the valley. Not a foot of the precipice was passed without the most elaborate inspection being bestowed upon it; and of course the twin cliffs which hemmed in the gorge of the glacier were examined with the rest.

There proved to be no place offering such advantages for an ascent by ladders as that already discovered; and although there was no positive certainty that they might be able to accomplish their formidable task, they determined to make a trial, and without further delay set about preparing the ladders.

The preliminary step was to select and cut down a sufficient quantity of timber of the right length. They were about to have recourse to the beautiful Thibet pine—the sort which had served them for bridging the crevasse—when a new tree was discovered by them, equally beautiful, and more suitable for their purpose. It was the cedar (*Pinus deodara*). Ossaroo once more lamented the absence of his beloved bamboos—alleging that with a sufficient number of these he could have made ladders enough for scaling the cliff, in less than a quarter of the time it would take to construct them out of the pines. This was no exaggeration: for the culm of the great bamboo, just as it is cut out of the brake, serves for the side of a ladder, without any pains taken with it, further than to notch out the holes in which to insert the rounds. Moreover, the bamboo being light, would have served better than any other timber for such ladders as they required—enabling them with less trouble to get them hoisted up to the ledges—an operation in which they apprehended no little difficulty. But although there was a species of cane growing in the valley—that known to the hill people as the "ringall"—its culms were neither of sufficient length nor thickness for their purpose. It was the great bamboo of the tropical jungles that Ossaroo sighed for; and which on their way up through the lower ranges of the Himalayas they had seen growing in vast brakes, its tall stems often rising to the height of a hundred feet.

The deodar, under favourable circumstances, attains to vast dimensions, trunks being often met with in the mountains upwards of ten feet in diameter, and rising to the height of one hundred feet. A few sticks of this description would have made their labour both short and easy.

Failing the bamboo, therefore, they selected the second best material which the forest afforded them—the tall "deodar." This tree, which is known to the Anglo-Indian residents of the Himalayan countries as the "cedar," has long since been introduced into English parks and arboretums, under the name of *deodara*—its specific botanical appellation. It is a true pine and is found in most of the hills and valleys of the Himalayan chain, growing at almost any elevation and on any kind of ground—in the low warm valleys, as well as near the line of everlasting snow. Its favourite habitat, however, is on the lower hills, and though by no means a beautiful tree, it is valuable on account of the great quantity of tar which can be extracted from its sap.

Where many deodar trees are growing together, they shoot up in long tapering shafts, with short branches, and present the acute conical form characteristic of the pines. When individual trees stand singly, or at some considerable distance apart, their habit is different. They then stretch out long massive arms in a horizontal direction; and as the separate twigs and leaves also extend horizontally, each branch thus presents a surface as level as a table. The deodar often reaches the height of one hundred feet.

The wood of the deodar is everywhere esteemed throughout the countries where it is found. It is excellent for building purposes, easily worked, almost imperishable, and can be readily split into planks—an indispensable requisite in a country where saws are almost unknown. In

Cashmere, bridges are built of it: and the long time that some of these have been standing, affords a proof of its great durability. A portion of these bridges are under water for more than half the year; and although there are some of them nearly a hundred years old, they are still in good preservation, and safe enough to be crossed.

When the deodar is subjected to the process by which tar is extracted from other pines, it yields a much thinner liquid than tar—of a dark red colour, and very pungent smell. This liquid is known as "cedar oil;" and is used by the hill people as a remedy for skin diseases—as also for all scrofulous complaints in cattle.

The deodar is of very slow growth; and this unfits it for being introduced into European countries—except as an ornamental timber for parks and pleasure grounds.

It was chiefly on account of its property of being easily split into planks, or pieces of light scantling, that the deodar was selected for making the sides of the ladders. To have cut down the trunks of heavy trees to the proper thickness for light ladders—with such imperfect implements as they were possessed of—would have been an interminable work for our inexperienced carpenters. The little axe of Ossaroo and the knives were the only tools they possessed available for the work. As the deodar could be split with wedges, it was just the timber wanted under these circumstances.

While engaged in "prospecting" among the deodar trees, a pine of another species came under the observation of our adventurers. It was that known as the "cheel."

It might have been seen by them without attracting any particular notice, but for Karl; who, upon examining its leaves, and submitting them to a botanical test, discovered that within the body of the "cheel" there existed qualities that, in the circumstances in which they were placed, would be of great value to them. Karl knew that the "cheel" was one of those pines, the wood of which, being full of turpentine, make most excellent torches; and he had read, that for this very purpose it is used by all classes of people who dwell among the Himalaya mountains, and who find in these torches a very capital substitute for candles or lamps. Karl could also have told his companions, that the turpentine itself—which oozes out of the living tree—is used by the people as an ointment for sores—and that for chapped hands it is a speedy and effectual cure. The "cheel" pine is nearly always found side by side with the deodar—especially where the latter forms the chief growth of the forest.

Karl could also have informed them that the deodar and the cheel are not, the only pines indigenous to the Himalayas. He could have mentioned several other species, as the "morenda," a large and handsome tree, with very dark foliage, and one of the tallest of the *coniferae*—often rising to the stupendous height of two hundred feet; the "rye" pine, of almost equal height with the morenda, and perhaps even more ornamental; and the "Kolin," or common pine, which forms extensive forests, upon the ridges that rise from six to nine thousand feet above sea-level. The last thrives best in a dry, rocky soil and it is surprising in what places it will take root and grow. In the perpendicular face of a smooth granite rock, large trees of this species may be seen. In the rock there exists a little crevice. Into this a seed in some manner finds its way, vegetates, and in time becomes a great tree—flourishing perhaps for centuries, where, to all appearance, there is not a particle of soil to nourish it, and probably deriving sustenance from the rock itself!

It was with no slight gratification that Karl beheld the "cheel" growing so near. He knew that from it they would obtain brilliant torches—as many as they might stand in need of; so that during the dark nights, instead of sitting idle for the want of light, they could occupy themselves till a late hour within the hovel, in making the "rounds" of the ladders, and doing such other little "chores" as the occasion might require.

Chapter Twenty Six.
The scaling ladders.

The cutting down of the trees did not occupy them a very long time. They chose only those of slender girth—the more slender the better, so long as they answered the requirements as to length. Trees of about fifty feet in total height were the best: as these, when the weaker part of the tops was cut off, yielded lengths of thirty or more feet. Where they were only a few inches in diameter, there was very little trouble in reducing them to the proper size for the sides of the ladders—only to strip off the bark and split them in twain.

Making the rounds was also an easy operation—except that it required considerable time, as there were so many of them.

The most difficult part of the work—and this they had foreseen—would be the drilling of the holes to receive the rounds; and it was the task which proved the most dilatory—taking up more time in its accomplishment than both the cutting of the timber, and reducing it to its proper shapes and dimensions.

Had they owned an auger or a mortising chisel, or even a good gimlet, the thing would have been easy enough. Easier still had they possessed a "breast bit." But of course not any of these tools could be obtained; nor any other by which a hole might be bored big enough to have admitted the points of their little fingers. Hundreds of holes would be needed; and how were they to be made? With the blades of their small knives it would have been possible to scoop out a cavity—that is, with much trouble and waste of time; but vast time and trouble would it take to scoop out four hundred; and at least that number would be needed. It would be a tedious task and almost interminable, even supposing that it could be accomplished; but this was doubtful enough. The blades of the knives might be worn or broken, long before the necessary number of holes could be made.

Of course, had they been possessed of a sufficient number of nails, they might have done without holes. The steps of the ladders could have been nailed upon the sides, instead of being mortised into them. But nails were a commodity quite as scarce with them as tools. With the exception of those in the soles of their shoes, or the stocks of their guns, there was not a nail in the valley.

It is not to be denied that they were in a dilemma. But Karl had foreseen this difficulty, and provided against it before a stick of timber had been cut. Indeed, close following on the first conception of the scaling ladders, this matter had passed through his mind, and had been settled to his satisfaction. Only theoretically, it is true; but his theory was afterwards reduced to practice; and, unlike many other theories, the practice proved in correspondence with it.

Karl's theory was to make the holes by fire—in other words, to bore them with a red-hot iron.

Where was this iron to be obtained? That appeared to offer a difficulty, as great as the absence of an auger or a mortise-chisel. But by Karl's ingenuity it was also got over. He chanced to have a small pocket pistol: it was single-barrelled, the barrel being about six inches in length, without any thimbles, beading, or ramrod attached to it. What Karl intended to do, then, was to heat this barrel red-hot, and make a boring-iron of it. And this was exactly what he *did* do; and after heating it some hundreds of times, and applying it as often to the sides of the different ladders, he at last succeeded in burning out as many holes as there were rounds to go into them, multiplied exactly by two.

It is needless to say that this wonderful boring operation was not accomplished at a single "spell," nor yet in a single day. On the contrary, it took Karl many an hour and many a day, and cost him many a wet skin— by perspiration, I mean—before he had completed the boring of those four hundred holes. Numerous were the tears drawn from the eyes of the plant-hunter—not by grief, but by the smoke of the seething cedar wood.

When Karl had finished the peculiar task he had thus assigned to himself, but little more remained to be done—only to set each pair of sides together, stick in the rounds, bind fast at each end, and there was a ladder finished and ready to be scaled.

One by one they were thus turned off; and one by one earned to the foot of the cliff, up which the ascent was to be *attempted*.

Sad are we to say that it was still only an attempt; and sadder yet that that attempt proved a failure.

One by one were the ladders raised to their respective ledges—until three-fourths of the cliff had been successfully scaled. Here, alas! was their climbing brought to a conclusion, by a circumstance up to this time unforeseen. On reaching one of the ledges—the fourth from the top of the cliff—they found, to their chagrin, that the rock above it, instead of receding a little, as with all the others, *hung over*—projecting several inches beyond the outer line of the ledge. Against that rock no ladder could have been set; none would have rested there—since it could not be placed even perpendicularly. There was no attempt made to take one up. Though the projection could not be discerned from below, Karl, standing on the topmost round of the last ladder that had been planted, saw at once, with the eye of an engineer, that the difficulty was insurmountable. It would be as easy for them to fly, is to stand a ladder upon that ill-starred ledge; and with this conviction fully impressed upon his mind, the young plant-hunter returned slowly and sorrowfully to the ground to communicate the disagreeable intelligence to his companions.

It was no use for either Caspar or Ossaroo to go up again. They had been on the ledge already; and had arrived at the same conviction. Karl's report was final and conclusive.

All their ingenuity defeated—all their toil gone for nothing—their time wasted—their hopes blighted—the bright sky of their future once more obscured with darkest clouds—all through that unforeseen circumstance.

Just as when they returned out of the cavern—after that patient but fruitless search—just as then, sate they down upon the rocks—each staggering to that which was nearest him—sad, dispirited, forlorn.

There sate they, with eyes now fixed upon the ground, now turning towards the cliff and gazing mechanically upon that serried line, like the stairway of some gigantic spider—those long ladders, planted with so much pains, climbed only once, and never to be climbed again!

Chapter Twenty Seven.
An empty larder.

Long sat they in this attitude, all three, observing a profound silence. The air was keenly cold, for it was now mid-winter, but none of them seemed to feel the cold. The deep disappointment, the bitter chagrin that filled their minds, hindered them from perceiving bodily pain; and at that moment had an avalanche threatened to slide down upon them from the snowy summit above, not one of the three would have much cared to escape out of its way.

So tired had they become of their aerial prison—so terrified by the prospect of its continuing for ever—or at least as long as they might live—they could have contemplated even death without additional terror.

The straw, to which they had so long and so fondly clung, was snatched from their grasp. Again were they drowning.

For nearly an hour sat they thus, moody and desponding. The purple-coloured tints, that began to play over the surface of the eternal snows above, admonished them that the sun was far down in the heavens, and that night was approaching.

Karl was the first to become conscious of this—the first to break silence.

"Oh, brothers!" said he, under the impress of their common misfortune including Ossaroo in the fraternal appellation. "Come away! It is useless to stay longer here. Let us go home!"

"Home!" repeated Caspar, with a melancholy smile. "Ah! Karl, I wish you had not spoken the word. So sweet at other times, it now rings in my ears like some unearthly echo. Home, indeed! Alas, dear brother! we shall ne'er go home."

To this pathetic speech Karl made no reply. He could offer no word of hope or consolation; and therefore remained silent. He had already risen to his feet—the others following his example—and all three walked moodily away from the spot, taking the most direct route towards their rude dwelling, which now more than ever they had reason to regard as their *home*.

On reaching the hut they found still another cause of inquietude. Their stock of provisions, which had survived the destructive onset of the elephant, had been economised with great care. But as they had been too busy in making the ladders to waste time on any other species of industry, nothing had been added to the larder—neither fish, flesh, nor fowl. On the contrary, it had dwindled down, until upon that clay when they issued forth to try their ladders against the cliff, they had left behind them only a single piece of dried yâk-beef—about enough to have furnished them with a single meal.

Hungry after the day's fruitless exertion, they were contemplating a supper upon it, and not without some degree of pleasant anticipation: for nature under all circumstances will assert her rights, and the cravings of appetite are not to be stifled even by the most anguished suffering of the spirit.

As they drew nearer to the hut, but more especially when they came in sight of it, and perceived its rude but hospitable doorway open to receive them—as from the chill atmosphere through which they were passing they beheld its sheltering roof of thatch, and thought of its snug, cosy interior— as, keenly experiencing the pangs both of cold and hunger, they beheld in fancy a bright faggot fire crackling upon the hearth, and heard the yâk-beef hissing and sputtering in the blaze, their spirits began to return to their natural condition, and if not actual joy, something that very much resembled cheerfulness might have been observed in the demeanour of all.

It is ever thus with the mind of man, and perhaps fortunate that it is so. The human soul finds its type in the sky—cloud and sunshine, sunshine and cloud.

With our adventurers the dark cloud had for the moment passed; and a gleam of light was once more shining upon their hearts.

It was not destined to shine long. A light had been struck, and a fire kindled that soon blazed brightly. So far one desire had been satisfied. They could warm themselves. But when they came to think of gratifying an appetite of a far more craving character—when they essayed to search for that piece of yâk flesh that was to furnish forth their supper—they found it not!

During their absence, the burglar had also been abroad. Their larder had been assailed. The *hung* beef was hanging there no longer.

Some wild animal—wolf, panther, or other predatory creature—had entered by the open doorway,—left open in the excitement of that hopeful departure—found open upon their return—but, like the door of that oft-quoted stable, not worth shutting, since the steed had been stolen.

Not a morsel, not a mouthful remained—either of yâk-beef or food of any other kind—and all three, Fritz making the fourth, had to go supperless to sleep.

Chapter Twenty Eight.
Going abroad for breakfast.

The exertions which they had made in carrying and erecting the ladders had so wearied them, that, despite their empty stomachs, all three were able to sleep. Their slumber, however, was neither profound nor prolonged; and one and another of them awoke at intervals during the night and lay awake, reflecting upon the miserable fate that had befallen them, and the poor prospects now before them.

They were even without the ordinary consolation of knowing that they might find something to eat in the morning. Before they could have any breakfast, they knew they would first have to find it in the forest. They would have to search, find, and kill, before they could eat.

But they had reason now not only to be in doubt about procuring their breakfast, but their dinner and supper—in short, their whole future subsistence. Circumstances had become changed. The larder, hitherto amply provided by Caspar's hunting skill, was now quite empty; and although he could soon have replenished it had their ammunition not been destroyed, it was now quite a different thing. Caspar's power was gone along with his powder; and the deer and other quadrupeds, which were known to be yet numerous in the valley—to say nothing of the winged creatures that frequented it, could now smile at any attempt on the part of Caspar to trouble them any longer with his double-barrelled detonator. The gun would hereafter be as useless as a bar of iron.

Only one charge of powder for each barrel remained, and one more for Karl's rifle. When these three should be fired off, not another shot might ever again be heard ringing through that silent valley, and waking the echoes of the surrounding cliffs.

But it had not yet entered their minds that they might be unable to kill any of the wild animals with which the place abounded. Had they thought so, they would have been unhappy indeed—perhaps so anxious as not to have slept another wink for that night. But they did not yet contemplate the future so despondingly. They hoped that, even without their guns, they would still be enabled to procure sufficient game for their support; and as they all lay awake, just before the breaking of the day, this became the subject of their conversation.

Ossaroo still felt full confidence in his bow and arrows; and should these fail, there was his fishing-net; and if that also were to draw blank, the experienced shikaree knew a score of other schemes for circumventing the beasts of the earth, the birds of the air, and the finny denizens of the water. Karl expressed his determination, as soon as spring should return, to commence cultivating certain edible roots and plants, which grew rather sparsely around, but, by the careful propagation of which, a crop might be procured of sufficient abundance. Moreover, they resolved that in the following year they should store up such wild fruits and berries as were fit for food; and thus insure themselves against any chance of famine for months to come. The failure of their late attempt with the ladders had reproduced within them the firm though fearful conviction, that for the rest of their lives they were destined to dwell within the mountain valley—never more to go beyond the bounds of that stupendous prison-like wall that encircled them.

With this impression now freshly stamped upon their minds, they returned to speculate on the means of present existence, as also on that of their more immediate future; and in this way did they pass the last hour of the night—that which was succeeded by the daybreak.

As the first streaks of dawning day appeared upon the snowy summits— several of which were visible from the door of the hut—all three might have been seen outside preparing themselves for the execution of some important design. Their purpose might easily be told from the character of their preparations. Caspar was charging his double-barrelled gun; and carefully too—for it was the "last shot in his locker."

Karl was similarly employed with his rifle, while Ossaroo was arming himself in his peculiar fashion, looking to the string of his bow, and filling the little wicker bag, that constituted his quiver, with sharp-pointed arrows.

From this it was evident that the chase was the occupation immediately intended, and that all three were about to engage in it. In truth, they were going out in search of something for their breakfast; and if a keen appetite could ensure success, they could scarce fail in procuring it: for they were all three as hungry as wolves.

Fritz, too, was as hungry as any of them; and looked as if he meant to do his best in helping them to procure the material for a meal. Any creature, beast or bird, that should be so unfortunate as to come within clutching distance of his gaunt jaws, would have but little chance on that particular morning of escaping from them.

It had been resolved upon that they should go in different directions: as by that means there would be three chances of finding game instead of one; and as something was wanted for breakfast, the sooner it could be procured the better. If Ossaroo should succeed in killing anything with his arrows, he was to give a shrill whistle to call the others back to the hut; while if either of them should fire, of course the shot would be heard, and that would be the signal for all to return.

With this understanding, and after some little badinage about who would be the successful caterer, they all set forth, Caspar going to the right, Ossaroo to the left, and Karl, followed by Fritz, taking the centre.

Chapter Twenty Nine.
Caspar on a stalk.

In a few minutes the three hunters had lost sight of one another, Karl and Caspar proceeding round the lake by opposite sides, but both keeping under cover of the bushes; while Ossaroo wended his way along the bottom of the cliff—thinking he might have a better chance in that direction.

The game which Caspar expected first might fall in his way was the "kakur," or barking-deer. These little animals appeared to be more numerous in the valley than any other creatures. Caspar had scarcely ever been abroad upon a shooting excursion without seeing one; and on several occasions a kakur had constituted his whole "bag." He had learnt an ingenious way of bringing them within range of his gun—simply by placing himself in ambush and imitating their call; which, as may be deduced from one of their common names, is a sort of bark. It is a sound very much resembling the bark of a fox, only that it is much louder. This the kakur sends forth, whenever it suspects the presence of an enemy in its neighbourhood; and keeps repeating it at short intervals, until it believes either that the danger has been withdrawn, or withdraws itself from the danger.

The simple little ruminant does not seem to be aware that this sound— perhaps intended as a note of warning to its companions—too often becomes its own death-signal, by betraying its whereabouts to the sportsman or other deadly enemy. Not only the hunter, man, but the tiger, the leopard, the cheetah, and other predatory creatures, take advantage of this foolish habit of the barking-deer; and stealing upon it unawares, make it their victim.

The bark is very easily imitated by the human voice; and after a single lesson, with Ossaroo as instructor, not only could Caspar do the decoy to a nicety, but even Karl, who only overheard the shikaree instructing his pupil, was able to produce a sound precisely similar.

Present hunger prompted Caspar to go in search of the kakur, as that would be the game most likely to turn up first. There were other quadrupeds, and some birds too, whose flesh would have served better, as being of superior delicacy: for the venison of the barking-deer is none of the sweetest. In the autumn it is not bad—nor up to a late period in the winter—though it is never very delicious at any season.

On that morning, however, Caspar was not at all fastidious; and he knew that neither were the others—hunger having robbed them of all delicacy of appetite. Even kakur venison would be palatable enough, could he procure it; and for this purpose was he going in a particular direction, and not wandering hither and thither, as sportsmen usually do when in search of game.

He knew of a spot where kakur were almost sure of being found. It was a pretty glade, surrounded by thick evergreen shrubbery—not far from the edge of the lake, and on the side opposite to that where the hut was built.

Caspar had never entered this glade—and he had gone through it several times—without seeing kakur browsing upon the grassy turf, or lying in the shade of the bushes that grew around its edge. It was but fair to presume, therefore, that on that morning, as upon others, the glade would furnish him with this species of game.

Without making stop anywhere else, he walked on till he had got within a few rods of the spot where he expected to procure the materials of the breakfast; and then, entering among the underwood, he advanced more slowly and with greater caution. To ensure success, he even dropped upon his knees, and crawled cat-like, using his arms as forelegs and his hands as paws! After this fashion he worked his way forward to the edge of the opening—all the while keeping a thick leafy bush before his body to screen himself from the eyes of any creature—kakur or other animal—that might be within the glade.

On getting close up behind the bush, he came to a halt; and then, cautiously raising his shoulders, he peeped through between the leafy branches.

It took him some seconds of time to survey the whole surface of the glade; but when he had finished his scrutiny, a shadow of disappointment might have been seen passing over his countenance. There was no game there—neither kakur nor animals of any other kind.

Not without a certain feeling of chagrin did the young hunter perceive that the opening was empty: for, to say nothing of the annoyance he felt on not being able to procure a joint of venison for breakfast, he had been flattering himself that, from his superior knowledge of the ground, he would be the first to find the material for their matutinal meal—about which he had some little feeling of hunter-pride and rivalry.

He did not permit this preliminary disappointment to rob him of all hope. If there were no kakur within the glade, there might be some in the bushes near its edge; and perhaps, by adopting the decoy he had several times already practised—that of imitating their call—he might entice one out into the open ground.

Acting upon this idea, he squatted close behind the bush, and commenced barking, as near as he could, *à la kakur*.

Chapter Thirty.
The double decoy.

It was some considerable time before he heard any response to cheer him, or observed any sign that indicated the presence or proximity of an animal.

He repeated his bark many times, with intervals of silence between— and was about yielding to the conviction, that not only the open ground, but the bushes around it, were going to draw blank.

He had uttered his last bark, with all the alluring intonation that he could throw into the sound; and was about starting to his feet to proceed elsewhere, when just then the real cry of the kakur responded to his feigned one—apparently coming from out the thicket on the opposite side of the glade.

The sound was heard only faintly, as if the animal was at a great distance off; but Caspar knew that if it was a response to his call—which he believed it to be—it would soon draw nearer. He lost no time, therefore, in giving utterance to a fresh series of barks of the most seductive character; and then once more strained his ears to listen for the reply.

Again the barks of the kakur came back upon the breeze—repeated serially, and so resembling his own, that had Caspar not known that they proceeded from the throat of a deer, he might have fancied them to be echoes. He did not allow many seconds to elapse before barking again, and again, with an equal straining at allurement.

This time, to the surprise of the young hunter, there was no response. He listened, but not a sound came back—not even an echo.

He barked again, and again listened. As before, silence profound, unbroken.

No—it was not unbroken. Although it was not the call of the kakur, another sound interrupted the stillness—a sound equally welcome to the ear of the young hunter. It was a rustling among the leaves on the opposite side of the glade; just such as might indicate the passage of an animal through the bushes.

Directing his eye towards the spot where the sound appeared to proceed, Caspar saw, or fancied he saw, some twigs in motion. But it was no fancy: for the moment after he not only saw the twigs move, but behind the bush to which they belonged he could just make out a darkish-coloured object. It could be nothing else than the body of the kakur. Although it was very near—for the glade was scarce twenty yards across, and the deer was directly behind the line of low shrubs which formed a sort of selvedge around it—Caspar could not get a good view of the animal. It was well screened by the foliage, and better perhaps by the absence of a bright light: for it was yet only the grey twilight of morning. There was light enough, however, to take aim; and as the intervening branches were only tiny twigs, Caspar had no fear that they would interfere with the direction of his ballet. There was no reason, therefore, why he should delay longer. He might not get a better chance; and if he waited longer, or barked again, the kakur might discover the decoy, and run back into the bushes.

"Here goes, then!" muttered Caspar to himself; at the same time placing himself firmly on one knee, raising his gun and cocking it.

It was a splendid lock—that upon the right-hand barrel of Caspar's gun—one in which the cock, on being drawn to the full, gives tongue to tell that the spring is in perfect order.

In the profound stillness of the morning-air the "click" sounded clear enough to have been heard across the glade, and much further. Caspar even feared that it might be loud enough to affright the deer; and kept his eye fixed upon the latter as he drew back the cock. The animal stirred not; but instead—almost simultaneous with the click of his gun, and as if it had been its echo—another click fell upon the hunter's ear, apparently coming from the spot on which the kakur was standing!

Fortunate was it for Caspar that his own spring had clicked so clear— and fortunate also he had heard that apparent echo—else he might either have shot his brother, or his brother him, or each might have shot the other!

As it was, the second click caused Caspar to start to his feet. Karl at the same instant was seen hurriedly rising erect upon the opposite side of the glade, while both with cocked guns in their hands stood eyeing each other, like two individuals about to engage in a deadly duel of rifles!

Had any one seen them at that moment, and in that attitude, their wild looks would have given colour to the supposition that such was in reality their intent; and some time would have elapsed before any action on the part of either would have contradicted this fearful belief: for it was several seconds before either could find speech to express their mutual surprise.

It was something more than surprise—it was awe—a deep tragical emotion of indefinable terror, gradually giving way to a feeling of heartfelt thankfulness, at the fortunate chance that had made them aware of each other's presence, and saved them from a mutual fratricide.

For some seconds I have said not a word was spoken; and then only short exclamations of similar import came trembling from the lips of both. Both, as if acting under a common impulse, flung their guns to the ground. Then, rushing across the glade, they threw their arms around each other; and remained for some moments locked in a brotherly embrace.

No explanation was needed by either. Karl, after passing round the lake by the other side, had strayed by chance in the direction of the glade. On nearing it, he had heard the barking of a kakur—not dreaming that it was Caspar acting as a decoy. He had answered the signal; and finding that the kakur still kept its place, he had advanced toward the opening with the intention of stalking it. On getting nearer he had ceased to utter the call, under the belief that he should find the deer out in the open ground. Just as he arrived by its edge, Caspar was mimicking the kakur in such an admirable manner, and so energetically, that Karl could neither fail to be deceived as to the character of the animal, nor remain ignorant of its position. The darkish disc visible behind the evergreen leaves could be no other than the body of the deer; and Karl was just about cocking his rifle, to bore it with a bullet, when the click of Caspar's double-barrel sounding ominously in his ear, fortunately conducted to a far different *dénouement* than that fatal *finale* which was so near having occurred.

Chapter Thirty One.
The signal of the Shikaree.

As if sent to cheer and distract their minds from the feeling of dread awe which still held possession of them, just then the shrill whistle of Ossaroo came pealing across the lake, reverberating in echoes from the cliff toward which he had gone. Shortly after the signal sounded again in a slightly different direction—showing that the shikaree had succeeded in bagging his game, and was returning towards the hut.

On hearing the signal, Karl and Caspar regarded each other with glances of peculiar significance.

"So, brother," said Caspar, smiling oddly as he spoke, "you see Ossaroo with his despised bow and arrows has beaten us both. What, if either of us had beaten him?"

"Or," replied Karl, "what if we had both beaten him? Ah! brother Caspar," added he, shuddering as he spoke, "how near we were to making an end of each other! It's fearful to think of it!"

"Let us think no more of it then," rejoined Caspar; "but go home at once and see what sort of a breakfast Ossy has procured for us. I wonder whether it be flesh or fowl."

"One or the other, no doubt," he continued, after a short pause. "Fowl, I fancy: for as I came round the lake I heard some oddish screaming in the direction of the cliff yonder, which was that taken by Ossaroo. It appeared to proceed from the throat of some bird; yet such I think I have never heard before."

"But I have," replied Karl; "I heard it also. I fancy I know the bird that made those wild notes: and if it be one of them the shikaree has shot, we shall have a breakfast fit for a prince, and of a kind Lucullus delighted to indulge in. But let us obey the signal of our shikaree, and see whether we're in such good luck."

They had already regained possession of their guns. Shouldering them, they started forth from the glade—so near being the scene of a tragical event—and, turning the end of the lake, walked briskly back in the direction of the hut.

On coming within view of it, they descried the shikaree sitting upon a stone, just by the doorway; and lying across his knee, a most beautiful bird—by far the most beautiful that either flies in the air, swims in the water, or walks upon the earth—the peacock. Not the half turkey-shaped creature that struts around the farmyard—though *he* is even more beautiful than any other bird—but the wild peacock of the Ind—of shape slender and elegant—of plumage resplendent as the most priceless of gems—and, what was then of more consequence to our adventurers, of flesh delicate and savoury as the choicest of game. This last was evidently the quality of the peacock most admired by Ossaroo. The elegant shape he had already destroyed; the resplendent plumes he was plucking out and casting to the winds, as though they had been common feathers; and his whole action betokened that he had no more regard for those grand tail feathers and that gorgeous purple corselet, than if it had been a goose, or an old turkey-cock that lay stretched across his knee.

Without saying a word, when the others came up, there was that in Ossaroo's look—as he glanced furtively towards the young sahibs, and saw that both were empty-handed—that betrayed a certain degree of pride— just enough to show that he was enjoying a triumph. To know that he was the only one who had made a *coup*, it was not necessary for him to look up. Had either succeeded in killing game, or even in finding it, he must have heard the report of a gun, and none such on that morning had awakened the echoes of the valley. Ossaroo, therefore, knew that a brace of empty game-bags were all that were brought back.

Unlike the young sahibs, he had no particular adventure to relate. His "stalk" had been a very quiet one—ending, as most quiet stalks do, in the death of the animal stalked. He had heard the old peacock screeching on the top of a tall tree; he had stolen up within bow range, sent an arrow through his glittering gorget, and brought him tumbling to the ground. He had then laid his vulgar hands upon the beautiful bird, grasping it by the legs, and carrying it with draggling wings—just as if it had been a common dunghill fowl he was taking to the market of Calcutta.

Karl and Caspar did not choose to waste time in telling the shikaree how near they had been to leaving him the sole and undisputed possessor of that detached dwelling and the grounds belonging to it. Hunger prompted them to defer the relation to a future time; and also to lend a hand in the culinary operations already initiated by Ossaroo. By their aid, therefore, a fire was set ablaze; and the peacock, not very cleanly plucked, was soon roasting in the flames—Fritz having already made short work with the giblets.

Chapter Thirty Two.
The ibex.

Big as was the body of the peacock, there was not much of it left after that *déjeuner aux doigts*! Only the bones; and so clean picked were they, that had Fritz not already been made welcome to the giblets, he would have had but a scanty meal of it.

The savoury roast did a good deal towards restoring the spirits of the party; but they could not help dwelling upon the indifferent prospect they now had of procuring a fresh stock of provisions—so much changed were circumstances by their powder having been destroyed.

The bow and arrows of Ossaroo were still left, and other bows could be made, if that one was to get broken. Indeed, Caspar now determined on having one of his own; and practising archery under the tutelage of the shikaree, until he should be able to use that old-fashioned and universal weapon with deadly effect. Old-fashioned we may well term it: since its existence dates far beyond the earliest times of historical record; and universal: for go where you will into the most remote corners of the earth, the bow is found in the hands of the savage, copied from no model, introduced from no external source, but evidently native to the country and the tribe, as if when man was first created the weapon had been put into his hands by the Creator himself!

Indeed, the occurrence of the bow—with its necessary adjunct, the arrow—among tribes of savages living widely apart, and who, to all appearance, could never have communicated the idea to one another—is one of the most curious circumstances in the history of mankind; and there is no other way of explaining it, than by the supposition that the propelling power which exists in the recoil of a tightly-stretched string must be one of the earliest phenomena that presents itself to the human mind; and that, therefore, in many parts of the world this idea has been an indigenous and original conception.

The bow and arrow is certainly one of the oldest weapons on the earth—as well as one of the most universally distributed. It is a subject that, in the hands of the skilled ethnologist, might become one of the most interesting chapters in the history of the human race.

I have said that after eating the peacock our adventurers were in better spirits; but for all that, they could not help feeling some little apprehension as to how their food was to be obtained for the future. Ossaroo's skill had provided their breakfast; but how about their dinner? And after that their supper? Even should something turn up for the next meal, they might not be so fortunate in obtaining the next after that; and this precarious way of subsistence—living, as it were, from hand to mouth—would be a constant exposure of their lives to the chances of starvation.

As soon, therefore, as they had finished with the flesh of the peacock— and while Ossaroo, who continued eating longer than any of them, was still engaged in polishing off the "drumsticks"—the point of replenishing the larder became the subject of their conversation; and all agreed that to get up a stock of provisions had now become a matter of primary importance. They resolved, therefore, to devote themselves entirely to this business—using such means as were in their power for capturing game, and devising other means should these prove insufficient.

First and foremost, then, what were they to have for dinner? Was it to be fish, flesh, or fowl? They did not think of having all three: for in their situation they had no desire for a fashionable dinner. One course would be sufficient for them; and they would only be too thankful to have one course assured to them.

Whether they would choose to go fishing with Ossaroo's net, and have fish for their dinner, or whether they would try for another peacock, or an argus pheasant, or a brace of Brahminy geese; or whether they would take to the woods and search for grander game, had not become a decided point; when an incident occurred that settled the question, as to what they were to have for dinner. Without any exertion on their part—without the wasting of a single shot, or the spending of an arrow, they were provided with meat; and in quantity sufficient, not only for that day's dinner, but to ration them for a whole week, with odds and ends falling to the share of Fritz.

They had gone out of the hut again; and were seated, as oft before, on some large stones that lay upon the ground in front. It was a fine bright morning; and, although cold in the shade, the sun shining down upon them, reflected from the white snow on the mountains above, made it warm enough to be pleasant. For that reason, and because there was some smoke inside the hut, where they had cooked their breakfast, they had preferred eating it in the open air; and here also they were holding council as to their future proceedings.

While thus engaged, a sound fell upon their ears that bore some resemblance to the bleating of a goat. It appeared to come down from the sky above them; but they knew that it must be caused by some animal on the cliffs overhead.

On looking upwards, they beheld the animal; and if its voice had already appeared to them to be like that of a goat, the creature itself in its *personal* appearance, to a very great extent, carried out the resemblance.

To speak the truth, it *was* a goat; though not one of the common kind. It was an *ibex*.

Once more Karl had the advantage of his companions. His knowledge of natural history enabled him to identify the animal. At the first glance he pronounced it an ibex; although he had never seen a living ibex before. But the goat-like shape of the animal, its shaggy coat, and above all, the immense ringed horns curving regularly backward over its shoulders, were all characteristic points, which Karl was able to identify by a comparison with pictures he had seen in books, and stuffed skins he had examined in a museum.

Ossaroo said it was a goat—some kind of a wild goat, he supposed; but as Ossaroo had never before been so high up the mountains, and therefore never in the regions frequented by the ibex, he knew it not. His conjecture that it was a goat was founded on the general resemblance which it bore to a goat; and this Caspar had observed as well as Ossaroo.

They could see the creature from head to foot, standing in a majestic attitude on a prominent point of the cliff; but although it was in reality much larger than the common domestic goat, it was so distant from them as not to appear bigger than a kid. It was *en profile*, however, to their eyes; and against the blue sky they could trace the outlines of the animal with perfect distinctness, and note the grand sweeping curvature of its horns.

The first thought of Caspar was to lay hold of his gun with the idea of taking a shot at it; but both the others interposed to prevent this—pointing out the impossibility of hitting at such a distance. Although seemingly much nearer, the ibex was considerably more than a hundred yards from where they were seated: for the point of the precipice upon which it stood was quite four hundred feet above the level.

Caspar, reflecting upon this, was easily dissuaded from his design; and the next moment was wondering why he had been so near playing the fool as to throw away a shot—his penultimate one, too—at an animal placed full fifty yards beyond the carry of his gun!

Chapter Thirty Three.
Goats and sheep.

As the ibex kept its ground, without showing any signs of retreating, or even moving a muscle of its body, they remained watching it. Not, however, in silence: for as the animal was standing as if to have its portrait painted, Karl, in words addressed to his two companions, but chiefly intended for the instruction of Caspar, proceeded to execute that very task.

"The ibex," said he, "is an animal whose name has been long famous, and about which the closet naturalists have written a great deal of nonsense—as they have about almost every other animal on the earth. After all that has been said about it, it is simply a goat—a wild goat, it is true, but still only a goat—having all the habits, and very much of the appearance characteristic of the domestic animal of this name.

"Every one knows that the common goat exists in as many varieties as the countries it inhabits. Indeed, there are more kinds of goats than countries: for it is not uncommon to meet with three or four sorts within the boundaries of a single kingdom—as in Great Britain itself. These varieties differ almost as much from each other as the 'breeds' of dogs; and hence there has been much speculation among zoologists, as to what species of wild goat they have all originally sprung from.

"Now, it is my opinion," continued the plant-hunter, "that the tame goats found among different nations of the earth have not all descended from the same stock; but are the progeny of more than one wild species— just as the domesticated breeds of sheep have sprung from several species of wild sheep; though many zoologists deny this very plain fact."

"There are different species of wild goats, then?" said Caspar, interrogatively.

"There are," replied the plant-hunter, "though they are not very numerous—perhaps in all there may be about a dozen. As yet there are not so many known to zoologists—that is, not a dozen that have been identified and described as distinct species; but no doubt when the central countries, both of Asia and Africa—with their grand chains of mountains—have been explored by scientific naturalists, at least that number will be found to exist.

"The speculating systematists—who decide about genera and species, by some slight protuberance upon a tooth—have already created a wonderful confusion in the family of the goats. Not contented with viewing them all as belonging to a single genus, they have divided them into five genera—though to most of the five they ascribe only *one species!*—thus uselessly multiplying names, and rendering the study of the subject more complicated and difficult.

"There can be no doubt that the goats, both wild and tame—including the ibex, which is a true wild goat—form of themselves a separate family in the animal kingdom, easily distinguishable from sheep, deer, antelopes, or oxen. The wild goats often bear a very close resemblance to certain species of wild sheep; and the two are not to be distinguished from each other, by the goats being covered with hair and the sheep with wool—as is generally the case with tame breeds. On the contrary, both sheep and goats in a wild state have *hairy* coats—the sheep as much as the goats; and in many instances the hair of both is quite as short as that of antelopes or deer. Even where there are almost no external marks to distinguish wild goats from certain kinds of wild sheep, there are found *moral* characteristics which serve as guides to the genus. The goat is bolder, and of a fiercer nature; and its other habits, even in the wild state, differ essentially from those of the wild sheep.

"The ibex which we see above us," continued Karl, looking up to the quadruped upon the cliff, "is neither more nor less than a wild goat. It is not the only species of wild goat inhabiting the Himalayas; for there is the 'tahir,' a stronger and larger animal than it; and it is believed that when these great mountains have been thoroughly *ransacked* (Karl here smiled at the very unscientific word he had made use of), there will turn up one or two additional species.

"It is not the only species of ibex neither," continued he, "for there is one found in the European Alps, known by the name of 'steinboc;' another, in the Pyrenees, called the 'tur;' a third, in the Caucasus, the 'zac;' and one or two others in the mountains of Africa.

"With regard to the animal now before, or rather above us," continued Karl, "it differs very little from others of the same family; and as both its appearance and habits have been very ably described by a noted sportsman, who was also an accomplished naturalist, I cannot do better than quote his description: since it gives almost every detail that is yet authentically known of the Himalayan ibex.

"'The male,' writes this gentleman author, 'is about the size of the *tahir* (here he speaks of the other well-known species of Himalayan wild goat, and which is itself much larger than any of the domesticated kinds).

Except just after changing their coats, when they are of a greyish hue, the general colour of the ibex is a dirty yellowish brown. I have, however, killed the younger animals, both male and female, with their coats as red as that of a deer in his red coat; but never saw an old male of that colour, for the reason, I imagine, that he lives much higher, and sheds his hair much later in the season. The hair is short, something in texture like that of the *burrell* and other wild sheep; and in the cold weather is mixed with a very soft downy wool, resembling the shawl-wool of Thibet. This and the old hair is shed in May and June; and in districts occupied by the flocks at that season the bushes and sharp corners of rocks are covered with their cast-off winter coats. The striking appearance of the ibex is chiefly owing to the noble horns: which nature has bestowed upon it. In full-grown animals the horns, which curve gracefully over the shoulders, are from three to four feet in length along the curve, and about eleven inches in circumference at the base. Very few attain a greater length than four feet; but I have heard of their being three inches longer. Their beards, six or eight inches in length, arc of shaggy black hair. The females, light greyish-brown in colour, are hardly a third the size of the males; and their horns are round and tapering, from ten inches to a foot in length. Their appearance upon the whole is clean-made, agile, and graceful.

"'In the summer they everywhere resort to the highest accessible places where food can be found—often to a part of the country several marches distant from their winter haunts. This migration commences as soon as the snow begins to disappear; and is very gradually performed—the animals receding from hill to hill, and remaining a few days upon each.

"'At this season the males keep in large flocks, apart from the females; and as many as a hundred may occasionally be seen together. During the heat of the day they rarely move about, but rest and sleep—either on the beds of snow in the ravines, or on the rocks and shingly slopes of the barren hill-sides, above the limits of vegetation. Sometimes, but very rarely, they will lie down on the grassy spots where they have been feeding. Towards evening they begin to move, and proceed to their grazing-grounds— which are often miles away. They set out walking slowly at first; but, if they have any considerable distance before them, soon break into a trot; and sometimes the whole flock will go as hard as they can lay legs to the ground. From what we could gather from the natives, we concluded that they remain in these high regions until the end of October; when they begin to mix with the females, and gradually descend to their winter resorts. The females do not wander so much or so far—many remaining on the same ground throughout the year—and those that do visit the distant hills are generally found lower down than the males, seldom ascending above the limits of vegetation. They bring forth their young in July, having generally two at a birth; though, like other gregarious animals, many are frequently found barren.

"'The ibex are wary animals, gifted with very sharp sight and an acute sense of smell. They are very easily alarmed, and so wild, that a single shot fired at a flock is often sufficient to drive them away from that particular range of hills they may be upon. Even if not fired at, the appearance of a human being near their haunt is not unfrequently attended with the same result. Of this we had many instances during our rambles after them, and the very first flock of old males we found gave us a proof. They were at the head of the Asrung valley, and we caught sight of them just as they were coming down the hill to feed—a noble flock of nearly a hundred old males. It was late in the day, and we had a long way to return to camp. Prudence whispered, "Let them alone till to-morrow," but excitement carried the day, and we tried the stalk. Having but little daylight remaining, we may have hurried, and consequently approached them with less caution than we should have done had we had time before us. However it might be, we failed; for long before we got within range, some of them discovered us, and the whole flock decamped without giving us the chance of a shot. Not having fired at, or otherwise disturbed them, more than by approaching the flock, we were in great hopes of finding them the next day; but that and several succeeding ones were passed in a fruitless search. They had entirely forsaken that range of hills.

"'All readers of natural history are familiar with the wonderful climbing and saltatory powers of the ibex; and, although they cannot (as has been described in print) make a spring and hang on by their horns until they gain footing, yet in reality, for such heavy-looking animals, they get over the most inaccessible-looking places in an almost miraculous manner. Nothing seems to stop them, nor to impede in the least their progress. To see a flock, after being fired at, take a direct line across country, which they often do, over all sorts of seemingly impassable ground; now along the naked face of an almost perpendicular rock, then across a formidable landslip, or an inclined plane of loose stones or sand, which the slightest touch sets in motion both above and below; diving into chasms to which there seems no possible outlet, but instantly reappearing on the opposite side; never deviating in the slightest from their course; and at the same time getting over the ground at the rate of something like fifteen miles an hour, is a sight not easily to be forgotten. There are few animals, if any, that excel the ibex in endurance and agility.'"

Chapter Thirty Four.
A battle of bucks.

Karl had scarcely finished speaking, when, as if to illustrate still further the habits of the ibex, a curious incident occurred to the animal upon, which their eyes were fixed.

It ceased to be a solitary individual: for while they were gazing at it another ibex made its appearance upon the cliff, advancing towards the one first seen. The new comer was also a male, as its huge scimitar-shaped horns testified; while in size, as in other respects, it resembled the one already on the rock as much as if they had been brothers. It was not likely they were so. At all events the behaviour of the former evinced anything but a fraternal feeling. On the contrary, it was advancing with a hostile intent, as its attitudes clearly proved. Its muzzle was turned downward and inward, until the bearded chin almost touched its chest; while the tips of its horns, instead of being thrown back upon its shoulders—their usual position when the animal stands erect—were, elevated high in the air. Moreover, its short tail, held upright and jerking about with a quick nervous motion, told that the animal meditated mischief. Even at so great a distance the spectators could perceive this: for the forms of both the ibex were so clearly outlined against the sky, that the slightest motion on the part of either could be perceived with perfect distinctness.

The new comer, when first observed, appeared to be approaching by stealth—as if he intended to play the cowardly assassin, and butt the other over the cliff! Indeed, this was his actual design, as was discovered in the sequel; and had the other only remained for six seconds longer in the attitude in which he had been first seen, his assailant would no doubt have at once succeeded in his treacherous intent.

We are sorry to have to say that he *did* succeed—though not without a struggle, and the risk of being himself compelled to take that desperate leap which he had designed for his antagonist.

It was probably the voice of Caspar that hindered the immediate execution of this wicked intention; though, alas! it only stayed it for a short time. Caspar, on seeing the treacherous approach, had involuntarily uttered a cry of warning. Though it could not have been understood by the imperilled ibex, it had the effect of startling him from his dreamy attitude, and causing him to look around. In that look he perceived his danger, and quick as thought, took measures to avert it. Suddenly raising himself on his hind-legs, and using them as a pivot, he wheeled about, and then came to the ground on all fours, face to face with his adversary. He showed no sign of any desire to retreat, but seemed to accept the challenge as a matter of course. Indeed, from his position, it would have been impossible for him to have retreated with any chance of safety. The cliff upon which he had been standing, was a sort of promontory projecting beyond the general line of the precipice; and towards the mountain slope above his escape had been already cut off by his challenger. On all other sides of him was the beetling cliff. He had no alternative but fight, or be "knocked over." It was less a matter of choice than necessity that determined him upon standing his ground.

This determination he had just time to take, and just time to put himself in an attitude of defence, when his antagonist charged towards him. Both animals, at the same instant, uttered a fierce, snorting sound, and rising upon their hind-legs, stood fronting each other like a brace of bipeds. In this movement the spectators recognised the exact mode of combat practised by common goats; for just in the same fashion does the ibex exhibit his prowess. Instead of rushing *horizontally*, head to head, and pressing each other backwards, as rams do in their contests, the ibex after rearing aloft, come down again, horns foremost, using the weight of their bodies as the propelling power, each endeavouring to crush the other between his massive crest and the earth. Several times in succession did the two combatants repeat their rearings aloft, and the downward strokes of their horns; but it soon became evident, that the one who had been the assailant was also to be the conqueror. He had an advantage in the ground: for the platform which his adversary occupied, and from which he could not escape, was not wide enough to afford room for any violent movements; and the imminent danger of getting a hoof over the cliff, evidently inspired him with fear and constraint. The assailant having plenty of space to move in, was able to "back and fill" at pleasure, now receding foot by foot, then rushing forward, rising erect, and striking down again. Each time he made his onslaught with renewed impetus, derived from the advantage of the ground, as well as the knowledge that if his blow failed, he should only have to repeat it; whereas, on the part of his opponent, the failure of a single stroke, or even of a guard, would almost to a certainty be the prelude to his destruction.

Whether it was that the ibex attacked was the weaker animal of the two, or whether the disadvantage of the ground was against him, it soon became evident that he was no match for his assailant. From the very first, he appeared to act only on the defensive; and in all likelihood, had the road been open to him, he would have turned tail at once, and taken to his heels.

But no opportunity for flight was permitted him at any moment from the beginning of the contest; and none was likely to be given him until it should end. The only chance of escape that appeared, even to him, was to make a grand leap, and clear his adversary, horns and all.

This idea seemed at length to take possession of his brain: for all on a sudden he was keen to forsake his attitude of defence, and bound high into the air—as if to get over his adversary's horns, and hide himself among the safer snowdrifts of the mountains.

If such was his intent it proved a sad failure. While soaring in the air— all his four feet raised high off the ground—the huge horns of his adversary were impelled with fearful force against his ribs, the stroke tossing him like a shuttlecock clear over the edge of the cliff!

The blow had been delivered so as to project his body with a revolving impetus into the air; and turning round and round, it fell with a heavy concussion into the bottom of the valley; where, after rebounding full six feet from the ground, it fell back again dead as a stone.

It was some seconds before the spectators could recover from surprise at an incident so curious, though it was one that may often be witnessed by those who wander among the wild crags of the Himalayas—where combats between the males of the ibex, the tahir, the burrell or Himalayan wild sheep, and also the rams of the gigantic *Ovis ammon*, are of common occurrence.

These battles are often fought upon the edge of a beetling precipice—for it is in such places that these four species of animals delight to dwell—and not unfrequently the issue of the contest is such as that witnessed by our adventurers—one of the combatants being "butted" or pushed right over the cliff.

It does not follow that the animal thus put *hors de combat* is always killed. On the contrary, unless the precipice be one of stupendous height, an ibex, or tahir, or burrell, will get up again after one of those fearful falls;

and either run or limp away from the spot—perhaps to recover, and try his luck and strength in some future encounter with the same adversary. One of the most remarkable instances of this kind is related by the intelligent sportsman, Colonel Markham, and by him vouched for as a fact that came under his own observation. We copy his account verbatim:—

"I witnessed one of the most extraordinary feats performed by an old tahir, that I, or any other man, ever beheld. I shot him when about eighty yards overhead upon a ledge of rocks. He fell perpendicularly that distance, and, without touching the ground or the sides of the precipice, rebounded, and fell again about fifteen yards further down. I thought he was knocked to atoms, but he got up and went off; and although we tracked him by his blood to a considerable distance, we were after all unable to find him!"

My young readers may remember that many similar feats have been witnessed in the Rocky Mountains of America, performed by the "bighorn"—a wild sheep that inhabits these mountains, so closely resembling the *Ovis ammon* of the Himalayas, as to be regarded by some naturalists as belonging to the same species. The hunters of the American wilderness positively assert that the bighorn fearlessly flings himself from high cliffs, alighting on his horns; and, then rebounding into the air like an elastic ball, recovers his feet unhurt, and even unstunned by the tremendous "header!"

No doubt there is a good deal of exaggeration in these "hunter stories;" but it is nevertheless true that most species of wild goats and sheep, as well as several of the rock-loving antelopes—the chamois and klipspringer, for instance—can do some prodigious feats in the leaping line, and such as it is difficult to believe in by any one not accustomed to the habits of these animals. It is not easy to comprehend how Colonel Markham's tahir could have fallen eighty yards—that is, 240 feet—to say nothing of the supplementary descent of forty-five feet further—without being smashed to "smithereens." But although we may hesitate to give credence to such an extraordinary statement, it would not be a proper thing to give it a flat contradiction. Who knows whether there may not be in the bones of these animals some elastic principle or quality enabling them to counteract the effects of such great falls? There are many mechanical contrivances of animal life as yet but very imperfectly understood; and it is well-known that Nature has wonderfully adapted her creatures to the haunts and habits for which she has designed them. It may be, then, that these wild goats and sheep—the Blondins and Leotards of the quadruped world—are gifted with certain saltatory powers, and furnished with structural contrivances which are altogether wanting to other animals not requiring them. It would not be right, therefore, without a better knowledge of the principles of animal mechanism, to contradict the statement of such a respectable authority as Colonel Markham—especially since it appears to be made in good faith, and without any motive for exaggeration.

Our adventurers had entered into no discussion of this subject on observing the descent of the ibex. Indeed, there was nothing to suggest such speculations; for the creature had fallen from such an immense height, and come down with "such a thump" upon the hard turf, that it never occurred to any of them to fancy that there was a single gasp of breath left in its body. Nor was there; for on reaching the ground after its rebound, the animal lay with limbs loose and limp, and without sign of motion—evidently a carcass.

Chapter Thirty Five.
The Bearcoots.

Our adventurers were congratulating themselves on this unexpected accession to their larder; which, like the manna of old, had, as it were, rained down from the sky.

"Our dinner!" shouted Caspar, gleefully, as the "thump" of the falling ibex sounded in their ears. "Our supper, too," he added. "Ay, more! In such a large carcass there must be provision to last us for a week!"

All three rose to their feet, and were about starting forward to secure the prize; when a shrill scream twice repeated fell upon their ears—coming down apparently from the top of the cliffs, or rather from the mountain that trended still higher above them.

Could it be the cry of the conquering ibex—his slogan of triumph? No; it was not his voice, nor that of a quadruped of any kind. Neither did the spectators for an instant believe it to be so. On turning their eyes upward, they saw the creature, or the creatures—for there were two of them—from whose throats those screams had proceeded.

The victorious ibex was still standing conspicuously upon the cliff. During the few seconds that the attention of the spectators had been occupied elsewhere, he appeared to have been contemplating the dire deed of destruction he had just accomplished, and perhaps indulging in the triumph he had obtained over his unfortunate rival. At all events he had stepped forward upon the projecting point of the rock—to the very spot so lately occupied by his adversary.

The cry, however, which had been heard in the valley below had reached his ears at the same time, and perhaps a little sooner: for as the spectators looked up, they saw that he had been startled by it, and was looking around him with evident alarm. In the air above and not many yards distant from him, were two dark objects, easily recognisable as birds upon the wing. They were of large size, nearly black in colour, and with that peculiar sharpness of outline and sweep of wing that distinguish the true birds of prey. There was no mistaking their kind—they were eagles—of a species known in the Himalayas and the steppes of Thibet as the "bearcoot."

They were swooping in short, abrupt curves, at intervals repeating their shrill screams, both crying out together, and from their excited mien, and the character of their movements, no doubt could be entertained as to the object of their noisy demonstrations. They were about to assault an enemy, and that enemy was no other than the ibex.

The animal appeared to be fully aware of their intent; and seemed for a moment to be irresolute as to how it should act. Instead of placing itself in a bold, defiant attitude—such as it had lately assumed towards an antagonist of its own kind—it stood cowering, and apparently paralysed with fear. It was this very effect which the eagles, by their screaming, had designed to produce; and certainly the fierce birds were succeeding to the utmost of their expectations.

The spectators kept their eyes fixed upon the actors of this new drama— watching every movement, both of the birds and the beast, with intense interest. All were desirous of seeing the latter punished for the cruel act he had just committed, and which they regarded as savouring very strongly of fratricide.

It was written in the book of fate that their desire should be gratified, and that the destroyer should himself be destroyed. They were expecting to witness a somewhat prolonged combat; but in this expectation they were disappointed. The duration of the conflict was as brief as the preliminaries that led to it; and these were of the shortest kind: for scarce ten seconds had elapsed, after they had uttered their first scream, before the bearcoots swooped down to the level of the cliff, and commenced a joint attack upon the ibex, striking at him alternately with beak and claws.

For a short time the quadruped was shrouded—almost hidden—under the broad, shadowy wings of the birds; but even when its figure could be traced, it appeared to be making no very energetic efforts at defending itself. The sudden attack made by such strange enemies seemed to have completely disconcerted the ibex; and it remained as if still under the paralysis of fear.

After a moment or two had passed, the ibex appeared to recover self-possession; and then he, rearing up, struck out with his horns. But the bearcoots were on the alert; and each time that the animal attempted a forward movement, they easily avoided the blow by shying to one side or the other; and then quickly wheeling, they would swoop back upon it from behind.

In this way was the conflict progressing, the ibex holding the ground upon which he had been first attacked, turning round and round, with his two fore hoofs held close together, or else rearing aloft on his hind-legs, and using them as a pivot.

It would have been better for the ibex had he kept to his fore-feet altogether; as in that attitude he might have held his ground a little longer — perhaps until he had either beaten off his winged assailants, or wearied them out by a prolonged defence.

But to fight on "all fours" did not chance to be his fashion. It was contrary to the traditions of his family and race — all of whose members, from time immemorial, had been accustomed, when battling with an enemy, to stand erect upon their hind-legs.

Following this fashion, he had raised himself to his full perpendicular, and was about aiming a "butt" against the breast of one of the bearcoots that was tantalising him in front, when the other, that had made a short retrocession in order to gain impetus, came swooping back with the velocity of an arrow, and seizing the ibex under the chin, by a quick, strong jerk of its talons, it struck the head of the animal so far backward that it lost its balance, and went toppling over the cliff. In another instant the ibex was in mid-air — falling — falling — through that same fearful space that had just been traversed by his own victim.

The spectators looked to see him strike the ground without receiving further molestation from his winged assailants. Not so, however, did it result. Just as the ibex had got about half-way down the face of the precipice, the second eagle was seen shooting after him with the velocity of a flash of lightning; and before he could reach the ground, the bearcoot was seen striking him once more, and causing him to diverge from his vertical descent. The body came to the ground at length — but at a considerable distance from where the other was lying — the eagle descending with it to the earth, and even remaining over it with wings and limbs extended, as if still clutching it in his talons!

Why the bearcoot was thus retaining the ibex in his clutch was not quite so clear: for the animal was evidently dead; and apparently had been so long before reaching the earth. There was something strange about this proceeding on the part of the bird—as there had also been in its mode of descent through the last forty or fifty yards of space. From the manner in which it had extended its wings after striking its prey, and from the way in which it still kept exercising them, the spectators began to think that its singular descent, and its remaining over the carcass in that cowering attitude, were neither of them voluntary acts on its part.

The truth was soon made clear—proving the contrary to be the case: for as the bearcoot continued to flap its wings, or rather, flutter them in a violent irregular motion, it became evident that instead of desiring to remain by the fallen body of its victim, it was doing its very best to get away from it! This was all the more easily believed, when it commenced uttering a series of wild screams; not as before indicating rage or menace, but in tones expressive of the greatest terror!

The spectators, who had already risen from their seats, ran towards the spot—surmising that there was something amiss.

On getting close up to the still screaming and fluttering bird, they were able to understand what had appeared so incomprehensible.

They saw that the bearcoot was in a dilemma; that its talons were buried in the body of the ibex, and so firmly fixed, that with all the strength of its sinewy legs, backed by the power of its elastic pinions, it was unable to free itself!

In striking the ibex in his descent, the bird had buried its crooked claws deeply into the soft abdomen of the animal, but in attempting to draw them out again, had found—no doubt to its great chagrin—that the thick coating of "poshm" which covered the skin of the ibex, had become entangled round its shanks; and the more it fluttered to free itself, turning round and round in the effort, the stronger and tighter became the rope which it was twisting out of that celebrated staple—the shawl-wool of Cashmere!

Beyond a doubt the bearcoot was in a bad fix; and, although it was soon relieved from its tether of *poshm*, it was only to find itself more securely tied by a stronger string taken out of the pocket of Ossaroo.

The other bearcoot having followed close after, seemed determined upon rescuing its mate out of the hands of its captors; and uttering loud screams, it flew, first at one, then at another of them—with its long pointed talons menacing each of them in turn.

As all of them had weapons in their hands, they succeeded in keeping the angry bird at bay, but it might not have fared so well with Fritz—who in turn became the object of its furious attack, and who had no weapon but his teeth.

These would scarce have been sufficient protection against the talons of an eagle; and Fritz would very likely have lost one of his eyes, or perhaps both of them, had it not been for an arrow springing from the bow of the shikaree; which, transfixing the great bird right through the gizzard, brought it down with a "flop" upon the surface of the earth.

It was not killed outright by the arrow; and the dog, on seeing it bite the dust, would fain have "jumped" it. But perceiving the strong curving beak and the sharp talons extended towards him, Fritz was easily persuaded to remain at a prudent distance, and leave the shikaree to make a finish of the bearcoot with his long boar-spear.

Chapter Thirty Six.
A hope built upon the bearcoot.

In this unexpected supply of food—which might be said almost literally to have descended from heaven—Karl could not help recognising the hand of Providence, and pointing it out to his companions. Even the less reflecting mind of Caspar, and the half-heathen heart of the Hindoo, were impressed with a belief that some other agency than mere chance had befriended them; and they were only too willing to join with Karl in a prayerful expression of their gratitude to that Being who, although unseen, was with them even in that lone valley.

For a time they stood contemplating with curiosity, not only the two ibex, but also the eagles—interesting on account of the knowledge that all four animals had but lately been roaming freely beyond the boundaries of that mountain prison—and had just arrived, as it were, from the outside world, with which they themselves so eagerly longed to hold communication. What would they not have given to have been each provided with a pair of wings like that bearcoot—the one that still lived? Furnished in that fashion, they would soon have sought escape from the valley—to them a valley of tears—and from the snowy mountains that surrounded it.

While reflecting thus, a thought shaped itself in the mind of the philosophic Karl, which caused his face to brighten up a little. Only a little: for the idea which had occurred to him was not one of the brightest. There was something in it, however; and, as the drowning man will clutch even at straws, Karl caught at a singular conception, and after examining it a while, communicated it to the others.

It was the bearcoot that had brought forth this conception. The bird was a true eagle, strong of wing and muscle like all of his tribe, and one of the strongest of the genus. Like an arrow, he could fly straight up towards the sky. In a few minutes—ay, in a few seconds—he could easily shoot up to the summits of the snowy mountains that towered above them.

"What is to hinder him?" asked Karl, pointing to the bird, "to carry—"

"To carry what?" said Caspar, interrupting the interrogation of his brother, who spoke in a hesitating and doubtful manner. "Not us, Karl?" continued he, with a slight touch of jocularity in his manner—"you don't mean that, I suppose?"

"Not us," gravely repeated Karl, "but *a rope* that may carry *us*."

"Ha!" exclaimed Caspar, a gleam of joy overspreading his face as he spoke. "There's something in that."

Ossaroo, equally interested in the dialogue, at the same moment gave utterance to a joyous ejaculation.

"What do *you* think of it, shikaree?" inquired Karl, speaking in a serious tone.

The reply of Ossaroo did not bespeak any very sanguine hope on his part. Still he was ready to counsel a trial of the scheme. They could try it without any great trouble. It would only need to spin some more rope from the hemp—of which they had plenty—attach it to the leg of the bearcoot, and give the bird its freedom. There was no question as to the direction the eagle would take. He had already had enough of the valley; and would no doubt make to get out of it at the very first flight he should be permitted to make.

The scheme superficially considered appeared plausible enough; but as its details were subjected to a more rigorous examination, two grand difficulties presented themselves—so grand that they almost obliterated the hope, so suddenly, and with too much facility, conceived.

The first of these difficulties was, that the bearcoot, notwithstanding his great strength of wing, might not be able to carry up a rope, which would be strong enough to carry one of themselves. A cord he might easily take to the top of the cliff, or even far beyond; but a mere cord, or even a very slender rope, would be of no use. It would need one strong enough to support the body of a man—and that, too, while engaged in the violent exertion of climbing. The rope would require to be of great length—two hundred yards or more; and every yard would add to the weight the eagle would be required to carry up.

It is not to be supposed that they intended to "swarm" up this rope hand by hand. For the height of a dozen yards or so, any of them could have accomplished that. But there would be a hundred and fifty yards of "swarming" to be done before they could set foot upon the top of the cliff; and the smartest sailor that ever crawled up a main-stay—even Sinbad himself—could not have done half the distance. They had foreseen this difficulty from the very first; and the ingenuity of Karl had at once provided a remedy for it—as will be seen in the sequel.

The second question that presented itself was:—admitting that the bearcoot might bear up a rope stout enough for the purpose, whether there would be any possibility of getting this rope stayed at the top?

Of course, they could do nothing of themselves; and that point would be a matter of mere chance. There was a chance—all acknowledged that. The bird, in fluttering over the mountain to make its escape, might entangle the rope around a rock, or some sharp angle of the frozen snow. There was a chance, which could be determined by trying, and only by trying; and there were certain probabilities in favour of success.

The first difficulty—that relating to the strength and weight of the rope—admitted of rational discussion and calculation. There were *data* to go upon, and others that might be decided conjecturally, yet sufficiently near the truth for all preliminary purposes. They could tell pretty nearly what stoutness of rope it would take to *hang* any one of them; and this would be strong enough to carry them up the cliff. The strength of the eagle might also be presumed pretty nearly; and there was no doubt but that the bearcoot would do his very best to get out of the valley. After the rough handling he had already experienced, he would not require any further stimulus to call forth his very utmost exertions.

On discussing the subject in its different bearings, it soon became evident to all, that the matter of supreme importance would be the making of the rope. Could this be manufactured of sufficient fineness not to overburden the bearcoot, and yet be strong enough to sustain the weight of a man, the first difficulty would be got over. The rope therefore should be made with the greatest care. Every fibre of it should be of the best quality of hemp— every strand twisted with a perfect uniformity of thickness—every plait manipulated with an exact accuracy.

Ossaroo was the man to make such a cord. He could spin it with as much evenness as a Manchester mill. There would be no danger that in a rope of Ossaroo's making the most critical eye could detect either fault or flaw.

It was finally determined on that the rope should be spun—Ossaroo acting as director, the others becoming his attendants rather than his assistants.

Before proceeding to work, however, it was deemed prudent to secure against a hungry day by curing the flesh of the brace of ibex. The dead bearcoot was to be eaten while fresh, and needed no curing.

And so indeed it was eaten—the bird of Jove furnishing them with a dinner, as that of Juno had given them a breakfast!

Chapter Thirty Seven.
The log on the leg.

As soon as they had hung the ibex-meat upon the curing strings, and pegged out the two skins for drying, they turned their attention to the making of the rope by which they were to be pulled out of their prison. By good fortune they had a large stock of hemp on hand all ready for twisting. It was a store that had been saved up by Ossaroo—at the time when he had fabricated his fish-net; and as it had been kept in a little dry grotto of the cliff, it was still in excellent preservation. They had also on hand a very long rope, though, unfortunately, not long enough for their present purpose. It was the same which they had used in projecting their tree-bridge across the crevasse; and which they had long ago unrove from its pulleys, and brought home to the hut. This rope was the exact thickness they would require: for anything of a more slender gauge would scarcely be sufficient to support the weight of a man's body; and considering the fearful risk they would have to run, while hanging by it against the face of such a cliff, it was necessary to keep on the safe side as regarded the strength of the rope. They could have made it of ample thickness and strength, so as to secure against the accident of its breaking. But then, on the opposite hand, arose the difficulty as to the strength of the eagle's wing. Should the rope prove too heavy for the bearcoot to carry over the top of the cliff, then all their labour would be in vain.

"Why not ascertain this fact before making the rope?"

This was a suggestion of Karl himself.

"But how are we to do it?" was the rejoinder of Caspar.

"I think we can manage the matter," said the botanist, apparently busying his brain with some profound calculation.

"I can't think of a way myself," replied Caspar, looking inquiringly at his brother.

"I fancy I can," said Karl. "What is to hinder us to ascertain the weight of the rope before making it, and also decide as to whether the bird can carry so much?"

"But how are you to weigh the rope until it is made? You know it's the trouble of making it we wish to avoid—that is, should it prove useless afterwards."

"Oh! as for that," rejoined Karl, "it is not necessary to have it finished to find out what weight it would be. We know pretty near the length that will be needed, and by weighing a piece of that already in our hands, we can calculate for any given length."

"You forget, brother Karl, that we have no means of weighing, even the smallest piece. We have neither beam, scales, nor weights."

"Pooh!" replied Karl, with that tone of confidence imparted by superior knowledge. "There's no difficulty in obtaining all these. Any piece of straight stick becomes a beam, when properly balanced; and as for scales, they can be had as readily as a beam."

"But the weights?" interrupted Caspar. "What about them? Your beam and scales would be useless, I apprehend, without proper weights? I think we should be 'stumped' for the want of the pounds and ounces."

"I am surprised, Caspar, you should be so unreflecting, and allow your ingenuity to be so easily discouraged and thwarted. I believe I could make a set of weights under any circumstances in which you might place me—giving me only the raw material, such as a piece of timber and plenty of stones."

"But how, brother? Pray, tell us!"

"Why, in the first place, I know the weight of my own body."

"Granted. But that is only one weight; how are you to get the denominations—the pounds and ounces?"

"On the beam I should construct I would balance my body against a lot of stones. I should then divide the stones into two lots, and balance these against one another. I should thus get the half weight of my body—a known quantity, you will recollect. By again equally dividing one of the lots I should find a standard of smaller dimensions; and so on, till I had got a weight as small as might be needed. By this process I can find a pound, an ounce, or any amount required."

"Very true, brother," replied Caspar, "and very ingenious of you. No doubt your plan would do—but for one little circumstance, which you seem to have overlooked."

"What is that?"

"Are your data quite correct?" naïvely inquired Caspar.

"My data!"

"Yes—the original standard from which you propose to start, and on which you would base your calculations. I mean the *weight of your body*. Do you know that?"

"Certainly," said Karl; "I am just 140 pounds weight—to an ounce."

"Ah, brother," replied Caspar, with a shake of the head, expressive of doubt, "you *were* 140 pounds in London—I know that myself—and so was I nearly as much; but you forget that the fret and worry of this miserable existence has reduced both of us. Indeed, dear brother, I can see that you are much thinner since we set out from Calcutta; and no doubt you can perceive the like change in me. Is it not so?"

Karl was forced to give an affirmative reply to the question, at the same time that he acknowledged the truth of his brother's statement. His data were not correct. The weight of his body—which, not being a constant quantity, is at all times an unsafe standard—would not serve in the present instance. The calculation they desired to make was of too important a character to be based upon such an untrustworthy foundation. Karl perceived this plainly enough; but it did not discourage him from prosecuting his purpose to make the attempt he had proposed.

"Well, brother!" said he, looking smilingly towards the latter, and apparently rather pleased at Caspar's acuteness; "I acknowledge you have had the better of the argument this time; but that's no reason why I should give up my plan. There are many other ways of ascertaining the weight of an object; and no doubt if I were to reflect a little I could hit upon one; but as luck has it, we need not trouble ourselves further about that matter. If I mistake not, we have a standard of weight in our possession, that is just the thing itself."

"What standard?" demanded Caspar.

"One of the leaden bullets of your own gun. They are ounce bullets, I've heard you say?"

"They are exactly sixteen to the pound, and therefore each of them an ounce. You are right, Karl, that is a standard. Certainly it will do."

The subject required no further sifting; and without delay they proceeded to ascertain the weight of two hundred yards of rope. A balance was soon constructed and adjusted, as nicely as if they had meant to put gold in the scale. Twenty yards of the rope already in hand was set against stones—whose weight they had already determined by reduplicating a number of bullets—and its quantity ascertained in pounds and ounces.

Eight times that gave one hundred and sixty yards—the probable amount of cord they should require.

This being determined upon, the next thing was to find out whether the eagle could carry such a burden into the sky. Of course, the bird would not have the whole of it to carry at first, as part would rest upon the ground; but should it succeed in reaching the top of the cliff—even at the lowest part—there would then be the weight of at least one hundred yards upon its leg; and if it ascended still higher, a greater amount in proportion.

It was natural to suppose that the bearcoot in going out would choose the lowest part of the precipice—especially when feeling his flight impeded by the strange attachment upon his leg; and if this conjecture should prove correct, there would be all the less weight to be sustained. But, indeed, by the cord itself they could guide the bearcoot to the lowest part—since by holding it in their hands, they could hinder him taking flight in any other direction.

Considering all these circumstances, and rather cheered by the many points that appeared to be in their favour, they proceeded to make trial of the eagle's strength.

It would not take long to decide; but conscious of the great importance of the result, they set about it with due deliberation.

A log of wood was procured, and chopped down, till it was exactly the weight of the rope to be used. To this the piece of twenty yards—already employed for a different purpose—was attached at one end—the other being tightly knotted around the shank of the eagle.

When all was ready, the bird was stripped of his other fastenings; and then all retired to a distance to give him space for the free use of his wings.

Fancying himself no longer under restraint, the bearcoot sprang up from the rock on which he had been placed; and, spreading his broad wings, rose almost vertically into the air.

For the first twenty yards he mounted with a vigorous velocity; and the hopes of the spectators found utterance in joyful ejaculations.

Alas! these hopes were short-lived, ending almost on the instant of their conception. The rope, carried to its full length, became suddenly taut—jerking the eagle several feet back towards the earth. At the same time the log was lifted only a few inches from the ground. The bird fluttered a moment, taken aback by this unexpected interruption; and, after recovering its equilibrium, again essayed a second flight towards the sky.

Once more the rope tightened—as before raising the log but very little from the ground—while the eagle, as if this time expecting the pluck, suffered less derangement of its flight than on the former occasion. For all that, it was borne back, until its anchor "touched bottom." Then after making another upward effort, with the like result, it appeared to become convinced of its inability to rise vertically, and directed its flight in a horizontal line along the cliffs. The log was jerked over the ground, bounding from point to point, occasionally swinging in the air, but only for a few seconds at a time.

At length the conviction forced itself upon the minds of the spectators—as it seemed also to have done upon that of the performer—that to reach the top of the cliff—with a cord upon its leg, equal in weight to that log—was more than a bearcoot could accomplish.

In short, the plan had proved a failure; and, no longer hoping for success, our adventurers turned their disappointed looks upon each other—leaving the eagle free to drag his wooden anchor whithersoever he might wish.

Chapter Thirty Eight.
Further experiments.

The usual silence which succeeds a disappointment was for some time preserved by the three individuals who had been spectators of the unsuccessful attempt of the eagle. Caspar seemed less cast down than the others; but why it was so, neither of them thought of asking him.

It was not a silence of very long duration, nor was the chagrin that had caused it of much longer continuance. Both were evanescent as the summer cloud that for a moment darkens the sky, and then glides off—leaving it bright and serene as ever.

It was to Caspar the party was indebted for this happy change of feeling. An idea had occurred to the young hunter—or rather a new scheme—which was at once communicated to his companions.

Strictly speaking, Caspar's scheme could not be termed a *new* one. It was only supplementary to that already set before them by Karl; and the bearcoot, as before, was to be the chief actor in it.

While calculating the length of rope it would take to reach to the top of the cliff, Caspar had already bethought him of a way by which it might be shortened—in other words, how it might be arranged, that a shorter rope would suffice. He had for some time carried this idea in his mind; but had declined communicating it, to the others, until after witnessing the test of the eagle's strength. Now that the bearcoot had been "weighed and found wanting," you might suppose that the creature would be no longer cared for—excepting to furnish them with a meal. This was the reflection of Karl and Ossaroo; but Caspar thought differently. He was impressed with a belief, that the bird might still do them a service—the very one which he had undertaken so unsuccessfully.

Caspar reflected, and very correctly: that it was the extra weight that had hindered the eagle from ascending. It was not so much beyond his strength neither. Perhaps had it been only half as heavy, or even a little more, he might have succeeded in carrying it over the cliff.

What if the weight should be reduced?

To make the rope more slender did not enter into Caspar's calculations. He knew this could not be done: since it was a point already discussed and decided upon.

But how if the rope were to be *shorter,* than that which had been theoretically considered? How if it were to be only fifty yards, instead of one hundred and fifty? Of course, then the eagle might fly with it, to whatever height its length would allow.

Caspar felt satisfied of this fact; nor did either of the others question its truth—but what then?

"What," inquired Karl, "would be the use of a rope of fifty yards, though the eagle might carry it up to the moon? Even at the lowest part of the cliffs—should the bearcoot take one end over, the other would be fifty yards above our heads?"

"Not a yard, brother—not a foot. The other end would be in our hands—in our hands, I tell you."

"Well, Caspar," calmly rejoined the philosopher, "you appear to be confident enough; though I can't guess what you are driving at. You know this hideous precipice is at no point less than a hundred yards in sheer height?"

"I do," replied Caspar, still speaking in the same tone of confidence; "but a rope of only fifty—ay, of not more than half that length—may be held in our hands, while the other end is over the top of the cliff."

Karl looked perplexed; but the shikaree, on this occasion quicker of perception than the philosopher, catching at Caspar's meaning, cried out:—

"Ha, ha! young sahib meanee from top ob da ladder! Dat meanee he."

"Exactly so," said Caspar; "you've guessed right, Ossy. I mean just that very thing."

"Oh! then, indeed," said Karl, in a drawling tone, at the same time lapsing into a reflective silence.

"Perhaps you are right, brother," he added, after a pause. "At all events, it will be easy to try. If your scheme succeed, we shall not require to make any more cord. What we have will be sufficient. Let us make trial at once!"

"Where is the bearcoot?" asked Caspar, looking around to discover the bird.

"Yonner be he, young sahib," answered Ossaroo, pointing towards the precipice; "yonner sitee he—ober da rock."

The eagle was perceived, perched, or rather crouching, on a low ledge of the cliff,—upon which it had dropped down after its unsuccessful attempt at flight. It looked crestfallen, and as if it would suffer itself to be caught by the hand. But as Ossaroo approached it with this intention, the bird seemed to fancy itself free, and once more rose, with a bold swoop, into the air.

It was only to feel the check-string tighten afresh upon his leg. It came fluttering down again, first drawn back by the weight of the log, and afterwards by the strong arm of the shikaree.

The log was now removed; and the whole rope they had on hand—a length of rather more than fifty yards—was knotted in its place.

The bearcoot was again set free—Ossaroo taking care to keep the leash well in hand; and now the beautiful bird of Jove rose into the air, as if not the summit of the cliff, but the proud peak of Chumulari, was to be the limit of its flight.

At the height of fifty yards its soaring ambition was suddenly curbed, by the check-string of Ossaroo, reminding it that it was still a captive.

The experiment had proved successful. Caspar's plan promised well; and they at once proceeded to take the necessary steps for carrying it into practical effect.

Chapter Thirty Nine.
The eagle's escape.

The first thing to be done, was to look to the quality of the rope, and test its strength. The ladders were already in place, just as they had been left. The rope once *proved*, there would be nothing further to do, but make it secure to the shank of the bearcoot; ascend the cliff to the highest ledge, reached by the ladders; and then fly the bird.

Should they succeed in getting the creature to go over the cliff—and by some means entangle the cord at the top—they might consider themselves free. The very thought of such a result—now apparently certain—once more raised their spirits to the highest pitch.

They did not count on being able to "swarm" up a piece of slender cord of nearly fifty yards in length—a feat that would have baffled the most agile tar that ever "slung the monkey" from a topgallant stay. They had no thoughts of climbing the rope in that way; but in another, long before conceived and discussed. They intended—once they should be assured that the cord was secure above—to make steps upon it, by inserting little pieces of wood between the "strands;" and these, which they could fix at long distances, one after the other, would form supports, upon which they might rest their feet in the ascent.

As we have said, all this had been settled beforehand; and no longer occupied their attention—now wholly absorbed in contriving some way to prove the reliability of the rope, upon which their lives were about to be imperilled.

It was not deemed sufficient to tie the rope to a tree, and pull upon it with all their united strength. Karl and Caspar thought this would be a sufficient test; but Ossaroo was of a different opinion. A better plan— according to the shikaree's way of thinking—was one which had generated in his oriental brain; and which, without heeding the remonstrances of the others, he proceeded to make trial of. Taking one end of the rope with him, he climbed into a tall tree; and, after getting some way out on a horizontal branch—full fifty feet from the ground—he there fastened the cord securely. By his directions the young sahibs laid hold below; and, both together, raising their feet from the ground, remained for some seconds suspended in the air.

As the rope showed no symptoms either of stretching or breaking under the weight of both, it was evident that it might, under any circumstances, be trusted to carry the weight of one; and in this confidence, the shikaree descended from the tree.

With the eagle carried under his right arm, and the coil of rope swinging over his left, Ossaroo now proceeded towards the place where the ladders rested against the cliff. Karl and Caspar walked close after, with Fritz following in the rear—all four moving in silence, and with a certain solemnity of look and gesture—as befitted the important business upon which they were bent.

The new experiment, like the trial of the eagle's strength, did not occupy any great length of time. Had it proved successful, our adventurers would have been longer occupied, and in the end would have been seen triumphantly standing upon the summit of the cliff—with Fritz frisking up the snowy slope beyond, as if he intended to chase the great *ovis ammon* upon the heaven-kissing crest of Chumulari.

Ah! how different was the spectacle presented on the evening of that eventful day! A little before sunset the three adventurers were seen slowly and sadly returning to their hut—that despised hovel, under whose homely roof they had hoped never to seek shelter again!

Alas! in the now lengthened list of their unsuccessful struggles, they had once more to record a failure!

Ossaroo, bearing the bearcoot under his arm, had climbed the ladders up to the highest ledge that could be attained. From it he had "flown" the eagle—freely dealing out all the cord in his possession. That was a perilous experiment for the shikaree to make; and came very near proving the last act in the drama of his life.

Thinking that the bearcoot would rise upward into the air, he had not thought of anything else; and as he stood balancing himself on that narrow shelf, he was but ill prepared for what actually came to pass. Instead of soaring upwards, the eagle struck out in a horizontal direction, not changing its course till it had reached the end of its tether; and then not changing it, nor even pausing in its flight, but with the fifty yards of rope trailing behind it—which, fortunately for Ossaroo, he was himself no longer at the end of— it continued on across the valley towards the cliffs on the opposite side— the summit of which it would have no difficulty in attaining by following the diagonal line in which it was making that unexpected escape from the clutches of the shikaree.

Not without chagrin did Karl and Caspar behold the spectacle of the bearcoot's departure; and for a while they were under the impression that Ossaroo had bungled the business with which he had been entrusted.

Ossaroo's explanations, however, were soon after received; and proved satisfactory. It was evident from these, that had he not let go in the right time, he would have been compelled to make a leap, that would have left him no opportunity for explaining the nature of the eagle's escape.

Chapter Forty.
Fritz and the falcons.

With feelings of sad and bitter disappointment did our adventurers turn their backs upon these ladders—that had once more deluded them—and make their way towards the hut.

As upon the former occasion, they walked with slow steps and downcast mien. Fritz, by his slouching gait and drooped tail, showed that he shared the general despondency.

They had arrived nearly at the hut, before any of the three thought of speaking; when the sight of that rude homestead, to which they had so often fancied themselves on the eve of bidding farewell—and to which as often had they been compelled to return—suggested a theme to Karl: causing him to break silence as they advanced towards the doorway.

"Our true friend," said he, pointing to the hovel, "a friend, when all else fails us. Rough it is—like many a friend that is nevertheless worthy. I begin to like its honest look, and feel regard for it as one should for a home."

Caspar said nothing in reply. He only sighed. The young chamois-hunter of the Bavarian Alps thought of another home—far away towards the setting sun; and, so long as that thought was in his mind, he could never reconcile himself to a forced residence in the Himalayas.

The thoughts of Ossaroo were equally absent from that spot. He was thinking of a bamboo hut by the borders of some crystal stream, overshadowed by palms and other tropical trees. He was thinking still more of rice curry and chutnee; but above all, of his beloved "betel," for which the "bang" of the *cannabis sativa* was but a poor substitute.

But Caspar had another thought in his mind; one which proved that he had not yet abandoned all hope of returning to the home of his nativity; and, after they had finished eating their supper of broiled venison, he gave utterance to it.

He had not volunteered to break the silence. It was done in obedience to a request of Karl who, having noticed the abstracted air of his brother, had asked for an explanation.

"I've been thinking," said Caspar, "ever since the eagle has escaped us, of another bird I know something about—one that might perform the service we want quite as well, if not better, than a bearcoot."

"Another bird!" inquired Karl; "of what bird are you speaking? Do you mean one of those Brahminy geese upon the lake? We might catch one alive, it is true; but let me tell you, brother, that their wings are constructed just strong enough to carry their own ponderous bodies; and if you added another pound or two, by tying a cord to their legs, they could no more mount out of this valley than we can. No—no. I fancy we may as well give up that idea. There's no bird but an eagle with wing strong enough to do what you wish."

"The bird I was thinking of," rejoined Caspar, "is of the same *genus* as the eagle. I believe that's correctly scientific language. Isn't it, my Buffon of a brother? Ha! ha! Well, shall I name it? Surely, you have already divined the sort of bird to which I allude?"

"No, indeed," replied Karl. "There are no other birds in this valley of the same genus as the eagle—except hawks; and according to the closet naturalists, they are not of the same genus—only of the same *family*. If you mean a hawk, there are several species in this place; but the largest of them could not carry anything over the cliff heavier than a string of twine. See, there's a brace of them now!" continued Karl, pointing to two birds that were circling in the air, some twenty yards overhead. "'Churk' falcons they are called. They are the largest of the Himalayan hawks. Are these your birds, brother?"

"A couple of kites, are they not?" interrogated Caspar, turning his eyes upward, and regarding the two winged creatures circling above, and quartering the air as if in search of prey.

"Yes," answered the naturalist, "they are of that species; and, correctly described, of the same genus as the eagles. You don't mean them, I suppose?"

"No—not exactly," replied Caspar, in a drawling tone, and smiling significantly as he spoke; "but if they be *kites*—Ho! what now?" exclaimed the speaker, his train of thought, as well as speech, suddenly interrupted by a movement on the part of the falcons. "What the mischief are the birds about? As I live, they seem to be making an attack upon Fritz! Surely they don't suppose they have the strength to do any damage to our brave old dog?"

As Caspar spoke, the two falcons were seen suddenly to descend—from the elevation at which they had been soaring—and then sweep in quick short circles around the head of the Bavarian boar-hound—where he squatted on the ground, near a little copse, some twenty yards from the hut.

"Perhaps their nest is there—in the copse?" suggested Karl; "That's why they are angry with the dog: for angry they certainly appear to be."

So any one might have reasoned, from the behaviour of the birds, as they continued their attack upon the dog—now rising some feet above him, and then darting downward in a sort of parabolic curve—at each swoop drawing nearer and nearer, until the tips of their wings were almost flapped in his face. These movements were not made in silence: for the falcons, as they flew, kept uttering their shrill cries—that sounded like the voice of a pair of angry vixens.

"Their young must be near?" suggested Karl.

"No, sahib," said Ossaroo, "no nest—no chickee. Fritz he hab suppa— de piece ob meat ob da ibex. Churk wantee take de dog suppa away."

"Oh! Fritz is eating something, is he?" said Caspar. "That explains it then. How very stupid of these birds, to fancy they could steal his supper from our valiant Fritz: more especially since he seems to relish it so much himself! Why he takes no notice of them!"

It was quite true that Fritz, up to this time, had scarcely noticed the brace of winged assailants; and their hostile demonstrations had only drawn from him an occasional "yir." As they swooped nearer, however, and the tips of their wings were "wopped" into his very eyes, the thing was growing unbearable; and Fritz began to lose temper. His "yirs" became more frequent; and once or twice he rose from his squatting attitude, and made a snap at the feathers that were nearest.

For more than five minutes this curious play was kept up between the boar-hound and the birds; and then the episode was brought to a somewhat singular—and in Fritz's estimation, no doubt—a very unpleasant termination.

From the first commencement of their attack, the two falcons had followed a separate course of action. One appeared to make all its approaches from the front; while the other confined its attacks exclusively to Fritz's rear. In consequence of these tactics on the part of his assailants, the dog was compelled to defend himself both before and behind: and to do this, it became necessary for him to look "two ways at once." Now, he would snarl and snap at the assailant in front—anon, he must sieve himself round, and in like manner menace the more cowardly "churk" that was attacking him in the rear. Of the two, however, the latter was the more demonstrative and noisy; and at length, not content with giving Fritz an occasional "wop" with its wing, it had the daring audacity to strike its sharp talons into a part of his posteriors approximate to the seat of honour.

This was something more than canine flesh and blood could bear; and Fritz determined not to submit to it any longer. Dropping the "quid" he had been chewing, he started up on all fours; wheeled suddenly towards the kite that had clawed him; and bounded aloft into the air with the design of clutching it.

But the wary bird had foreseen this action on the part of the quadruped; and, ere the latter could lay a fang upon it, had soared off—far beyond the highest leap that any four-footed creature might accomplish.

Fritz, with a disappointed growl, turned round again to betake himself to his piece of meat; but still more disappointed was his look, when he perceived that the latter was no longer within reach! Churk falcon number one had clawed him over the croup, but churk falcon number two had deprived him of his supper!

The last look Fritz ever had of that piece of ibex venison, was seeing it in the beak of the bird, high up in air, growing smaller by degrees and beautifully less—until it disappeared altogether in the dim distance.

Chapter Forty One.
Fritz offended.

This odd little episode, between the boar-hound and the churk falcons, had interrupted the conversation of the two brothers on the subject which Caspar had introduced. Nor was it resumed immediately, on the termination of the affair: for the look with which Fritz regarded the departure of the bird, that had so adroitly bilked him out of his bit of venison, was so supremely ludicrous, as to elicit long loud peals of laughter from the spectators.

Fritz's "countenance" betrayed the presence of rare emotions. Profound surprise and chagrin—strongly blended with a feeling of concentrated rage—were visible not only in his eyes, but his attitude, and, for some time, he stood with head erect and muzzle high in air, his glances speaking unutterable vows of vengeance, as they followed the flight of the falcons.

Never in all his life—not even when the trunk of the elephant was trumpeting at his tail—had Fritz so sensibly felt the want of wings. Never had he so regretted the deficiency in his structure that left him without those useful appendages; and had he been gifted with the "wand of a fairy," the use to which he would at that moment have applied it would have been to furnish himself with a pair, not of "beautiful wings"—for that was a secondary consideration—but of strong and long ones, such as would have enabled him to overhaul those churk falcons, and punish them for their unheard-of audacity.

For more than a minute Fritz preserved the attitude to which we have alluded: the demeanour of a dog that had been regularly duped and "sold" by a brace of beings, for whose strength and capacity he had exhibited supreme contempt; and it was this mingling of surprise and rage that imparted to him that serio-comic appearance that had set them all a-laughing. Nor was his countenance less ludicrous under the expression with which, on turning round, he regarded his trio of human companions. He saw that they were making merry at his expense; and his look of half-reproach half-appeal had no other effect than to redouble their mirth. Glancing from one to the other, he appeared to seek sympathy from each in turn—from Karl, Caspar, and Ossaroo.

It was an idle appeal. All three had equally surrendered themselves to hilarity—unsympathetic, as it was uncontrollable. Fritz had not a friend on the ground.

Full ten minutes must have elapsed before any of them could check his loud cachinnations; but long before that time, the butt of their ridicule had betaken himself out of sight—having moved away from the spot, where he had been robbed of his supper, and retired, with an offended and sneaking air, to the more friendly concealment of the hovel.

It was some time before our adventurers could recover their serious mood; but the subject of their mirth being now out of their sight, went gradually also out of their minds.

It might be wondered that, circumstanced as they were, they had thus given way to a fit of jollity. But, indeed, there was nothing wonderful about it. On the contrary, it was perfectly natural—perfectly true to the instincts of the human soul—to be thus stirred: joy and sorrow following each other in periodic succession—as certainly as day follows night, or fair weather succeeds to the storm.

Though we know not the why and the wherefore of this, we can easily believe that a wise Providence has ordered it so. A poet who has sung sweetly says, that:—

"Spring would be but gloomy weather,
If we had nothing else but Spring;"

and our own experience proclaims the truth conveyed in the distich.

He who has lived in the tropical lands of ever-spring—where the leaves never fall, and the flowers never fade—can well confirm the fact: that even spring itself may in time become tiresome! We long for the winter—its frost and snow, and cold bitter winds. Though ever so enamoured of the gay green forest, we like at intervals to behold it in its russet garb, with the sky in its coat of grey, sombre but picturesque. Strange as it may appear, it is true: the moral, like the natural atmosphere, stands in need of the storm.

Chapter Forty Two.
A Kite!

As soon as their mirth had fairly subsided, Karl and Caspar resumed the conversation, which had been broken off so abruptly.

"And so, brother," said Karl, who was the first to return to the subject, "you say there is a bird of the eagle genus, that might carry a rope over the cliff for us. Of what bird are you speaking?"

"Why, Karl, you are dull of comprehension this morning. Surely the presence of the two *kites* should have suggested what I mean."

"Ha! you mean a kite, then?"

"Yes, one with a very broad breast, a very thin body, and a very long tail: such as you and I used to make not so many years ago."

"A *paper kite*," said Karl, repeating the phrase mechanically, at the same time settling down, into a reflecting attitude. "True, brother," he added, after a pause; "there might be something in what you have suggested. If we had a paper kite—that is, a very large one—it is possible it would carry a rope over the summit of the cliff; but, alas!—"

"You need not proceed further, Karl," said Caspar, interrupting him. "I know what you are going to say: that we have no paper out of which to make the kite; and that, of course, puts an end to the matter. It's no use our thinking any more about it: since we have not got the materials. The body and bones we could easily construct; and the tail too. But then the wings— ah, the wings. I only wish we had a file of old newspapers. But what's the use of wishing? We haven't."

Karl, though silent, did not seem to hear, or at all events heed, what Caspar had been just saying. He appeared to be buried either in a reverie, or in some profound speculation.

It was the latter: as was very soon after made manifest by his speech.

"Perhaps," said he, with a hopeful glance towards the wood, "we may not be so deficient in the material of which you have spoken."

"Of paper, do you mean?"

"We are in the very region of the world where it grows," continued Karl, without heeding the interrogation.

"What! where paper *grows*?"

"No," replied Karl, "I do not mean that the paper itself grows here; but a 'fabric' out of which that useful article may be made."

"What is that, brother?"

"It is a tree, or rather a shrub, belonging to the order of the *Thymelaceae*, or 'Daphnads.' The plants of this order are found in many countries; but chiefly in the cooler regions of India and South America. There are even representatives of the order in England: for the beautiful 'spurge laurel' of the woods and hedges—known as a remedy for the toothache—is a true daphnad. Perhaps the most curious of all the Thymelaceae is the celebrated Lagetta, or lace-bark tree of Jamaica; out of which the ladies of that island know how to manufacture cuffs, collars, and berthas, that, when cut into the proper shapes, and bleached to a perfect whiteness, have all the appearance of real lace! The Maroons, and other runaway negroes of Jamaica, before the abolition of slavery, used to make clothing out of the lagetta; which they found growing in plenty in the mountain forests of the island. Previous also to the same abolition of slavery, there was another, and less gentle, use made of the lace-bark, by the masters of these same negroes. The cruel tyrants used to spin its tough fibres into thongs for their slave-whips."

"And you think that paper can be made out of these trees?" asked Caspar, impatient to know whether there might be any chance of procuring some for the covering of a kite.

"There are several species of daphnads," replied the botanist, "whose bark can be converted into paper. Some are found at the Cape of Good Hope, and others in the island of Madagascar; but the best kinds for the purpose grow in these very mountains, and in China. There is the 'Daphne Bholua,' in Nepaul; from which the Nepaulese make a strong, tough, packing-paper; and I have reason to believe that it also grows in the Bhotan Himalayas—at no very great distance from our position here. Besides, in China and Japan, on the other side of these mountains, there are two or three distinct kinds of the same plant—out of which the Chinese make the yellowish-coloured paper, you may have seen in their books, and pasted upon their tea-chests. So then," added the botanist, looking wistfully towards the woods, "since the paper-yielding daphne grows in China, to the east of us, and in Nepaul and Bhotan to the west, it is but reasonable to conclude that some species of it may be found in this valley—where the climate is just that which it affects. Its seed may have been transported hither by birds: since many species of birds are fond of its berries, and eat them without receiving any injury; though, strange to say, they are poisonous to all kinds of quadrupeds!"

"Do you think you would know the shrub, if you saw it, brother?"

"Well, to say the truth, I do not think I could recognise it by its general appearance; but if I had a flower of the *daphne*, I could no doubt tell it by its botanical characteristics. The leaves of the paper-yielding species are of a lanceolate form and purplish hue, glabrous and shining, like the leaves of laurels—to which genus the *daphne* is closely allied. Unfortunately, the shrub would not be in flower at this season; but if we can find one of the berries, and a leaf or two, I fancy I shall be able to identify it. Besides, the bark, which is very tough, would help to guide us. Indeed, I have some reason to think that we shall find it not far off; and that is why I speak with such confidence, in saying, that we might not be so deficient in the materials for paper-making."

"What reason, brother Karl? Perhaps you have seen something like it?"

"I have. Some time ago, when I was strolling about, I passed through a thicket of low shrubs—the tops of which reached up to my breast. They were then in flower—the flowers being of a lilac colour, and growing at the tops of the branches in little cymes. They had no corolla—only a coloured calyx. Now these characters correspond with those of the daphne. Besides, the leaves were lanceolate, velvety on the surface, and of purplish colour; and the flowers were of an exceedingly sweet scent—as is the case with all the daphnads. I did not think of examining them at the time; but, now that I recall these characteristics, I feel almost certain that the shrubs were of this genus."

"Do you think you can find the thicket again?"

"Oh! yes, easily enough. It is not very distant from the place, where we were so near fighting that fearful duel."

"Ha! ha! ha!" laughed Caspar, in reply to the significant remark of the botanist. "But, brother!" continued he, "suppose it should prove to be the shrub you speak of, what good would there be in our finding it, so long as we don't understand the process of manufacturing it into paper?"

"How do you know that we don't?" said Karl, challenging the too positive declaration of Caspar. "I am not so sure that we don't. I have read the whole account of the process, as given by one of the old writers upon China. It is very simple; and I think I remember enough to be able to follow it. Perhaps not to make fine paper, that one might write upon; but something that would serve our purpose just as well. We don't want the best 'cream-laid.' Unfortunately, we have no post-office here. I wish we had.

If we can fabricate anything as fine as the coarsest packing-paper, it will do well enough for a kite, I fancy."

"True," replied Caspar. "It would be all the better to be coarse and strong. But, dear Karl, suppose we go at once, and see if we can discover the trees."

"That is just what we shall do," replied Karl, rising as he spoke, and preparing to set out in search of the daphne.

All, of course, went together: for Ossaroo was as much interested in the result of the exploration as any of them; and Fritz, from within the hut, perceiving that they were about to depart upon some new expedition, managed partially to coax himself out of his ill-humour; and, sallying forth from his hiding-place, trotted silently after them.

Chapter Forty Three.
The paper-tree.

To the great delight of the party, it turned out just as Karl had conjectured. The thicket that he had spoken of was composed chiefly of daphne shrubs—judging by the appearance of the fallen leaves, and some berries that still remained on the branches, Karl believed them to be of this species. But the bark was also a characteristic: being exceedingly tenacious, and moreover of a strongly acrid taste—so much so as to cauterise he skin of Ossaroo's mouth, who had been foolish enough to chew it too freely.

After duly examining the leaves, berries, and bark, the botanist came to the conclusion that the shrub must be a true daphne; and so in reality it was—that species known in Nepaul as the *Daphne Bholua*—from which, as already stated, the Nepaulese manufacture a coarse, but soft paper.

As soon as this point was determined to their satisfaction, they resolved upon carrying Caspar's hint into execution—by trying the experiment of a paper kite.

But for Karl's practical education—which had made him acquainted not only with the botanical characters of plants and trees, but also with their uses—and in some cases with the mode of using them—the mere discovery of the daphne would have availed them nothing. As it stood in the thicket, it was no more like paper than any of the trees that grew around it. Indeed, there were many others that would have yielded bark in broader flakes than it, and much more resembling paper: for that of the daphne, stripping off as it did in narrow pieces, looked like the last thing in the world of which to make a kite out of. But Karl knew the process by which it could be metamorphosed into paper; and without further delay, he entered upon the performance—the others placing their services at his disposal, and acting in obedience to his orders.

The knife-blades of all three were called into requisition; and in an incredibly short space of time, some scores of the little trees were stripped of their bark—from their roots up to the lower branches. The trees themselves were not cut down; as that was not necessary. They could be peeled more readily, as they stood; and for this reason they were left standing.

Up to the hour of sunset did these "cascarilleros" work—with only a few minutes of interruption, while they went back to the hut, and ate a hurried luncheon of ibex-meat—and just as the sun was sinking behind the summit of the great Chumulari, they might have been seen trudging homeward—each bearing a heavy bundle of bark, with Fritz following gleefully at their heels.

The thicket from which they had taken their departure, gave evidence of the industry with which they had been working all day long. Over a space, of nearly half an acre in extent, the trees were seen standing, each with its tiny trunk completely divested of bark: as if a whole gang of goats had been browsing upon them!

On reaching the hovel, our bark-gatherers did not desist from their labour. They only entered upon a new branch of industry: by becoming *paper manufacturers*.

It was after night; and they had to work by the light of their torches of cheel-pine, already prepared. But as these burnt with a clear steady flame, they served quite as well as candles would have done.

The first process in the paper-making did not require much nicety in its execution; and, moreover, it could be performed as well inside the hut as in the largest room of a paper-mill. All they had to do was to pick the bark to shreds. This occupied them the whole evening—during which there was much conversation of a cheerful kind, with a joke or two about oakum-picking in a prison; and of this, not only the task in which they were engaged, but the situation in which they were executing it, did not fail to remind them.

When they had finished, they ate their frugal supper and retired to rest—full of the idea of continuing the paper manufacture in the morning.

When morning came, they had not much to do: for the next process was one which required the exercise of patience rather than of labour.

When the bark of the daphne has been thoroughly picked to pieces, it is put into a large pot or cauldron filled with water. A lixivium of wood-ashes is then thrown in along with it; and it is suffered to boil for several hours.

As our manufacturers were without pot or cauldron of any kind, there would have been here an interruption of an insurmountable kind: had it not been that they had plenty of water already on the boil, and perpetually boiling—in the hot-spring near the hut.

Apparently all they should have to do would be, to immerse the prepared bark in the spring, and there leave it for a proper length of time. But then the water, where it was hottest, was constantly in motion—bubbling up and running off; so that not only would the strings of bark be carried away, but the ashes would be separated from the mass, and consequently of no service in aiding to macerate it.

How was this difficulty to be got over? Easily enough. They had not proceeded thus far without thinking of a plan; and this plan was, to place the bark along with the ashes in one of the large yâk-skins still in good preservation, and after making it up into a sort of bundle—like clothes intended for the laundry—to plunge the skin and its contents into the spring, and there leave them—until the boiling water should perform its part. By this ingenious contrivance, did they get over the difficulty, of not being provided with a not.

When Karl thought that the bark was sufficiently boiled, it was taken out of the water, and also out of its yâk-skin wrapper. It was then placed, in mass, upon a flat rock near by—where it was left to drip and get dry.

During the time that it was in the water—and also while it was dripping and drying on the rock—none of them were idle. Caspar was engaged in fashioning a stout wooden mallet—a tool which would be needed in some after operations—while Ossaroo was equally busy upon an article of a very different kind. This was a sort of sieve made of thin splints of cane, set in a frame of thicker pieces of the same cane—ringall bamboo.

Ossaroo had undertaken this special task: as none of the others knew so well, how to fashion the bamboo into any required utensil; and although he was now making something altogether new to him, yet, working under the direction of Karl, he succeeded in making a sieve that was likely to serve the purpose for which plant-hunter designed it. That purpose will presently be spoken of.

As soon as the fibre was nearly dry, the mallet was brought into requisition; and with this the mass was pounded upon the flat surface of the rock—until it became reduced to a complete state of "pulp."

This pulp was once more put into the yâk-skin—which had been gathered up around the edges so as to form a sort of concavity or rude vat— and again immersed under water—not of the boiling spring, but the cool water of the lake—until the bag became full. The pulp was next stirred with a stick—which brought the coarse dirty parts to the surface. These were skimmed off, and thrown away as refuse; and the process was repeated with fresh water—until the whole substance, which was of a mucilaginous character, was rendered pure, and soft to the touch. The next and last operation was in fact the making of the paper; and was performed by Karl himself. It was simple enough, though requiring a certain dexterity, or sleight of hand, to do it well. It consisted in placing a quantity of the pulp upon the sieve before mentioned; and cradling the frame about—all the time held under water—until the substance became equally and uniformly spread over the whole surface. The sieve was then taken out of the water— being raised gently and kept in a horizontal position—so as not to derange the even stratum of pulp that severed it. This done, nothing more remained but to place the frame across a pair of bars, and leave the pulp to get drained and eventually become dry. When dry, it would be *paper*!

Of course, with one sieve, the whole quantity required could not be made at a single cast; but, as soon as one sheet became sufficiently dry to be taken off the frame, the sieve was again repulped; and so on, till the whole of the boiled bark was converted into paper; and they found themselves in possession of a sufficient number of broad sheets to make a kite as big as a coach-house-door.

In consequence of their having to wait for the drying of each sheet, the process occupied them for several days; but during this time they had not been either idle or inactive. Karl and Caspar had been hard at work, in getting up the "bones" of the kite; while Ossaroo had undertaken to fabricate the tail.

The rope with which it was to be "flyed," occupied more time, and required more care, than any other portion of their work. Every strand had to be twisted with the greatest exactness; and almost every fibre tested, as to its strength and fitness. Could they have used a rope of stouter build, it would not have been necessary to be so particular; but a thick rope would have been too heavy for the kite to carry—just as it had been too heavy for the strength of the eagle. A slender cord, therefore, like that they were obliged to make, required to be faultless—else the life of some one of them might be sacrificed while attempting the ascent.

With a foreknowledge of this, it is hardly necessary to say that Ossaroo did his best in the manufacture of that rope—every strand of it being twisted between his index finger and his thumb, as smoothly and evenly as if he had been spinning it for a fishing-line.

The framework of the kite was made out of split culms of the ringall bamboo; which, on account of its strength, elasticity, and lightness, was far superior for the purpose to any species of exogenous wood; while the glue for laying on the paper was procured from the root of an arum—grated, and then boiled into a glutinous starch.

In about a week after the notion of a kite had been "hatched" in the brain of Caspar, the bird itself might have been seen outside the door of the hut—full-fledged and ready for flight!

Chapter Forty Four.
Flying the kite.

The kite having been thus prepared, they only waited for an opportunity of flying it—for a day when the wind should be sufficiently strong, and blowing from the right quarter—that is, towards that portion of the precipice over which it appeared best that the paper-bird should be dispatched. This was the same place, where the ladders had been set, and where they had unsuccessfully endeavoured to send up the bearcoot.

They had already ascended one of the isolated cairns of rock, that stood within the valley nearly opposite this part of the cliff; and from its top they had been able to get a view—though not a very good one—of a portion of the sloping declivity of the mountain above. It appeared to be covered with snow—here and there supporting huge masses of something, either boulders of rock, or dark-coloured lumps of ice. The eyes of our adventurers rested on these with the greatest interest: as they had done upon a former occasion, when about to send the bearcoot among them. Now they had conceived higher hopes than ever—founded upon the presence of these masses. If they should succeed in flying the kite into their midst, and there dropping it, it was not only possible, but highly probable, that it might either get the rope warped around one of them, or itself become caught between two, so as to hold fast. To render this the more practicable, they had furnished its wings with spurs—in other words, they had left the cross-piece of bamboo to extend on each side about a foot beyond the edge of the paper; and near the end of each extension, they had placed other pieces transversely, and lashed them firmly—so that they might act as the flukes of an anchor.

They had spared neither pains nor ingenuity to ensure success. They had done all, that man could do, to deserve it.

Fortune was so far favourable, as not to keep them long in suspense. Only two or three days had passed, when one came, on which the wind blew in their favour—exactly as they wanted it. It was a stiff breeze, steady in the right direction, and strong enough to carry up the largest of paper kites.

Proceeding to the place, where the ladders were set, with the huge bird carried in the arms of Ossaroo, they made ready for its flight. Karl was to start the kite, and guide its ascent from the ground; while Caspar and the shikaree were to run out with the rope: as it would require the united strength of both to hold such a broad-breasted bird against the wind. They had taken the precaution to cut away the bushes to a long distance backwards from the cliff, and so clear the track: there was therefore nothing to impede them while paying out the string.

It was arranged that Karl should have direction of the movement, and give out the signal for them to start.

It was a moment of vivid emotion, as each of he three placed himself in the position assigned to him—Karl by the kite, with its backbone in one hand, and its tail in the other—Ossaroo clutching the rope—and Caspar by his side, holding the great coil in readiness for delivery.

Karl poised the creature upon the stump of its tail; and then, lifting with all his strength—so as to raise it several feet from the ground—he gave forth the signal at the highest pitch of his voice.

At the same instant, Caspar and the shikaree ran backward—tightening the rope as they went; and like a vast vulture with outspread wings, the bird soared silently upward into the air.

It rose with a regular majestic motion, soon overtopping the trees that grew near, and still mounting on towards the summit of the cliff.

Karl cheered as he saw it ascend. The others were too busy in the performance of their parts to find time for this expression of triumph; and not until the kite had soared high into the heavens, and appeared many yards above the brow of the beetling precipice, did Caspar and Ossaroo respond to the cheering of Karl. Then both together gave vent to their excited feelings in a long-continued hurrah!

"Let go now, Ossaroo!" cried Karl, shouting so as to be heard above the wind. "You, Caspar, keep hold of the end of the cord."

Ossaroo, obedient to the order, suddenly slackened his hold—at the same time springing towards Caspar, and prudently seizing the end along with him.

The kite, thus released, like some huge bird that had received its death-wound, turned head downwards towards the earth; and, after making various sinuous evolutions through the air, flouting its long tail first in one direction then in another—it was seen darting down towards the acclivity of the mountain. At length, passing behind the summit of the cliffs, it was no longer visible to the eyes of those who had aided it in its lofty flight, and then left it helplessly to fall.

So far they had succeeded to the utmost of their expectations. The kite had alighted, just where they wanted it.

But now arose the question—would it stay there? In other words, would it be caught among the rocks, and hold fast?

If not, they would have to fly it again and again, until it should get fastened above, or until the experiment should prove a failure.

Karl stepped forward to decide the point—the others looking on with an eagerness of glance, that betrayed how deep was their interest in the result.

Karl's hand trembled as he laid hold of the cord. At first he pulled upon it in a gentle way—hand over hand—so as merely to take in the slack.

At length it began to tighten, requiring greater strength to take it in: as if the kite was still free, and dragging over the snow.

This produced anything but a pleasant anticipation; and as the rope came to hand, foot after foot, and yard after yard, a shadow, that had stolen over the countenances of all three, became sensibly darker.

Only for a short while did this shadow remain. It vanished, more suddenly than it had arisen: when they saw the running cord become abruptly checked, and then tighten as Karl continued to draw it in. He pulled upon it, at first exerting only a part of his strength, as if afraid that it might again come loose. After awhile, gaining confidence, he pulled with all his power. It still held fast!

Ossaroo and Caspar now joined their strength to his; and all three pulled together.

Hurrah! the kite would not come! The cord kept its place, stretching to the bottom of the cliff, as taut as the main-stay of a ship!

Ejaculations of joy escaped from all three at the same instant of time: and for some moments they stood, tightly clutching the rope, and holding it firmly: as if in dread of its being dragged out of their grasp by some hostile and invisible hand.

At length Karl suggested the propriety of making the cord secure, by fastening it to some object. A large upright stone, close by the bottom of the cliff, appeared to be the most proper thing; and to this they determined upon tying it.

Still keeping it taut—lest by slackening it they might disturb the anchor aloft—they moved hand over hand along the rope, until they had got close to the bottom of the precipice. Then, while Karl and Caspar still held on, Ossaroo gathered up the slack; and, turning it several times round the stone, securely *belayed* it.

Nothing more remained but to make the steps—which had been already designed—adjust them in their places—climb up to the top of the cliff—and be free as the mountain breeze, which would there be blowing around them!

The thought of such a lucky deliverance filled them once more with joyous imaginings; and they stood around the stone, to which the rope had been attached—congratulating themselves, as if they had already escaped.

They knew there would still be some time required to make the steps, and fix them in their places; but, since they no longer doubted their ability to accomplish the ascent, the interval of time might be passed cheerfully enough; and, with this pleasant anticipation, they went back to their workshop in the best of spirits, and cooked themselves a more careful dinner than they had eaten since the discovery of the daphne trees.

Chapter Forty Five.
The rope-ladder.

It took them another day—with their blades all busy from morning till night—to prepare the pegs which were to constitute the "rounds" of their rope-ladder. More than a hundred were required: as the cliff where the rope passed up was over a hundred yards in height; and the steps were intended to be placed at equal distances of about two feet apart.

It had been their design at first to insert the steps in the rope—between the strands of which it was composed; but, on reflection, a better plan suggested itself. By opening the strands to let in the pieces of wood, the rope might be weakened, so much as to endanger its breaking; and this alone, above all things, was to be avoided. It was deemed more prudent to leave the cord untouched, and place the sticks crosswise outside of it. Whipped round with strong pieces of other cord, they could easily be made to keep their places—more especially as, with the hands of the climber grasping the rope above, no one stick would have to carry the full weight of his body; and, even should one of them slip a little out of place, there would be no great danger of an accident arising out of the circumstance.

It occupied them a second day in twining the pieces of string, required for tying the sticks in their places; and, upon the morning of the third, they returned to the cliff, with the intention of transforming the cord, that the kite had carried up, into a rope-ladder.

The mode by which they intended to effect this purpose will be easily understood—after what has been already said respecting it. The little sticks were to be laid transversely against the rope, and then so tightly tied in their places, as to prevent them from slipping down. The first was to be attached about the height of a man's waist from the ground; and the second on a level with his chin. Then with the feet resting upon the first, and the left hand grasping the rope above, it would be possible to fix another at the height of the chin, as it would then be. By climbing up to the second, a fourth could be placed at a little distance above; and thus in succession, till the top of the cliff should be attained.

It was not supposed, that any one could continue the process of attaching the steps, till all were set in their places; nor did they contemplate being able to complete the work in a little time. On the contrary, they expected it to occupy them for days; and they knew, moreover, that long intervals of rest would be required by any one who should have to execute it. Standing upon such unstable footing, for any considerable length of time, would be both irksome and fatiguing; and they were about to enter upon the task with a full knowledge of its difficulties.

On reaching the cord they at once set to work upon it. Rather should it be said, that one of them did so: for only one could work at a time in this, the last labour, as they supposed, they would have to perform in that lone valley.

In attaching the steps to the rope, Ossaroo was allowed to act as sole operator: since neither of the others understood the handling of cordage so well as he. They could but act as spectators and the only purpose which their presence could serve, was to cheer the shikaree by their company and conversation.

By good fortune it was not necessary for Ossaroo to fix any steps to the first thirty feet of the kite cord. One of the long ladders which they had made enabled him to ascend that far without using the sticks; and, indeed, all of the ladders might have served in this way, had the kite carried its cord up the cliff within reach of them. Unfortunately, this did not happen to be the case; and only the first ladder could be made available.

Placing it nearly parallel with the rope, Ossaroo mounted up; and, when near its top, commenced attaching the steps. He had carried up along with him about a dozen of the little sticks, with cords to correspond—in a sort of pouch, which he had formed with the skirts of his cotton tunic.

Karl and Caspar below, seated upon stones, and Fritz squatted on the ground, watched the movements of the shikaree with deep and speechless interest.

It was not a very long time, before he had adjusted the first two pegs in their proper places; and, then letting himself off the ladder, and placing both his feet upon the first cross-piece, in a way that they balanced one another and kept the stick in a horizontal position—he proceeded to attach the third about the height of his chin.

To do this required, a good deal of adroitness; but Ossaroo was gifted with this quality to a high degree; and, so far as his footing was concerned, the Hindoo was as much at home upon a rope, as would have been one of those monkeys sacred to the believers in his Brahministic creed.

Any other feet would soon have become tired—resting upon such a slender support; but Ossaroo had been accustomed to climbing the tall lofty palms, until his toes had acquired a certain degree of prehensile power; and the smallest branch or protuberance on the trunk of a tree, or even a knot on a rope, was footing enough to enable him to hold on for many minutes at a time. He had no difficulty, therefore, in balancing himself upon the sticks, which he had already attached; nor ascending from one to the other, as each was got into its place. In this way he proceeded, until the stock which he had taken up with him was exhausted, and his apron hung empty. Then, letting himself down from step to step, and cautiously returning to the wooden ladder, he descended to the bottom of the cliff.

Karl or Caspar might have rendered his coming down unnecessary, as either could have carried so light a "hod" up the ladder; but there was good reason why Ossaroo should make the descent—that was, to rest and refresh himself.

He did not remain very long below—just long enough to let the blood circulate along the soles of his naked feet—and then, with his apron distended—being once more full of sticks—he reclimbed the ladder, swung himself out upon the cord, and clambered up the steps he had already fixed in their places.

His second stock of sticks becoming exhausted as the first, he again revisited the earth; again allowed himself an interval of rest; and then ascended as before.

With Ossaroo proceeding in this fashion, the remainder of the day was spent—a long interval being allowed for dinner; which Karl and Caspar, having nothing else to do, had cooked with extra care. They did not go home to the hut to perform their culinary operations. There would have been no advantage in doing so: since the kitchen accommodation there was not a whit better than where they were at work; and the larder contained nothing more than what they had brought along with them—some dried ibex-meat. But Karl had not been idle for a portion of the time; and had collected various roots and fruits that, when roasted, not only helped out the meal, but rendered it sufficiently luxurious for stomachs like theirs, no longer fastidious.

After dinner, Ossaroo indulged in a long smoke of his favourite "bang;" and, stimulated by this, returned to his task with renewed energy.

So successful was he in its accomplishment, that, before sunset he had full fifty steps in place; which, along with the wooden ladder, enabled him to climb nearly a third of the way up the cliff.

Of course darkness put an end to his operations for that day; and with the intention of continuing them on the morrow, both the operator and spectators wended their way back to the hut—Karl and Caspar showing as much respect to Ossaroo, as if he had been the master architect, and they only his assistants or labourers. Even Fritz appeared to be impressed with the belief that the shikaree was the most important personage in the party: for every time that the latter descended from the cliff the dog had paid his "devoirs" to him, frisking around, leaping up, and looking steadfastly in his face, as if congratulating him on being their deliverer!

On the road home Fritz continued these demonstrations—springing against the legs of the shikaree so as occasionally to impede his progress, evidently convinced—either from his own observation or from the respect which he saw the others were paying him—that the Hindoo was the hero of the day!

Chapter Forty Six.
Ossaroo makes a quick descent.

Next morning, as soon as they had despatched an early meal, they returned to their work—that is, Ossaroo to work, the others to watch.

Unfortunately on this day the weather was unfavourable for operations. There was a high wind, not continuous, but blowing in short, quick puffs—gusty and violent.

As Ossaroo hung upon the rope half-way up the precipice, the wind acting upon his body, carried him at times several feet out from the face of the cliff—causing him also to oscillate violently from side to side, notwithstanding that the rope was fast at both ends.

It was fearful to look at him thus suspended, and swinging in mid-air. At times the hearts of the spectators were filled with consternation, lest the brave shikaree should either have his brains dashed out against the beetling cliff; or, being forced to let go his hold, be flung far out, and falling upon the rocks below, get crushed to atoms.

Often during the earlier part of the day were the alarms of Karl and Caspar raised to such a height, that they shouted to Ossaroo to come down; and when down, entreated him not to go up again until, by the lulling of the wind, the danger should become diminished.

Their entreaties, however, were of no avail. The shikaree, accustomed all his life to braving the elements, felt no fear of them; but on the contrary, seemed to feel a pride, if not an actual pleasure, in thus daring danger.

Even while swinging out from the cliff, and oscillating along its *façade*—like the pendulum of some gigantic clock—he was seen tying the strings and adjusting the pieces of stick, as coolly, as if he had been standing upon *terra firma* at the bottom!

Thus, nearly to the hour of noon, did Ossaroo continue his arduous undertaking—of course with the usual intervals of rest, during each of which Karl and Caspar reiterated their entreaties for him to desist and leave the work to be executed at a more favourable opportunity. Fritz, too, while lavishing his caresses on the daring climber, seemed to look persuadingly into his face—as if he knew there was danger in what the Hindoo was doing.

It was all in vain. The shikaree, while resisting all their efforts to restrain him, seemed to scorn the danger which they dreaded; and, without hesitation, returned to his perilous task.

And no doubt he would have succeeded in accomplishing it, allowing due time for its completion. It was not the wind that would have shaken him from that rope, to which he clung with the tenacity of a spider. Had the support proved true, he could have held on, even though it had been blowing a hurricane!

It was not in this that his chief danger lay; nor from such source was it to come; but from one altogether unexpected and unthought-of.

It was near the hour of noon, and Ossaroo had already succeeded in setting the steps up to about half the height of the cliff. He had descended for a fresh supply of sticks; and, having gone up the tree-ladder, and swung himself back upon the kite cord, was just commencing to clamber up it—as he had already done nearly a score of times.

The eyes of Karl and Caspar were upon him, following his movements, as they had been doing all along; for, despite his frequent repetition of the ascent, it was always a perilous performance, and interesting to behold.

Just as he had got free from the ladder, and fairly out upon the rope, a cry came from his lips that thrilled the hearts of the spectators with alarm: for they knew that the utterance was one of terror. They needed no explanation of that cry; for at the same moment that it reached their ears, they perceived the danger that had caused Ossaroo to utter it. He was descending along the façade of the cliff—not gliding down the rope of his own free will, but as if the kite had got loose at the top, and, yielding to the weight of his body, was being dragged over the surface of the snow!

At first, he appeared to be descending only very slowly; and, but for the cries he was putting forth, and the slackening of the rope below, they upon the ground might not have been aware of what was going on. But they had not regarded his movements for many seconds, before perceiving the true state of the case, and the fearful peril in which their faithful shikaree was now placed.

Beyond doubt the kite had become detached above; and, yielding to the strain upon the rope, caused by Ossaroo's weighty was being pulled towards the edge of the precipice!

Would the resistance be equal to the weight of the man's body? Would it let him down easily? Or would the dragging anchor arrive at a place where the surface was smooth, and then gliding rapidly over it, increase the velocity of the descent? In other words, was the shikaree about to be projected through a fall of thirty feet to the bottom of the cliff?

The spectators were left but little time to speculate on probabilities. Not a moment was allowed them to take measures for securing the safety of their companion. Before they could recover from the surprise, with which his first shout had inspired them, they saw that his descent was every moment becoming more accelerated: now in gradual declination, then in quick, short jerks—until he had got within about twenty-feet of the ground. They were in hopes that he might continue to descend in this fashion for a few yards further, and then the danger would be over; but, just at that moment, the broad breast of the kite was seen poising itself over the top of the cliff; and like a great living bird, it sprang off from the rocks, and soared out over the valley!

Ossaroo, still clinging to the cord, was carried some distance from the cliff; but, fortunately for him, the weight of his body overbalanced the resistance which the atmosphere offered to the broad surface of the kite; else he might have been carried much higher into the air. Equally fortunate was it, that the amount of overbalance was exceedingly slight—otherwise he might have been dashed with violence to the earth!

As it was, he came down as gently as a dove, alighting upon his legs, and remaining erect upon them, like Mercury upon the top of his "sky-kissing mountain."

The moment that the shikaree felt his feet touching *terra firma*, he sprang nimbly to one side, at the same instant letting go the rope, as if it had been a rod of red-hot iron!

The great kite, no longer held in poise against the wind, commenced darting hither and thither; at each turn descending lower and lower—until by one last swoop, in which it seemed to concentrate all its failing strength, it came down towards Ossaroo like a gigantic bird of prey descending upon its victim!

It was just as much as the shikaree could do to get out of the way; and, had he not ducked his head in the very nick of time, he would certainly have received a blow upon his skull, that would have endangered its entirety.

Chapter Forty Seven.
The escape of the kite.

The joy, which all felt at the miraculous escape of Ossaroo, more than compensated for their chagrin at the circumstance of the kite having returned to them: more especially, as they believed that the accident was not without remedy. It might be attributed to the wind: which no doubt had lifted the kite from where it lay, detaching it from the rock, or whatever other object that had for the time entangled it.

They doubted not, but that they might again succeed in sending it up, and getting it fast as before; and this confidence hindered them from grieving over the unfortunate occurrence, as they might otherwise have done.

As the wind on that day was in the wrong quarter for flying a kite towards the cliff, they determined to postpone the attempt, till a more favourable opportunity; and, in order that their kite should not be in danger of getting spoiled by the rain, they once more shouldered, and carried it back, rope and all, to the shelter of the hut.

Nearly a week elapsed, before there was a breeze that blew in their favour; but during this interval, they had not been altogether unemployed. Still uncertain of the length of time they might be detained in the valley, they had passed almost every hour of the daylight in increasing their stock of provisions—so as not to encroach upon the cured venison of the ibex, of which a considerable quantity was still to the good.

Their guns were no longer used for procuring food. The last loads still remained in the barrels; and were not to be fired off—until every other means of capturing game should fail them.

Indeed, they were now so confident of being able to get out of their prison, that at times they almost fancied themselves already on their way down the mountains; and talked of keeping their guns loaded, against any danger from large animals they might encounter on their homeward journey. For procuring food they knew that firearms were not necessary. Ossaroo's bow was sufficient weapon for that. Often might it be heard twanging among the trees; and as often did the shikaree's arrow pierce the breast of some fine bird—a peacock, or argus pheasant, or one of the beautiful Brahminy geese that frequented the waters of the lake.

Ossaroo's nets and lines, too, were not without their use. Fish were caught of various kinds, and excellent quality; and there was one sort in particular, should all else fail, that promised to furnish them with an inexhaustible supply. This was a large species of eel, in which the lake abounded, to such an extent, that it was only necessary to cast in a hook, with a worm upon it, and an eel of nearly six feet in length would be instantly landed.

As they did not always relish to dine upon eels, but little of their time was spent in procuring them. For all that, they were gratified on discovering the abundance of these slippery creatures—knowing that, should other resources fail, they would find in them a staple article of wholesome food, that could never become scarce, no matter how much they should eat of it.

A favourable wind at length came on to blow; and the kite was once more shouldered, and carried to the same place as before. Just in the same way did they proceed to fly it; and in the same style it again rose soaring above the cliff; and—the cord having been suddenly slacked—sank to rest upon the slope of the mountain.

So far were they once more successful; but alas! it proved to be just so far and no farther.

Pulling upon the rope, to ascertain whether their anchor had "bit," they were chagrined to receive an answer in the negative. The cord came back to them with scarce any resistance; or only such, as was caused by friction over the edge of the cliff, and by the drag of the kite itself along the snowy surface.

Hand over hand, they drew it back: foot by foot, and yard by yard, it came yieldingly towards them—until they saw the broad curving breast of the pseudo-bird projecting over the parapet edge of the precipice!

Once more was it launched out into the air; once more was rope given it, till it had ascended to the full length of its tether; and once more was it allowed to alight.

Again the pull downward and inward—again the cord came freely to hand—and again was the rounded bow seen upon the brow of the precipice, and outlined against the blue sky above; not like the beautiful bow of the iris—a thing of promise—but one of disappointment and chagrin.

Again the flight—again the failure—again and again; until the patience of the operators—to say nothing of their strength—was well nigh exhausted.

But it was no mere play for the sake of pastime. They were not flying that kite for their amusement; nor yet for the purpose of making some scientific experiment. They were flying it as a means of obtaining their personal liberty; and they were all of them interested in the success or failure of the attempt—almost as much as if their lives rested on the issue.

However tried their strength, or worn out their patience, it would not do to give up; and therefore—although at each unsuccessful effort, with hopes constantly becoming diminished—they continued their exertions.

For more than a score of times they had sent up the kite, and as often dragged it back to the brow of the cliff; not always at the same point: for they had themselves changed their ground, and tried the flight in different places.

In all cases, the result was the same. The bird refused to take hold with its claws—either on rocks, or blocks of ice, or banks of frozen snow—all of which lay scatter over the slope of the mountain.

Considering that it had caught hold on the very first trial, so many failures were regarded by our adventurers with some surprise. Had it never held, there would have been no cause for this; and after so many attempts, they would have been the more inclined to yield up their plan, deeming it impracticable. But the fact of their first success sustained them in the hope that success might again be obtained; and, in this belief, they were encouraged to "keep on trying."

Half a dozen additional flights were made, but fortune still declining to favour them, they desisted from their efforts, leaving the paper-bird with its breast protruding over the cliff: as if perched there in preparation for a further flight.

By this time the kite had become sadly damaged—its *plumage* having received rough usage by constant trailing over the rocks and sharp angles of ice. While up in the air, daylight could be seen shining through it in several places; and it no longer exhibited that majesty of flight that had originally characterised it. It was evident that repairs would soon be needed; and to discuss this question, as also to consider the propriety of proceeding to make trial at some other place, our adventurers, for a time, discontinued their efforts.

All three were standing together, but at several paces distant from the end of the rope; which they had for the moment abandoned, and which lay negligently along the ground.

They had not taken the slightest precaution to secure it: for it had not occurred to them that there was any risk in leaving it loose.

It was only when too late, that they perceived the mistake they had committed—only when they saw the cord suddenly jerked up from the ground, as if some invisible hand was lifting it aloft into the sky!

All three rushed towards it at the same instant. They were too late. Already the end of the rope was dangling at such a height above their heads, that even the tallest of them could not touch it with the tips of his fingers.

Ossaroo leaped high into the air in an endeavour to clutch the string. Caspar ran to procure a pole which lay near, in hopes of retaining it in that way: while Karl ran up the ladder that was resting against the cliff, near which the rope was yet trailing.

The efforts of all three were alike vain. For a second or two, the end of the cord hung oscillating above their heads—just sufficiently out of reach to tantalise them; and then, as if the invisible hand above had given it another gigantic jerk, it was drawn rapidly and vertically upward, till it finally disappeared over the crest of the cliff!

Chapter Forty Eight.
No more paper-trees!

There was nothing mysterious in the disappearance of the cord. The kite was no longer visible on the summit of the cliff. The wind had carried it away; and, of course, its rope along with it.

When the first moment of surprise had passed, our adventurers turned towards each other with glances that spoke something more than disappointment. Notwithstanding the number of times that the kite had failed to fix itself, still it had once taken a fast hold, and it was but reasonable to suppose it would have done so again. Besides, there were other places where the precipice was as low, and even lower, than where they had made the trials; and at some of these they might have been more successful. Indeed, there was every probability that, had they not lost that kite, they would have been able in due time to have climbed out of their rock-bound prison by a ladder of rope; but now all chance of doing so was gone for ever—swept off by a single puff of wind.

You may be fancying, that the misfortune was not irremediable. Another kite, you will be saying, might be constructed out of similar materials as those used in making the one carried away. But to say this, would be to speak without a full knowledge of the circumstances.

The same thought had already passed through the minds of our adventurers, when they perceived that the kite they were flying was getting torn and otherwise damaged.

"We can easily make another," suggested Caspar at that crisis.

"No, brother," was the answer of Karl; "never another, I fear. We have paper enough left to patch this one; but not enough to make another."

"But we can make more paper, can we not?" urged Caspar, interrogatively.

"Ah!" again replied Karl, with a negative shake of the head, "no more—not another sheet!"

"But why? Do you think there are no more daphne trees?"

"I think there are not. You remember we stripped all there were in the thicket; and since then, thinking we might need more bark, I have gone all through the valley, and explored it in every direction, without meeting with a single shrub of the daphne. I am almost certain there are none."

This conversation between the brothers had occurred, long before the losing of the kite. When that event came to pass, it was not necessary for them to repeat it; and, both being thus acquainted with the fact that it was impossible for them to construct another, they felt that they had sustained an irreparable loss.

In what direction had the kite been carried off? Might it not be blown along the line of cliffs, and tossed back again into the valley?

As there appeared some probability that such a chance might arise, all three ran outward from the rocks—in order to command a better view of the precipice, on each side.

For a long time they stood watching—in hopes that they might see the great paper-bird returning to the scene of its nativity. But it never came back; and they became at length convinced, that it never would. Indeed, the direction of the wind—when they paused to consider it—rendered the thing not only improbable, but impossible. It was blowing *from* the cliffs, and *towards* the snowy ridge. No doubt the kite had been carried up the sloping acclivity; and had either passed clear over the mountains, or become lodged in some deep defile, where the wind could no longer reach it. At all events, it was certain, that both kite and cord were lost to them for ever.

"Ach! how very unfortunate!" exclaimed Caspar, in a vexed tone, when they had finally arrived at this conviction. "What ill-starred luck we have, to be sure!"

"Nay! brother," remarked Karl, in a tone of reproval; "do not chide Fortune for what has happened just now. I acknowledge it is a great misfortune; but it is one for which we may justly blame ourselves, and only ourselves. By sheer negligence we have lost the kite, and along with it, perhaps, the last chance of regaining our liberty."

"Yes, you speak truly," rejoined Caspar, in a tone of mingled regret and resignation. "It *was* our fault, and we must suffer for it."

"But are you quite sure, brother Karl," resumed he, after a pause, and referring to the conversation that had already passed between them—"are you quite sure there are no more of these paper-bearing trees?"

"Of course," replied the plant-hunter, "I am not positive—though I fear it is as I have said—that there are no more. It will be easy for us to determine the point, by making a complete exploration of the valley. It may be that something else might turn up which would answer the purpose equally as well. There is a birch-tree indigenous to the Himalaya mountains, found both in Nepaul and Thibet. Its bark can be stripped off in broad flakes and layers, to the number of eight or ten—each almost as thin as common paper, and suitable for many purposes to which paper is usually applied."

"Do you think it would do for a kite?" inquired Caspar, without waiting for Karl to finish his explanation.

"I am sure of it," replied the botanist. "It would serve even better than the daphne paper; and had I believed there was a chance of finding it here, I should have preferred it to that. But I do not think we shall find it. I have observed no species of birch; and I know that this one, like most of the *Betulaceae*, affects a much colder climate than there is in this valley. Likely enough, it grows on the mountains above; but there it is out of our reach. Could we reach it there, we should not need to be robbing it of its manifold envelope. But let us not despair," added Karl, endeavouring to appear cheerful; "perhaps it may be found growing down here; or, if not, we may still find another grove of the daphne trees. Let us proceed on and search!"

Karl was far from being sanguine in either conjecture; and it was as well for him that he was not: for after a minute and careful exploration of the valley—which occupied nearly three whole days—neither the wished-for birch, nor the desired daphne trees—nor any other material out of which a kite might be manufactured—rewarded their search.

It was of no use, therefore, to think any longer of a kite; and the subject was at length dismissed from their minds.

Chapter Forty Nine.
Aerostatics.

It is scarce possible to talk of a paper kite, without thinking of that other and greater aerostatic contrivance—a balloon.

Karl had thought of it, long before this time; and so had Caspar, just as long: for the kite had suggested it simultaneously to the minds of both.

It may be asked why they had not entertained the thought, and endeavoured to carry it into practical effect: since a balloon would have been far more likely to have delivered them out of their "mountain prison" than a paper kite?

But they *had* entertained the thought—at least, Karl had done so—and examined it in all its bearings. Caspar had permitted it to pass out of his mind, under the impression that *they could not make a balloon*; and Karl had arrived at the same conclusion; but only from a belief that they *had not the materials* with which to make one. Given the materials, Karl felt quite equal to the construction of a balloon—a rude one, it is true; but one which might have served the purpose for which they required it.

During the days when they had been occupied in making the paper-bird, he had given his thoughts a good deal to this subject; for, to say the truth, he had never been very sanguine about the success of the kite experiment. He had pondered long and patiently on the subject of balloons—endeavouring to recall to mind what little he had studied of aerostatics—and had mentally examined all the material objects within reach, in the hope of discovering some substance out of which one might be constructed.

Unfortunately, he had not been able to think of anything that appeared to be suitable. The daphne paper—even had it been in abundance—would not do: for paper of itself, however close in texture, is not strong enough to withstand the pressure of the outside air—that is, in a balloon of sufficient size to carry any considerable weight. But it was of no use to talk of paper: since there was not enough; and Karl had given over thinking of a balloon: because there was nothing within reach likely to serve for its construction.

He knew that that great sphere would require to be air-proof. He had thought of the skins of animals; but such of these as might have been obtained in sufficient quantity, were entirely too thick and heavy to make the covering of a balloon. The hemp, of which there *was* an abundance, might be woven into a cloth, and then coated over by gum obtained from some tree; for in the valley were several species of gum-exuding trees. But the question was, could they manufacture a cloth out of hemp that would be light enough when thus coated over? It was very doubtful whether they could—at all events they would have to practise the weaving trade for a long time, before they should arrive at a sufficient expertness to accomplish such a feat. The plan was too unpromising to be seriously entertained; and Karl had dismissed it, along with the whole subject of the balloon.

That had been previous to the experiment of the kite, and its unfortunate ending. But now that all hope from this quarter had been brought to an end, the balloon once more began to shape itself in his mind, as well as in that of Caspar; and for the first time they proceeded to talk over the subject together.

"Cords we could have in plenty," remarked Caspar, "but they'd be of no use, without the stuff to cover the great globe. They make it of silk, don't they?"

"Yes," replied Karl, "silk is the best material for the purpose."

"And why?" inquired Caspar.

"Because it combines the three properties of lightness, strength, and closeness of texture, in a greater degree than any other known substance."

"Would nothing else do?"

"Oh, yes; many things would answer to make a balloon, that might carry up a certain amount of weight. Even a paper balloon can be constructed to take up a few pounds—a cat, or a small dog; and people in many countries have been cruel enough to dispatch such creatures into the air, not caring what became of them."

"Very cruel indeed!" assented Caspar, who, although a hunter, was far from having an unfeeling heart. "Such people should be sent up themselves in paper balloons."

"Yes, if paper balloons would carry them; which, unfortunately for us, they wouldn't. Even if we had an unlimited supply of paper, it would be of no use to us. We require something stronger, and more tenacious."

"Can we not think of something? Let us try, Karl!"

"Ah! dear brother, I have been trying for days, and in vain. There is nothing within this valley at all suitable for the purpose."

"Would canvas do? Have you thought of that?"

"I have. It would be too coarse and heavy."

"But, with great pains, could we not make it light enough? We might choose the finer fibres of the hemp; and spin and weave it with scrupulous care. Ossaroo here is a perfect Omphale in his way. I'll warrant he could beat Hercules with the distaff."

"Ho! brother!" exclaimed Karl, a little astonished. "You are quite classical in your speech this morning. Where learnt you the history of Hercules—you who have never seen the inside of a university?"

"You forget, brother Karl, that you yourself have been my instructor in these classical themes, as you call them. Though I must tell you that, with the exception of their occasionally lending a little ornament to my speech, I have derived not the slightest advantage from them; nor is it likely I ever shall."

"Well, Caspar," answered the botanist, "I am not going to stand up for the classics, as you are well aware. Although I have taught you a little of their lore, it was when I had nothing to do, and you were equally idle; otherwise I should have considered that both of us were wasting time. You already know my opinions on that subject—which are: that a knowledge of what is usually termed 'the classics' is of about as much use to a reasoning man as might be an equally profound knowledge of Chinese *mnemonics*. The time I have spent in the study of the *dead* languages has been sheer waste; and all I have learnt wont raise us a foot higher here. My knowledge of Jupiter and Juno is not likely to gain us the means of getting out of our difficulty, no more than my acquaintance with Mercury will help me to a pair of wings. So a truce to classical ideas, and let us see whether scientific ones may not serve us better just now. You have a quick invention, brother Caspar; can you think of anything—I mean anything within our reach—that would make the air-bag of a balloon?"

"But could you make the balloon, if you had the stuff?" inquired Caspar, still in doubt whether any other than an experienced aeronaut could construct so wonderful a machine.

"Pooh!" replied the philosopher, "the making of a balloon is almost as easy as making a soap-bubble. Any air-tight bag, filled with heated atmosphere, becomes a balloon. The question is, what weight it can be made to carry—including the materials out of which it may be constructed."

"But how are you to get the heated air into it?"

"Simply by making a fire under an aperture left open below."

"But would not this air soon become cold again?"

"Yes; and then the balloon would sink back to the earth from the air inside getting cooled, and becoming as heavy as that without. Of course," continued the philosopher, "you are aware that heated air is much lighter than the ordinary atmosphere; and that is why a balloon filled with the former, rises, and will continue rising, till it has reached that elevation, where the rarefied atmosphere is as light as the heated air. Then it can go no further, and the weight of the balloon itself will bring it down again. A bladder of ordinary air sunk in water, or a corked bottle, will illustrate this point to your comprehension."

"I comprehend it well enough," rejoined Karl, rather piqued at being treated too much *à l'enfant* by his learned brother. "But I thought that, in a balloon, it was necessary to keep a fire constantly burning—a sort of grate or fire-basket suspended below. Now, even if we had the silk to make the great spherical bag, how could we make a fire-basket without iron?"

"We should not need the fire-basket you speak of. That is only required, when you design to keep your balloon some length of time in the air. If you only wish to make a short ascent, once filling the bag with hot air is sufficient; as it would be for us here. Even if we wanted a suspended grate, surely, brother, you have enough ingenuity to get over such a trifling difficulty as that?"

"Well, I'm not so sure that I could. How would you get over it?"

"Why, by making a common basket, and lining it with clay. That would carry fire, as well as a vessel of either cast or wrought iron—at least sufficient to serve for a short excursion such as we should care to make. Now-a-days, fire is not used for inflating balloons. Inflammable gas has been found to be far superior for this purpose; but as we have no such thing in stock, we should have to proceed on the old original plan—that employed by the brothers Montgolfier—the first inventors of the balloon."

"You think, then, that the fire apparatus could be dispensed with, if we could only discover some material that would make the great globe-shaped bag to contain the heated air?"

"Ay," replied Karl; "think of something to do that, and I promise to make you a balloon."

Thus challenged, Caspar set his wits to work; and for a long while he sat in silence, as if buried in some very profound speculation. Probably, there was no material substance in that valley that did not pass in review before the retina of his mental vision; and all were considered in turn.

"It must be light, air-tight, and strong?" asked he, at length, as if there was something in his thoughts possessing these three requisites.

"Light, air-tight, and strong," answered Karl, simply repeating his words.

"The two last I am sure of," rejoined Caspar. "Of the first only have I my doubts."

"What is it?" asked Karl, in a tone that betrayed his interest in what Caspar had said.

"Eel-skins!" was the laconic answer.

Chapter Fifty.
The skin balloon.

"Eel-skins," said Caspar, repeating the phrase, as he saw that Karl hesitated before pronouncing an opinion. "Don't you think they would do?"

Karl had it on the tip of his tongue to cry out—"The very thing!" but something withheld him from making this unqualified declaration.

"They might—it is possible they might," said he, apparently debating the question within himself—"just possible; and yet I fear—"

"What do you fear?" asked Caspar.

"Do you think they would not be strong enough?"

"Strong enough," replied Karl. "That's not what I fear."

"The air can't pass through an eel-skin?"

"No—not that."

"At the seams, perhaps? We can stitch them neatly; and then gum them over at the joinings. I'll warrant Ossaroo can sew like a shoemaker."

The shikaree could do all that. Karl knew it. It was not there the difficulty lay.

"The weight, then?" pursued Caspar interrogatively.

"Precisely that," answered Karl; "I fear they will be too heavy. Bring one, Ossaroo; and let us have a look at it."

The shikaree rose from his seat; and going into the hovel, returned presently—bringing back with him a long shrivelled object, which any one could tell to be a dried eel-skin.

There were many like it inside: for they had carefully preserved the skins of the eels they had caught, induced to do so by a sort of presentiment, that some day they might find a use for them. In this case their prudent providence was likely to prove of service to them.

Karl took the skin; and, holding it out on the palm of his hand, appeared to make an estimate of its weight. Caspar watched his brother's countenance, and waited to hear what he would say; but Karl only expressed himself by a doubtful shake of the head, which seemed to show that his opin'on was *against* the eel-skins.

"They might be made much lighter, I fancy," suggested Caspar: "scraping would do a deal for them; and by the way, why would not boiling make them light enough? It would take all the fatty, oily substance out of them."

"There's something in what you say," rejoined Karl, apparently impressed by the last suggestion. "Boiling might render them a good deal lighter. We can easily try it."

As Karl said this, he proceeded to the boiling spring, and plunged the eel-skin under the water. There it was permitted to remain for about half an hour, when it was taken out; and, after being scraped with the blade of a knife, was spread upon a rock, under the sun, where it would soon get thoroughly dry.

They all waited patiently for the completion of this process. The result was of too interesting a character to allow of their occupying themselves with anything else.

In due time the eel-skin had become sufficiently dry, to be submitted to examination; and Karl, once more taking it up, balanced it upon his palm.

Tested, even in this inexact fashion, it was evidently much lighter than before; and, by the gratified look with which the philosopher regarded it, he appeared to be much better satisfied with its weight. Still, however, he was not sanguine: as his words testified. They were almost a repetition of what he had said before.

"It may do—it is just possible. At all events, there can be no harm in trying. Let us try it, then."

To say, "Let us try it," meant the same as to say, "Let us make the balloon." The others understood that; and of course acquiesced in the determination.

As there was nothing to interfere with the immediate commencement of the work, they resolved to set about it at once; and in fact did set about it without farther delay.

The number of eel-skins on hand, though very considerable, would not be near enough for covering a balloon; and therefore Ossaroo went to work with his hooks and lines to catch a few hundreds more. Karl was able to tell how many it would take; or he could at least make an estimate sufficiently exact for the purpose. He designed a balloon of twelve feet diameter: for he knew that one of less size would not have power enough to carry up the weight of a man. Of course, Karl knew how to calculate the surface of a sphere whose diameter should be twelve feet. He had only to multiply the diameter on the circumference; or the square of the diameter on the fixed number 3.1416; or find the convex surface of the circumscribing cylinder; or else find four times the area of a great circle of the said sphere. Any one of these methods would give him the correct result.

On making the calculation, he found that a sphere of 12 feet diameter would have a surface of 452 square feet, within a trifling fraction. Therefore 452 square feet of eel-skins would be required to cover it. In other words, that quantity would be required to make the balloon.

As the eels happened to be of large size—most of them being over a yard in length, and full four inches in average girth—the skin of one when spread out would yield about a square foot of surface. Taking large and small together—and allowing for waste, the heads and tails that would have to be chopped off—Karl calculated that he would get nearly a square foot each out of the eels; and that about five hundred skins would make the balloon bag. But as they would have to be cut occasionally with a slant, in order to get the globe shape, perhaps a few more would be needed; and therefore Ossaroo was to keep his baits in the water, until the requisite number of eels should be hooked out of it.

Ossaroo had another department assigned to him besides catching the fish; and one that took up more of his time: since the baiting of the hooks, and looking after them, required only his occasional attention. Spinning the thread by which the skins were to be sewed together, was a much more delicate operation: since in these both strength and fineness were absolutely necessary. But as Caspar had said, Ossaroo was an adept with the distaff; and several large skeins of the finest twist were soon turned off from his nimble fingers.

When enough thread had been thus produced, Ossaroo proceeded to making the cords and stronger ropes, that would be needed for attaching the "boat"—as well as to hold the balloon in its place, while being got ready for its ascent.

Caspar's employment was—first, the skinning of the eels; and afterwards the scraping, boiling, and drying of the skins; while Karl, who acted as engineer-in-chief, besides giving a general superintendence to the work, occupied himself in imparting the final dressing to the material, and cutting it into such shapes, that it could be closely and conveniently stitched together.

Karl had also made an excursion into the forest, and brought back with him large quantities of a gum, which he had extracted from a tree of the genus *ficus*—a sort of *caoutchouc*—which is yielded by many species of *ficus* in the forests of the Lower Himalayas. Karl had gone in search of this substance, because he knew it would be required for paying the seams, and rendering them air-tight.

When they had pursued their various avocations for about a week, it was thought that material enough of every kind was collected and made ready; and then Ossaroo was set to stitching. Fortunately, they were provided with needles: for these had formed a part of the *accoutrement* of the plant-hunters—when originally starting upon their expedition.

As neither Karl nor Caspar had any experience in handling such sharp tools, the sewing had all to be done by Ossaroo; and it took another full week to accomplish this Sartorean task.

At the end of that time, it was fully accomplished and complete; and the huge bag was ready to receive its coat of gum varnish. A day sufficed for "paying;" and nothing more remained but to attach the "boat," or "car," that was to carry them aloft in their daring flight into the "azure fields of air."

Chapter Fifty One.
Making ready for the ascent.

Karl was the only one of the three who knew anything about a balloon, or the mode of inflating it. Had it been their intention of navigating the air, an apparatus would have been required to carry up a fire. This Karl could easily have contrived. A basket of wicker-work, as he had said, well lined with clay, would have answered the purpose after a fashion; but as they did not intend to use the balloon for any purpose beyond making the single ascent to lift them over the cliffs, a continuous fire would not be required. The first inflation would answer that end well enough; and therefore a grate or fire-basket was not thought of.

The car to carry the passengers—or boat, as it is sometimes styled: since, for reasons easily understood, it is usually a boat—was quite another affair; and had it been designed for more than a mere temporary use, would have taken a considerable time in the making; but for what they wanted almost anything would serve; and all that they intended employing was a sort of wicker basket, or deep hamper, suspended by stout ropes. This had been already prepared; and only needed to be attached to the bottom of the air-bag.

In the present case, the "bottom of the bag" is quite a figure of speech— *lucus a non lucendo*. Strictly speaking, it had no bottom; but, where this should have been, there was a round aperture, formed by a stout hoop of ringall bamboo, to which the skin covering was lashed, and to which, also, the cords intended to sustain the afore-mentioned basket, as also the stay-ropes, were to be attached.

The object of this aperture will be easily understood. It was by it that the hot air was to be admitted inside the balloon, for the purpose of inflating it.

And how was this hot air to be obtained? That was a question which Karl alone could answer. Of course, fire was to be the agent for producing it: but how was it to be got into the bag? Karl could tell that, and Karl only; and, now that the time had arrived for trying the experiment, he condescended to explain to his coadjutors how he meant to proceed.

The bag was to be propped up between tall stakes set in the ground; its bottomless bottom turned towards the earth, so that the aperture would be below. Under this a fire was to be kindled—not, however, until everything else should be ready; and the hot air rising up into the aperture would enter the balloon, and cause it to swell out to its full globular dimensions. More hot air being admitted, the cooler atmosphere within would be expelled, the balloon would become lighter than the surrounding air, and by the simple principle of atmospheric pressure it would ascend into the air. It was expected it would do so—it was hoped it would.

To say the truth, the hopes of the engineer were far from being high— his expectations anything but sanguine. He had observed all along, that, notwithstanding the process employed for lightening the eel-skins, they were still far heavier than silk; and perhaps, after all, the experiment might not succeed. There was another circumstance that had as much *weight* on the mind of Karl as the eel-skins; and that was quite as likely to have a *bearing* upon the balloon. He had not overlooked the fact, that the spot, from which they proposed making the ascent, was nearly ten thousand feet above the level of the sea. He knew that the atmosphere in such a situation would be extremely rarefied, and that a balloon, which might easily ascend many thousand feet into the air starting from the level of the sea, would not stir from the ground if carried to the top of a mountain ten thousand feet high. This was the circumstance which preyed upon the spirit of the young philosopher, and hindered him from entertaining any very sanguine hopes of success in the experiment they were making.

The philosophical truth had been before his mind from the first, and at times had almost determined him to abandon the project. But as he was not sufficiently acquainted with the laws of aerostation as to be certain of failure, he had worked on with the determination to seek success, though it must be acknowledged with but faint hopes of finding it.

Thus stood matters on the morning when it was finally arranged to launch their great aerial ship, and ascertain whether it would swim.

All things were made ready at an early hour. The huge bag was set up between the supporting stakes the *car* was attached to it, as also several ropes to keep the balloon from being carried away; and these were fastened at their other ends to stout pegs, driven firmly into the ground; while a little furnace of stones was built underneath to hold the fire, whose ascending caloric was to expand the balloon, and raise it into the air.

The fuel out of which this fire was to be made had been already collected near the spot. It was not wood, nor faggots of any kind; for although these might have served after a fashion, Karl was acquainted with a better material. He remembered that the Montgolfiers, and other early aerostats—previous to the introduction of the inflammable gas—had used chopped straw and wool, and regarded these materials to be the best substances for inflating their balloons. Karl had adopted their idea; and had provided chopped grass as a substitute for the chopped straw, and in lieu of sheep's wool he had procured a quantity of the *poshm* of the ibex, and other animals, that had been killed—the rich shawl-wool of Cashmere!

The car, which has already been described as a sort of deep hamper, was not over three feet in diameter. It was evidently not equal to the holding of three persons—to say nothing of a large dog—for it is hardly necessary to say that Fritz was not going to be left behind. The faithful creature had too long followed the fortunes of our adventurers to be abandoned by them now.

But there was not the slightest danger of that. The dimensions of the car were large enough for what the "vehicle" was intended to carry, which was only *one*.

Karl believed that there would be little chance of the balloon having sufficient power to take up all three of them, their united weight being over four hundred pounds. He would be but too contented if one should be carried aloft; and if that one should succeed in effecting a landing on the summit of the cliff, it was of no importance what afterwards became of the aerial ship. Having completed that one voyage, it might make another on its own account—either south to Calcutta or eastward to Hong Kong, if it liked China better.

Of course, if any one of them should succeed in surmounting the cliff, it would be an easy matter to get over the mountain; and as they had passed native villages on their way upward, these could be reached in a day or two, and a party of men, with a proper rope-ladder, brought to the rescue of the others.

Even had there been no prospect of assistance from any one outside, it would not matter very much. If only one of them could get to the top of the cliffs, they could construct a rope-ladder of themselves—by which the other two would be able to make the ascent.

It is hardly necessary to say who was to make the attempt—Ossaroo was to be the aeronaut. Ossaroo had voluntarily offered himself for this perilous performance; and his offer had been accepted.

Not that either of the others were at all afraid to have run the risk. It was from no desire to shirk the danger that they had appointed Ossaroo to undertake it; but simply because, once outside, the shikaree would be far better able to find his way down the mountains: and in his native language could readily communicate with the villagers, and give a correct account of their situation.

Chapter Fifty Two.
Inflation and failure.

At length arrived the hour for making that important experiment—as to whether their aerial ship would prove herself air-worthy.

All three stood around the spot where the chopped grass and shawl-wool were to be set on fire. This fuel itself appeared underneath—in a little heap lightly laid, and ready for the touch of the tinder.

Karl had a piece of blazing torch in his hand; Caspar held one of the stay-ropes, to prevent the balloon from rising too rapidly; while Ossaroo, equipped as if for a journey, stood by the hamper, in readiness, when the proper time should arrive, to "pack" himself into it.

Alas! for the frailty of all human foresight! The most careful calculations often prove erroneous—not that in the present instance there was any unforeseen error: for from the very first, Karl had been distrustful of his data; and they were now to disappoint, rather than deceive him. It was not written in the book of destiny that Ossaroo should ever set foot in that wicker car or ever make an ascent by that balloon.

The torch was applied to the chopped grass and shawl-wool. Both blazed and smoked, and smouldered; and, more being thrown on, the blaze was kept up continuously. The heated air ascended through the aperture, causing the great sphere of stitched skins to swell out to its full dimensions.

It trembled and rocked from side to side, like some huge monster in pain. It rose to the height of a few inches from the ground, sank, and then rose again, sank once more, and so kept on rising and sinking and bobbing about, but alas! never exhibiting sufficient ascending power, to raise the hamper even as high as their heads!

Karl continued to feed the furnace with the chopped grass and poshm, but all to no purpose. The air within was sufficiently heated to have raised it for miles—had they only been as low as the sea-level, and the balloon constructed of lighter materials.

As it was, all their efforts were in vain. The gigantic globe could not be raised above six feet from the ground. It had not power enough to carry up a cat—much less a man. In short, it was a failure—one more added to the long list of their dark disappointments!

For more than an hour Karl continued to keep his fire ablaze. He even tried faggots of the resinous pine: in hopes that by obtaining a greater strength of caloric he might still succeed in causing the balloon to soar upward; but there was no perceptible difference in the effect. It bobbed about as before, but still obstinately refused to ascend.

At length, with patience exhausted and hopes completely crushed, the engineer turned away from the machine which he had taken so much pains in constructing. For a moment he stood irresolute. Then heaving a sigh at the recollection of his wasted labour, with sad, slow step he departed from the spot. Caspar soon followed him—fully participating in the feeling of grievous disappointment. Ossaroo took leave of the inflated monster in a different fashion. Drawing near to it, he stood for some seconds contemplating it in silence—as if reflecting on the vast amount of seam he had stitched to no purpose. Then uttering a native ejaculation, coupled with a phrase that meant to say, "No good either for the earth, the water, or the air," he raised his foot, kicked the balloon in the side—with such violence that the toe of his sandals burst a hole in the distended eel-skins; and, turning scornfully away, left the worthless machine to take care of itself.

This task, however, it proved ill adapted to accomplish: for the disappointed aeronauts had not been gone many minutes from the ground, when the heated air inside, which had for some time been gradually growing cooler, reached at length so low a temperature, that the great sphere began to collapse and settle down upon the embers of the pine faggots still glowing red underneath. The consequence was that the inflammable skins, cords, and woodwork coming in contact with the fire, began to burn like so much tinder. The flames ran upward, licking the oily eel-skins like the tongues of fiery serpents; and when the *ci-devant* aeronauts looked back from the door of their hut, they perceived that the balloon was ablaze!

Had the accident occurred two hours before, they would have looked upon it as the saddest of calamities. Now, however, they stood regarding the burning of that abandoned balloon, with as much indifference as is said to have been exhibited by Nero, while contemplating the conflagration of the seven-hilled city!

Chapter Fifty Three.
Another spell of despair.

Never, during all the days of their sojourn in that "Valley of Despond," did our adventurers feel more despondence, than on the afternoon that succeeded the bursting of their great air-bubble—the balloon. They felt that in this effort, they had exhausted all their ingenuity; and so firmly were they convinced of its being the last, that no one thought about making another. The spirits of all three were prostrate in the dust, and seemed at length to have surrendered to despair.

Of course, it was not that sort of despair which takes possession of one conscious of coming and certain death. It was far from being so dire as this; but for all it was a bitter feeling. They knew they could continue to live, perhaps as long there, as elsewhere upon the earth; but what would life be worth to them, cut off from all communication with the world?—for now, to the fulness of conviction, did they believe themselves thus isolated.

In disposition not one of the three had the slightest particle of the hermit. Not one of them, but would have shuddered at the thought of becoming a Simon Stylites. You might suppose that, with books and Nature to study, Karl could have made shift. True, with such companions he might have lived a less irksome life than either of the others; but even with these to occupy him, it is doubtful whether Karl could have passed the time; for it is not very certain, that a man—knowing himself alone in the world, and for ever to be alone—would care either for the books of men or the book of Nature.

As for Caspar, the thought that their lonely existence was to be perpetual, was enough at times to send the blood rushing coldly through his veins.

The Hindoo felt the affliction as much as either of his companions in misfortune; and sighed as much for his bamboo hut on the hot plains of Hindostan, as they for their home in the far fatherland of Bavaria.

It is true their situation was not so bad as if each had been left alone by himself. Many a poor castaway upon a desert island has been condemned to a far more unhappy fate. They knew and acknowledged this. Each had the other two for companions; but as they reflected thus, they could not hinder their thoughts from casting forward into the future—perhaps not distant—when one of them might leave that valley without the aid of either rope-ladders or balloons; and then another—leaving the last of the three lonely and forlorn!

With such sad reflections did they pass the evening of that day, and the morning and evening of that which followed. They took no heed of time; and could scarce summon sufficient energy to cook their frugal meals. The spirit to plan, and the energy to act, seemed both to have departed from them at once and for ever.

This state of things could not long continue. As already said, the soul of man holds within itself a power of resuscitation. So long as it continues to live, it may hope to recover from the heaviest blow. Broken hearts are more apparent than real; and even those that are worst shattered have their intervals in which they are restored to a perfect soundness. The slave in his chains, the prisoner within his dark dungeon, the castaway on his desert isle, all have their hours of joy—perhaps as vivid and lasting as those of the king upon his throne, or the conqueror in his car of triumph.

On earth there is no happiness unmingled with alloy; and, perhaps, there is no sorrow that may not in time find solace.

On the second clay succeeding their last great disappointment, the spirits of all three began to revive; and those natural wants—which, whether we will or not, force themselves upon our attention—commenced to claim their consideration.

Karl was the first to recognise these necessities. If they were to live there for life, he reasoned,—and this seemed no longer a doubtful supposition,—it would be of no use, giving way to despondency—moping out their days like mutes at a funeral. Better far to lead an active life; and live well too—by providing plenty to eat and plenty to drink—which with industry they could easily do. All this might not make them cheerful; but they would certainly be less a prey to melancholy while engaged in some active industry, than if they remained brooding over their fate.

These thoughts, as we have said, arose on the morning of the second day succeeding that on which the balloon had been abandoned. Karl gave words to them, in an attempt to cheer his brother Caspar—who had relapsed into a state of unusual despondency. Ossaroo equally required cheering; and therefore it devolved on the botanist to attempt enlivening the spirits of his companions.

For a time, he met with very slight success; but gradually the necessity of action forced itself upon the attention of all—if only to provide the means to keep them from starving; and without further loss of time, they resumed the various branches of industry, by which they had hitherto been enabled to supply their larder.

To Caspar, as before, the chase was entrusted; while Ossaroo attended to the fishing; as he, better than either of the others, understood the management of hooks, lines, and nets.

The botanist busied himself in the old way, exploring the valley, in search of such seeds, plants, and roots, as might be found wholesome for food—not neglecting others of a medicinal character, that might serve in case of sickness. Many such had the young plant-hunter encountered during his early researches; and had made note of them against the possibility of their being required.

Fortunately, up to that time there had been no real need for any of the party to make trial of the natural *Pharmacopoeia* which the valley afforded: and it was to be hoped they should never have occasion to test the virtues of the specifics which the plant-hunter had discovered. Karl nevertheless collected several kinds; and, after submitting them to a process necessary for their preservation, had stored them away within the hut.

Of those vegetable products adapted for food, the chief article obtained was the nutritive seed yielded by the edible pine (*Pinus Gerardiana*). The cones of this valuable tree were as large as artichokes; each yielding several seeds of the size and appearance of pistachio nuts.

The wild cockscomb (*Amaranthus Cruentus*) also furnished a portion of their supply. Its seeds when parched, and crushed between two stones, produced a kind of meal, of which cakes of bread were manufactured by Ossaroo. These, although very far inferior to the real home-bake, or even to the most ordinary production of the bakehouse, were nevertheless sufficiently palatable to those who had no other bread.

The lake, besides yielding fish to the nets of Ossaroo, also afforded a supply of vegetables. On searching it, the botanist discovered several edible kinds of plants; among others the curious *Trapa bicornis*, or horned water-nut—known among the natives of the Himalayan countries by the name *Singara*, and much used by them as an article of wholesome food.

There was also a splendid water-lily—with very broad leaves and large flowers of pink and white colour—the seeds and the stalks of which Karl knew to be edible; as he had read of their being used for this purpose by the poorer people in the country of Cashmeer. The lily in question, viz. the *Nelumbium speciosum*, grows plentifully in the lakes of the far-famed valley so named.

On first observing this beautiful plant growing luxuriantly, as it was, in their own little valley lake, Karl took occasion to inform his brother— Ossaroo at the same time listening attentively to his statement—of the various uses made of it by the inhabitants of Cashmeer. How the boys sailing about in their boats when the day chances to be very hot, are in the habit of plucking one of its large shining leaves out of the water, and spreading it over their crowns, to protect them from the fervid rays of the sun; and how the petiole of the leaf, being hollow inside, serves them as a tube for drinking out of. Many such interesting particulars, in regard to the economy of this fine aquatic plant, did the young botanist communicate to his companions; but none more interesting than the fact that both its seeds and stalks are edible: since this promised them additional security against the danger of running short in their supply of vegetable food.

Chapter Fifty Four.
The bean of Pythagoras.

The discovery of the water-lily was not a thing of recent occurrence. They had known of its existence before; and more than once had visited the little embayment in the lake, where it chiefly grew. In fact, it had attracted their attention a few days after their first arrival in the valley—not by its own conspicuousness, for its broad round leaves, spread horizontally upon the surface, could scarce be seen from the shore. Only when its beautiful pink-white flowers were in bloom, could it be observed at any great distance.

That which had first led them to approach the place where it grew, and examine the plant, was their having noticed a singular phenomenon connected with it; and which for awhile had puzzled all three of them to explain.

The *bed* of lilies, at that time in full bloom, was visible from the place where they had originally made their encampment; and every morning, just after daybreak, and sometimes also during the day, they were in the habit of seeing some birds disporting themselves near that place in a singular manner—very singular indeed: since these birds appeared to *walk upon the water*!

They were tall, long-legged, slender-bodied creatures, and easily distinguished by both Karl and Caspar, as belonging to the family of *rallidae* or water-hens.

There could be no doubt that they were walking on the water—sometimes slowly, at other times in a quick run—and, what was even more unaccountable than this, they were seen at times to *stand still upon the water*! Ay, and, what might be considered more surprising still, they performed this aquatic feat *upon only one leg*!

The thing might have been more mysterious, had not Karl from the first suspected the reason why the laws of specific gravity appeared to be thus contradicted. He suspected the existence of some plant, whose leaves, lying spread on the surface, perhaps offered a footing for the birds, sufficiently firm to support the weight of their bodies.

The botanist was only reasoning from remembrance. He had lately read the account published but a few years before of the discovery of the gigantic water-lily of tropical America—the *Victoria Regia*—and remembered how its discoverers had spoken of large birds of the crane family making their perch upon its huge leaves, and thus supported, playing about over the surface of the water, as if the firm earth had been under their feet.

With these facts fresh in his memory, Karl conjectured that the water-hens seen by him and his companions were supported on a similar pedestal, and playing themselves on a like platform. His conjecture proved correct: for on visiting the place shortly after, the broad orbicular leaves of the *Nelumbium speciosum* were perceived—almost as large as those of their South American congener.

Other interesting points relating to the great lily growing in the Himalayan lake, Karl had mentioned from time to time to his companions: for he knew that the *Nelumbium speciosum* was the celebrated Pythagorean bean mentioned in the writings of the Greeks—more especially by Herodotus and Theophrastes.

It is described by these writers as growing plentifully in Egypt; and no doubt was cultivated in that country in their day; though it is not known there at the present time. It is found represented on the Egyptian sculptures, and so accurately has it been described by the Greek writers, as to leave no doubt as to the identification of the species.

It is one of the plants supposed to be the celebrated "lotus" of antiquity; and this supposition is probable enough: since not only its succulent stalk, but its seeds or "beans," have been eaten in all times by the people in whose country it grows. It is a food that produces a strengthening effect upon the system; and is also very refreshing in cases of thirst. The Chinese call it "Lienwha," and its seeds with thin slices of its root, mixed with the kernels of apricots and walnuts, and placed between alternate layers of ice, constituted one of the select dishes offered by the great mandarins to the British ambassadors on the visit of the latter to the Celestial Empire.

These people store up the roots of the lienwha for winter use—preserving them in a pickle of salt and vinegar. The Japanese also make use of the plant as an esculent; and it is, moreover, regarded by them as sacred to their divinities—the images of which are often represented seated upon its large leaves.

The flowers of the *Nelumbium speciosum* when in full bloom, give out a most fragrant odour—somewhat resembling that of anise; while the seeds, shaped like acorns, have a flavour equal in richness and delicacy to that of the finest almonds.

Chapter Fifty Five.
An aquatic harvest.

It was not upon that occasion that Karl communicated to his companions all these interesting facts in relation to the great lily. Many of them he had made known long before—especially that the seeds of the plant were eatable; and both Caspar and Ossaroo had often proved to their own satisfaction that they were something more than eatable—in short, a great delicacy.

It was from a knowledge of this fact that the thoughts of all three were now turned upon the lilies—whose huge roseate corollas, no longer seen glistening above the surface of the water, proclaimed that the "beans" were ripe, and ready for "shelling."

The three were about starting from the hut to reap this aquatic harvest—which, judging from the quantity of seed-pods that appeared above the surface, promised to be abundant.

Each had provided himself with a rush basket—which the shikaree had woven, during the long winter nights, for other purposes; but as they were of just the size and shape to hold the Pythagorean beans they were now to be employed in that capacity.

Both Karl and Caspar had rolled up their trowsers to mid-thigh; so as not to wet them while wading among the lilies; but Ossaroo, not being provided with any nether garment entitled to the name of trowsers, had simply tucked up the skirt of his cotton tunic, making it fast under his girdle.

In this guise all three proceeded round the shore of the lake, to that side where they would be nearest the bed of lilies. The water-hens, seeing them make their approach, rose from their perch upon the leaves, and fluttered off to seek a more secure shelter among the sedge.

The aquatic gleaners at once waded in; and commenced picking off the pods, and shelling them into their rush baskets. They had been there before, and knew there was no danger in the depth of the water.

They had nearly filled their respective sacks with the Pythagorean beans, and were meditating a return to dry land, when a dark shadow passing over the tranquil surface of the lake—closely followed by another of similar size and shape—attracted their attention.

All three saw the shadows at the same instant of time; and all simultaneously looked up to ascertain what sort of creatures were casting them. In the sky above they beheld a spectacle, calculated to inspire them with feelings of a strange interest.

Right above the lake, and also over their heads, a brace of large birds was circling in the air. Each was borne up by a pair of huge wings full five yards from tip to tip; while from the body, between, a neck of enormous length was extended horizontally—prolonged into a tapering-pointed beak, in shape like the seed-pistil of a pelargonium.

Their beaks might well have been compared to the pistil of a pelargonium; or rather the latter should be assimilated to them; since it is from this species of birds, the flower has derived its botanical cognomen.

The birds were *storks*. Not the ordinary *Ciconia*, that makes its home among the Hollanders—or finds a still more welcome hospitality on the roof-tree of the Hungarian by the plains of the *Puszta*—but a stork of far grander dimensions; in short, a stork that is the *tallest* of his tribe—the *Adjutant*.

On looking up, Karl recognised the species; so did Caspar, and at a glance. It required no lengthened scrutiny—no profound knowledge of natural history, to identify the noted *adjutant*. It only needed to have seen him before either in *propria persona*, or in a picture; but both brothers had seen specimens of the bird, in full flesh and feather, on the plains of India—in the environs of Calcutta itself.

As to the shikaree, was it likely he should be mistaken about the character of those winged giants—those tall scavengers he had seen thousands of times stalking pompously along the sandy shores of the sacred Ganges? It was not possible for him, to have a doubt about the identity of the birds, who were now throwing their shadows over that lone lake of the Himalayas. He had no doubt. The very certainty that the birds above him were the gigantic cranes of the Ganges—the sacred birds of Brahma—caused him to utter a sort of frenzied shout, and at the same time, dropping his "sack of beans" into the water!

He needed not to look at the colour of the birds, to note that they were brown black above, and white underneath. The naked vulture neck with its pouch-like appendage of brick-red hue; the silken feathers of bluish white under the tail—those precious plumes well-known and worn by the ladies of many lands under the appellation of *marabout feathers*—all were recognised at a glance.

Even quicker than either of his youthful comrades had the Hindoo identified the birds. A single glance sufficed, and simultaneously with that glance had the cry fallen from his lips, and the sack of Pythagorean beans from his grasp.

The birds were flying slowly, and to all appearance *laboriously*: as if wearied of wing. They appeared to be in search of some roost on which to repose themselves.

That they had entered the valley with this intention was made evident a few moments after: for having made a circuit round the little lake, both at the same instant ceased to ply their long pinions, and drawing their wings suddenly in to their bodies, they settled down upon the shore.

The spot upon which they had chosen to alight was the prominence terminating a little peninsula that protruded out almost to the bed of lilies, and from which the three waders had themselves descended into the water. As the latter now stood knee-deep among the aquatic plants, they were distant not more than twenty paces from the point of this peninsula.

The storks, after alighting, stood upon the shore in erect attitudes— apparently as unconcerned about the presence of our three adventurers, as if the latter were only overgrown stalks of the Pythagorean bean—utterly incapable of doing them an injury.

Chapter Fifty Six.
The adjutants.

The brace of gigantic birds, that had thus alighted by the shore of the little lake, were, to say the least, uncouth creatures; for the whole ornithological world might be ransacked without finding a greater oddity than the *adjutant*.

In the first place, it stands six feet upon its long, straight shanks; though its actual length, measuring from the tip of its bill to the termination of its claws, is full seven and a half. The beak, of itself, is over a foot in length, several inches in thickness, with a gibbous enlargement near the middle, and having both mandibles slightly curved downwards.

The spread of a full-grown adjutant's wing is fifteen feet, or five yards, from tip to tip—quite equalling in extent either that of the Chilian condor or the "wandering" albatross.

In colour the adjutant may be described as black above and white underneath, neither (that) being very pure. The upper plumage is a dirty brownish black; while the belly and under parts present a dull white appearance,—partly from an admixture of greyish feathers, but also from the circumstance that the bird is usually bedaubed with dirt—as mud from the marshes, where it feeds, and other filth, in which it seems to take delight. But for this foulness, the legs of the adjutant would be of a dark colour; but in the living bird they are never seen of the natural hue—being always whitened by the dust shaken out of its plumage, and other excrement that attaches itself to the skin.

The tail is black above and white underneath—more especially the under coverts, which are of a pure white. These last are the plumes so highly prized under the name of "marabout feathers," an erroneous title, arising through a mistake—made by the naturalist Temminck in comparing the Indian adjutant with another and very different species of the same genus—the marabout stork of Africa.

One of the distinctive characteristics of the adjutant, or "argala," as it is better known to the Indians,—and one, too, of its ugliest "features,"—is a naked neck of a flesh-red colour the skin shrivelled, corrugated, and covered with brownish hairs. These "bristles" are more thickly set in young birds, but become thinner with age, until they almost totally disappear—leaving both head and neck quite naked.

This peculiarity causes a resemblance between the adjutant bird and the vultures; but indeed there are many other points of similarity; and the stork may in all respects be regarded as a vulture—the vulture of the *grallatores*, or waders.

In addition to the naked neck, the adjutant is furnished with an immense dew-lap, or pouch which hangs down upon its breast—often more than a foot in length, and changing from pale flesh colour to bright red, along with the skin of the throat. At the back of the neck is found still another singular apparatus—the use of which has not been determined by the naturalist. It is a sort of vesicular appendage, capable of being inflated with air; and supposed to serve as an atmospheric buoy to assist in sustaining the bird in its flight. The inflation has been observed to take place under exposure to a hot sun; and, therefore, it is natural to infer, that the rarefaction of the air has something to do in causing (the bird to use this organ). As the adjutant often flies to a great height, it is possible that this balloon-like apparatus is necessary to sustaining it in the rarefied atmosphere found at such an elevation. The annual migration of the bird over the lofty chain of the Himalayas might not be possible, or if possible, more difficult, without this power of decreasing the specific gravity of its body.

It is scarce necessary to say that the adjutant—like all birds of the family to which it belongs—is a filthy and voracious feeder; carnivorous in the highest degree; and preferring carrion and garbage to any other sort of food. It will kill and swallow live kind—such as frogs, snakes, small quadrupeds, and birds—the latter not so very small either: since it has been known to bolt a whole fowl at a single "swallow." Even a cat or a hare can be accommodated with a passage down its capacious gullet; but it will not attempt to kill either one or the other: since, notwithstanding its gigantic size, it is one of the veriest cowards in creation. A child, with a bit of a switch, can at any time chase the adjutant away; and an enraged hen will put it to flight whenever it strays into the neighbourhood of her young brood. It does not retreat, without first making a show of defiance—by placing itself in a threatening attitude—with reddened throat, and beak wide agape, from which latter proceeds a loud roaring, like that of a bear or tiger. All this, however, is mere braggadocio; for, on the enemy continuing the attack, it immediately cools down, and betakes itself to ignominious flight.

Such are a few peculiarities of the gigantic stork, known as the *adjutant* or *argala*. It only remains to be added, that there are at least two, perhaps three, other species of storks of very large dimensions—though not so large as this one—that for a long time have been confounded with it. One of these is the *marabou*; which inhabits the tropical regions of Africa, and which also produces the plumes so much prized in the world of fashion. The feathers of the African species, however, are far less beautiful and valuable than those from the tail of the adjutant; and it is these last that are really best known as *marabout feathers*, in consequence of the mistake made by Temminck, and propagated by the anatomist Cuvier.

Another great stork—differing both from the *argala* of Asia and the *marabou* of Africa—inhabits the Island of Sumatra. It is known to the natives as the "Boorong Cambay;" while in the neighbouring Island of Java is found either a fourth species of these gigantic birds, or the same that belongs to Sumatra.

It is somewhat singular that such creatures should have remained so long unknown to the scientific world. It is not much more than half a century since travellers began to describe them with any degree of exactness; and even at the present time their history and habits have received but very slight elucidation. This is the more surprising when we consider that on the banks of the Ganges—even in Calcutta itself—the adjutant is one of the most common birds—constantly stalking about the houses, and entering the enclosures with as much familiarity, as if it was one of the regular *domestics* of the establishment!

Its services as a "scavenger" procure for it an immunity from persecution; and it is not only tolerated by the people, but encouraged, in its advances towards fellowship with them; notwithstanding that at times it becomes rather troublesome in its attentions to the young ducklings, chicklings, and other denizens of the farmyard.

Sometimes they are not even contented with such fare as may be found outside; but have been known to enter the bungalow; snatch a smoking joint from the table; and swallow it, before either master or servant could rescue the dainty morsel from between their long and tenacious mandibles!

When seen in flocks, wading through the water,—with wings outstretched, as is their custom,—they may be taken for a fleet of small boats. At other times, when stalking about over the sandy shores; and picking up the *débris* strewed along the banks of the sacred river; they resemble a crowd of native women engaged in the like occupation.

Ofttimes may they be seen feeding voraciously upon the filthiest carrion of animals; and not unfrequently upon a human body in a state of putrefaction—the corpse of some deluded victim to the superstition of Juggernaut—which has been thrown into the so-styled *sacred* river, to be washed back on the beach, an object of contention between *pariah* dogs, vultures, and these gigantic cranes of the Ganges!

Chapter Fifty Seven.
The standing sleepers.

The advent of the adjutants produced a vivid impression on the minds of all three of our adventurers—more vivid, perhaps, upon Ossaroo than either of the others. To him they seemed like old friends who had come to visit him in his prison; and though it never occurred to the shikaree, that they could be in any way instrumental in obtaining his release, still the impression produced was one of a pleasant nature. He saw before him two creatures whose forms, however uncouth, were associated with the scenes of his earliest childhood; and he could not help a passing fancy, that the pair, that had thus unexpectedly made their appearance, might be the same old cock and hen he had so often seen roosted on the branches of a huge banyan tree, that overshadowed the bungalow in which he was born.

Of course this could be only fancy on the part of Ossaroo. Out of the thousands of storks, that annually make their migration from the plains of Hindostan to the northward of the Himalaya Mountains, it would have been a rare coincidence if the two that for years had performed the office of scavengers in the shikaree's native village, should be identical with those now hovering above his head—for it was while they were yet upon the wing that Ossaroo had indulged in this pleasant speculation. Though scarce serious in his thought—and only entertaining it for an instant—he was nevertheless gratified by the sight of the two storks, for he knew they must have come from his native plains—from the banks of that glorious river in whose waters he longed once more to wet his feet.

The sight of the huge birds suggested to Caspar a different train of thought. As he beheld their immense wings, extended in slow but easy flight, it occurred to him that one or other of the great creatures might have the power to perform that task which had proved too much for the bearcoot; and for which the "kite" had been "flyed" in vain.

"Oh!" exclaimed he, as the idea came across his mind, "don't you think, Karl, that either of those great creatures would be strong enough to carry the line aloft? They look as if they could lift even one of ourselves to the top of the cliff."

Karl made no reply; though his silence was only caused by Caspar's suggestion—which he was proceeding to ponder upon.

The young hunter continued: "If we could only catch one of them alive! Do you suppose they are going to alight? They look as if they would. What do *you* say, Ossaroo? You know more of these birds than we do."

"Yees, youngee Sahib; ee speakee de true. Dey go for come down. You savey dey make long fly. Dey both weary on de wing—no able fly furder. 'Sides, ee see, here am de lake—water—dey want drinkee—want eat too. Dey sure come down."

Ossaroo's prediction was fulfilled, almost as soon as it was uttered. The birds, first one and then the other, jerked in their spread wings; and dropped down upon the shore of the lake—as already stated, not over twenty paces from the spot where the three waders were occupied among the leaves of the lilies.

The eyes of all three were now directed with a fixed gaze upon the new-comers,—in whose behaviour they observed something irresistibly ludicrous.

Almost on the instant of their feet touching *terra firma*, instead of moving about over the ground in search of food, or striding down towards the water to drink—as the spectators were expecting them to do—the two long-legged bipeds acted in an entirely different manner. Neither of them seemed to care either for food or drink. If they did, both these appetites must have been secondary with them to the desire for rest; for scarce ten seconds had elapsed after their alighting, when each drew in its long neck, burying it between the shoulders as in a case, leaving visible only the upper half of the head, with its huge scythe-shaped beak—the mandibles resting against the prominence of the breast bone, and pointing diagonally downwards.

Simultaneous with this movement, the spectators perceived another— equally indicative of a desire on the part of the birds to betake themselves to repose. This was the drawing up of one of their long fleshless legs, until it was entirely concealed under the loose feathers of the belly—a movement made by both so exactly at the same instant, as to lead to the belief that they were actuated by like impulses, by some spiritual union that existed between them!

In ten seconds more both birds appeared to be asleep. At all events, their eyes were closed; and not a movement could be detected in the limbs, wings, bodies, or beaks of either!

It was certainly a ludicrous sight to see these huge creatures—each supporting itself on a single stalk, so straight and slender that nothing but the nicest balance could have ensured their equilibrium; and this, too, while neither seemed conscious of any danger of toppling over—of which, indeed, there was not the slightest reason to be afraid.

The Hindoo had been too long accustomed to this sort of spectacle, to see anything in it worthy of being laughed at. Not so Caspar—whose mirth was at once excited to the point of risibility. The unconcerned manner in which the storks had come to a stand—along with the picturesque *pose* in which they had composed themselves to sleep—was even too much for the stoical Karl; who at once echoed the laughter which his brother had inaugurated.

Their united cachinnations rang loudly over the lake—reverberating in repeated peals from the adjacent cliffs.

It might be supposed that the *fracas* thus created would have alarmed the new arrivals: and caused them once more to make an appeal to their wings.

Nothing of the sort. The only effect perceptible on either, was the opening of their eyes, a slight protrusion of the neck, a shake of the head, an upraising of the long beak, with a quick clattering of its mandibles—which soon becoming closed again, were permitted to drop into their original position of repose.

This cool behaviour of the birds only increased the hilarity of the boys; and for several minutes they remained in their places, giving way to loud and uncontrollable laughter.

Chapter Fifty Eight.
Fritz among the feathers.

Their hilarity could not be continued for ever. Even that of Caspar came to a termination; though not until his ribs ached with the agreeable exercise.

As their bean-sacks had been already filled, it was determined that they should first take them to the hut, and then return to the storks with the design of capturing them. Ossaroo was of the opinion, that they would have no difficulty in effecting this; declaring the birds to be so tame, that he might walk straight up to them, and throw a noose over their necks. This, in all probability, he might have done, had he been provided with a piece of cord proper for the making of such a noose. But there was no cord at hand—not even a bit of string—nothing but the rush baskets filled with the lotus beans. To obtain a snare, it would be necessary to make a journey to the hut.

In the minds of our adventurers there was no very clear conception of the object of capturing the storks: unless it might have been that the thought, to which Caspar had given speech, was still entertained by himself and his brother. That indeed would have justified them in their attempt to take the birds.

Another idea may have suggested itself—more especially to Ossaroo. If nothing else should come of it, there would be some pleasure in holding the birds in captivity—as pets and companions. Ossaroo had been involuntarily contemplating the prospect of a long lonely life in the solitude of that mountain valley. With such a prospect even the solemn stork might be regarded as a cheerful companion.

Stimulated by these thoughts—and some others of a more indefinite kind—our adventurers came to the determination to ensnare the *adjutants*!

All three commenced wading out of the lake—in a direction so as not to disturb the sleepers. Karl and Caspar—now that they had become inspired with a design—lifted their feet out of the water, and set them down again, as though they ere treading upon egg. Ossaroo sneered at their over-caution— telling them, that there was not the slightest fear of frightening the storks; and indeed there was truth in what he affirmed.

In most countries bordering upon the banks of the Ganges, these birds, protected alike by superstitious fears and edicts of law, have become so used to the proximity of man, that they will scarce stir out of their way to avoid him. It was possible that the brace in question might have belonged to some of the wilder flocks—inhabiting the swamps of the Sunderbunds— and therefore less accustomed to human society. In that case there might be some difficulty in approaching them; and it was for this reason that Ossaroo had consented to adopt the precautions for their capture which Karl had insisted should be taken.

The truth is, that Karl had conceived a deeper design than either of his companions. It had occurred to him—while engaged with his brother in that laughing duetto—and somewhat to the surprise of Caspar, it had caused a sudden cessation of his mirth, or at least the noisy ebullition of it.

The philosopher had become silent and serious; as if the thought had suddenly arisen, that hilarity under the circumstances was indecorous and out of place. From that moment Karl had preserved a mysterious silence— even refusing to explain it when interrogated by Caspar. He was only silent on this one theme. Otherwise his speech flowed freely enough—in counsel to his companions—charging both to adopt every precaution for ensuring the capture of the storks—and with an eagerness, which puzzled them to comprehend.

A few minutes' walk brought them back to the hut. It was rather a run than a walk—Karl going in the lead, and arriving before either of the others. The bean-sacks were flung upon the floor—as if they had been empty and of no value—and then the strings and lines that had been spun by Ossaroo were pulled out of their hidden places, and submitted to inspection.

It did not take long to make a running noose, which was accomplished by the nimble fingers of the shikaree. Easily also was it attached to the end of a long stem of the ringall bamboo; and thus provided, our adventurers once more sallied forth from the hut; and made their way towards the sleeping storks.

As they drew near, they were gratified at perceiving the birds still in the enjoyment of their meridian slumber. No doubt they had made a long journey, and needed rest. Their wings hung drooping by their sides, proclaiming weariness. Perhaps they were dreaming—dreaming of a roost on some tall fig-tree, or the tower of an antique temple sacred to the worship of Buddha, Vishna, or Deva—dreaming of the great Ganges, and its odorous waifs—those savoury morsels of putrefying flesh, in which they delighted to dig their huge mattocks of mandibles.

Ossaroo being entrusted with the noose, did not pause to think, about what they might be dreaming; or whether they were dreaming at all. Enough for him to perceive that they were sleeping; and, gliding forward in a bent attitude, silent as a tiger threading his native jungle, the shikaree succeeded in making approach—until he had got almost within *snaring distance* of the unconscious adjutants.

There is many a slip between the cup and the lip. The old saw was illustrated in the case of the shikaree while endeavouring to ensnare the storks; though it was not the snare, but the birds that now illustrated the adage.

After the attempt had been made, the snare could be still seen in its place, stiffly projecting from the point of the long bamboo rod; while the adjutants were soaring in the air, mounting still higher upward, their slender necks outstretched, their beaks cracking like castanets, and their throats emitting an angry sound like the roaring of a brace of lions.

The failure was not to be attributed to Ossaroo; but to the imprudence of one of his companions—an individual of the party close treading upon his heels. That individual was *Fritz*!

Just as Ossaroo was about casting his loop over the shoulders of a sleeping adjutant, Fritz—who had followed the party from the hut—now for the first time perceiving the birds, rushed forward and seized the tail of one of them between his teeth. Then, as if determined on securing the beautiful *marabout feathers*, he pulled a large mouthful of them clean out by the roots.

This was not exactly the motive that impelled Fritz to make such an unexpected attack—unexpected, because the well-trained animal would have known better than to fright the game which his masters were in the act of stalking; and such imprudence had never before been displayed by him. It was the particular kind of game that had provoked Fritz to act contrary to his usual habit of caution; for of all the creatures which he had encountered, since his arrival in the counted there, was none that had inspired him with a more profound feeling of hostility than these same adjutants. During Fritz's sojourn in the Botanic Gardens of Calcutta—where his masters, it will be remembered, were for some time entertained as guests—Fritz had often come in contact with a brace of these gigantic birds, that were also guests of that justly celebrated establishment: they habitually made their stay within the enclosure, where they were permitted to stalk about unmolested, and pick up such stray scraps as were cast out by the domestics of the *curator's* mansion.

These birds had grown so tame, as to take food freely out of the hand of anyone who offered it to them; and with like freedom, to take it where it was not offered, but found within reach of their long prehensile beaks. Often had they pilfered provisions to which they were anything but welcome; and, among other acts of their rapacity, there was one of which Fritz had been an interested spectator, and for which he was not likely ever to forgive them. That was, their robbing him of a dainty piece of meat, which one of the cooks had presented to Fritz himself; and upon which he had been going to make his dinner. One of the birds had the audacity to seize the meat in its mandibles, jerk it out of the dog's very teeth, and swallow it, before the latter had time to offer either interruption or remonstrance.

The consequence was, that, from that time, Fritz had conceived a most rancorous antipathy towards all birds of the genus *Ciconia*—and the species *Argala* in particular; and this it was that impelled him, on first perceiving the adjutant—for being by the hut on their arrival he had not seen them before,—to rush open-mouthed towards them, and seize the tail of one of them between his teeth.

It is not necessary to add that the bird, thus indecorously assailed, took to instant flight, followed by its more fortunate though not less frightened mate—leaving Fritz in a temper to treat Marabout feathers as they had never been treated before—even when by the hands of some scorned and jealous vixen they may have been torn from the turban of some hated rival!

Chapter Fifty Nine.
Capturing the storks.

Our adventurers witnessed the uprising of the birds with looks that betokened disappointment and displeasure; and Fritz was in danger of getting severely castigated. He merited chastisement; and would have received it on the instant—for Caspar already stood over him with an upraised rod—when an exclamation from Karl caused the young hunter to hold his hand, and saved Fritz from the "hiding" with which he was being threatened.

It was not for this that Karl had called out. The exclamation that escaped him was of a different import—so peculiarly intoned as at once to draw Caspar's attention from the culprit, and fix it on his brother.

Karl was standing with eyes upraised and gazing fixedly upon the retreating stork—that one with whose tail Fritz had taken such an unwarrantable liberty.

It was not the ragged Marabout feathers, hanging half plucked from the posterior of the stork, upon which Karl was gazing; but its long legs, that, as the bird rose in its hurried flight, hung, slantingly downward, extending far beyond the tip of its tail. Not exactly these either was it that had called forth that strange cry; but something attached to them—or one of them at least—which, as it came under the shining rays of the sun, gleamed in the eyes of Karl with a metallic lustre.

It had a yellowish sheen—like gold or burnished brass—but the scintillation of the sun's rays, as they glanced from its surface, hindered the spectators from making out its shape, or being able to say exactly what it was.

It was only Caspar and Ossaroo who were thus perplexed. Karl knew that glittering meteor, that for a moment had flashed before his eyes like a beam of hope—now slowly but surely departing from him, and plunging him back into the old misery.

"Oh! brother!" he exclaimed, as the stork flew upward, "what a misfortune has happened!"

"Misfortune! what mean you, Karl?"

"Ah! you know not how near we were to a chance of being delivered. Alas! alas! it is going to escape us!"

"The birds have escaped us, you mean?" inquired Caspar. "What of that? I don't believe they could have carried up the rope anyhow; and what good would it be to catch them? They're not eatable; and we don't want their feathers valuable as they may be."

"No, no!" hurriedly rejoined Karl; "it is not that—not that."

"What then, brother?" inquired Caspar, somewhat astonished at the incoherent speeches of the plant-hunter. "What are you thinking of?"

"Look yonder!" said Karl, now for the first time pointing up to the soaring storks. "You see something that shines?"

"Ha! on the leg of one of the birds? Yes; I do see something—like a piece of yellow metal—what can it be?"

"I know what it is!" rejoined Karl, in a regretful tone; "right well do I know. Ah! if we could only have caught that bird, there would have been a hope for us. It's no use grieving after it now. It's gone—alas! it's gone; and you, Fritz, have this day done a thing that will cause us all regret—perhaps for the rest of our lives."

"I don't comprehend you, brother!" said Caspar; "but if it's the escape of the storks that's to be so much regretted, perhaps it will never take place. They don't appear to be in such a hurry to leave us—notwithstanding the inhospitable reception Fritz has given them. See! they are circling about, as if they intended to come down again. And see also Ossaroo—he's holding out a lure for them. I warrant the old shikaree will succeed in coaxing them back. He knows their habits perfectly."

"Merciful Father!" exclaimed Karl, as he looked first at the flying storks and then at Ossaroo; "be it permitted that he succeed! You, Caspar, lay hold upon Fritz, and give Ossaroo every chance! For your life don't let the dog get away from you; for your life—for the lives of all of us!"

Caspar, though still under surprise at the excited bearing of his brother, did not allow that to hinder him from obeying his command, and rushing upon Fritz, he caught hold of the dog. Then placing the hound between his legs, he held him with both hands and knees as tightly as if Fritz had been screwed in a vice.

The eyes of all—the dog included—were now turned upon Ossaroo. Caspar contemplated his movements with an undefined interest; while Karl watched them with feelings of the keenest anxiety.

The cunning shikaree had not come to the spot unprepared. Having anticipated some difficulty in getting hold of the storks, he had providentially provided a lure, which, in the event of their proving shy, might attract them within reach of his *ringall*. This lure was a large fish—which he had taken out of the larder before leaving the hut, and which he was now holding out—as conspicuously as possible, to attract their attention. He had gone some distance apart from the others, and especially from Fritz, whom he had scolded away from his side; and, having stationed himself on a slight eminence near the edge of the lake, he was using all his wiles to coax back the birds that had been so unwittingly compelled to take wing.

It was evident to Ossaroo—as well as to the others—that the flight of the storks had been against their will; and that they had reluctantly ascended into the air. They were no doubt wearied, and wanted rest.

Whether this desire would have brought them to the earth again, Ossaroo did not stay to determine. As soon as by their actions he became convinced that they saw the fish held out in his hand, he flung the tempting morsel to some distance from him, and then stood awaiting the result.

It proved a success—and almost instantaneously.

There was nothing in the appearance or attitude of Ossaroo to excite the suspicion of the adjutants. His dark skin and Hindoo costume were both well-known to them; and though now observed in an odd, out-of-the-way corner of the world, that was no reason for regarding him as an enemy.

Fritz was alone the object of their fear, but Fritz was a good way off, and there appeared no longer any reason for dreading him.

Reasoning thus—and perhaps with empty stomachs to guide them to a conclusion—the sight of the fish—lying unguarded upon the grass—put an end to their fears; and, without further hesitation, both dropped down beside it.

Both at the same instant clutched at the coveted prize—each endeavouring to be the first in securing it.

As one of the birds had got hold of the fish by the head and the other by its tail, a struggle now arose as to which should be the first to swallow its body. Each soon passed a portion of it down its capacious throat, until its mandibles met in the middle, and cracked against each other.

As neither would yield to the other, so neither would consent to disgorge, and let go; and for some seconds this curious contention was kept up.

How long it might have continued was not left to the determination of the parties themselves; but to Ossaroo, who, while they were thus occupied, rushed upon the spot; and, flinging wide his arms, enfolded both the birds in an embrace, from which they vainly struggled to get free.

With the assistance of Karl and Caspar—who had in the meantime tied Fritz to a tree—the huge creatures were soon overpowered, and pinioned beyond the possibility of escaping.

Chapter Sixty.
A labelled leg.

"It is! it is!" cried Karl, stooping suddenly down, and grasping the shank of one of the birds.

"What?" inquired Caspar.

"Look, brother! See what is there, round the stork's leg! Do you not remember having seen that bit of jewellery before?"

"A brass ring! Oh yes!" replied Caspar; "now I do remember. In the Botanic Gardens there was an adjutant with a ring round its ankle; a brass ring, too—just like this one. How very odd!"

"Like!" echoed Karl. "Not only like, but the very *same*! Stoop down, and examine it more closely. You see those letters?"

"*R.B.G., Calcutta,*" slowly pronounced Caspar, as he read the inscription graven upon the ring. "'*R.B.G.*' What do these initials stand for, I wonder?"

"It is not difficult to tell that," knowingly answered Karl. "*Royal Botanical Garden*! What else could it be?"

"Nothing else. For certain, these two birds must be the same we used to see there, and with which we so often amused ourselves!"

"The same," asserted Karl. "No doubt of it."

"And Fritz must have recognised them too—when he made that unprovoked attack upon them! You remember how he used to quarrel with them?"

"I do. He must not be permitted to assail them any more. I have a use for them."

"A use?"

"Ah, a most important one; so important that these birds, ugly and unamiable as they are, must be cared for, as if they were the prettiest and most prized of pets. We must provide them with food and water; we must tend them by day, and watch over them by night—as though they were some sacred fire, which it was our duty to keep constantly burning."

"All that, indeed!"

"Verily, brother! The possession of these storks is not only important—it is essential to our safety. If they should die in our hands, or escape out of them—even if one of them should die or get away—we are lost. Our last hope lies in them. I am sure it is our last."

"But what hope have you found in them?" interrogated Caspar—puzzled to make out the meaning of his brother's words, and not without wonder at their apparent wildness.

"Hope? Every hope. Ay, something more than hope: for in this singular incident I cannot fail to recognise the finger of a merciful God. Surely He hath at length taken compassion upon us! Surely it is He who has sent these birds! They are messengers from Heaven!"

Caspar remained silent, gazing earnestly in the eyes of his brother, that were now sparkling with mingled gratitude and joy. But although Caspar could perceive this expression, he was utterly unable to interpret it.

Ossaroo was alike puzzled by the strange looks and speeches of the Sahib Karl; but the Hindoo gave less heed to them—his attention being almost wholly taken up by the adjutants, which he fondled in turns—talking to them and embracing them, as if they had been his brothers!

As soon as the cord had been looped round their ankles, and there was no longer any danger of their getting away, Ossaroo cut up the fish into slices convenient for their gullets; and proceeded to feed them with as much fondness as he could have shown to a brace of human beings, who had arrived from a long journey in a state of starvation.

The storks exhibited no signs of shyness—not the slightest. It was not in their nature to do so. They gobbled up the morsels flung before them, with as much avidity and unconcern, as if they were being fed by the side of the great tank in the Garden at Calcutta.

The sight of Fritz alone had a disturbing influence upon them; but, by the command of Karl, the dog was kept out of view, until they had finished the meal with which Ossaroo had provided them.

Caspar, still in a cloud, once more interrogated the plant-hunter as to his purpose.

"Ho, brother!" answered Karl, "you are not wont to be so dull of comprehension. Can you not guess why I am so joyed by the presence of these birds?"

"Indeed I cannot—unless—"

"Unless what?"

"You expect them to carry a rope up the cliff."

"Carry a rope up the cliff! Nothing of the sort. Yes; perhaps it is something of the sort. But since you have made such a poor guess, I shall keep you in suspense a little longer."

"O, brother!—"

"Nay, I shall not tell you. It is news worth guessing at; and you and Ossaroo must make it out between you."

The two hunters, thus challenged, were about entering upon a series of conjectures, when they were interrupted by Karl.

"Come!" said he, "there is no time now. You can exercise your ingenuity after we have got home to the hut. We must make sure of the storks, before anything else be attended to. This cord is too slight. They may file it in two with their bills, and get free. The very strongest rope we have got will not be more than sufficient. Come, Ossaroo, you take one. Lift it up in your arms. I shall carry the other myself; while you, Caspar, see to Fritz. Lead the dog in a leash. From this time forward he must be kept tied up—lest any misfortune should happen to spoil the best plan that has yet offered for our deliverance."

So saying, Karl flung his arms around one of the adjutants. Ossaroo at the same instant embraced the other; and, despite the roaring that proceeded from their throats, and the clattering made by their mandibles, the huge birds were borne home to the hut.

On arriving there, they were carried inside, and fastened with strong ropes—carefully attached to their legs, and tied to the heavy beams forming the rafters of the roof. The door was to be kept shut upon them at all times when the eyes of the captors were not watching them: for Karl, knowing the importance of having such guests, was determined to make sure of his "game."

Chapter Sixty One.
Mail-carriers on wings.

It was only after they had gone back for their baskets of beans, and once more returned to the hut, that Caspar and Ossaroo found time to indulge in their conjectures. Then both of them set to work in earnest—seated upon the great stones outside the door, where often before they had conjured up schemes for their deliverance. Neither communicated his thoughts to the other; each silently followed the thread of his own reflections—as if there was a rivalry between them, as to who should be the first to proclaim the design already conceived by Karl.

Karl was standing close by, apparently as reflective as either of his companions. But his thoughts were only occupied in bringing to perfection the plan, which to them was still undiscovered.

The storks had been brought out of the hut, and tied to a heavy log that lay near. This had been done, partly to accustom them to the sight of the place, and partly that they might be once more fed—the single fish they had swallowed between them not being deemed sufficient to satisfy their hunger.

Caspar's eyes wandered to that one that had the ring upon its leg; and then to the ring itself—R.B.G., *Calcutta*.

The inscription at length proved suggestive to Caspar, as the ring itself, on first seeing it, had to his brother. On that bit of brass there was information. It had been conveyed all the way from Calcutta by the bird that bore the shining circlet upon its shank. By the same means why might not information be carried back? Why—

"I have it! I have it!" shouted Caspar, without waiting to pursue the thread of conjecture that had occurred to him. "Yes, dear Karl, I know your scheme—I know it; and by Jupiter Olympus, it's a capital one!"

"So you have guessed it at last," rejoined Karl, rather sarcastically. "Well, it is high time, I think! The sight of that brass ring, with its engraved letters, should have led you to it long ago. But come! let us hear what you have got to say, and judge whether you have guessed correctly."

"Oh, certainly!" assented Caspar, taking up the tone of jocular badinage in which his brother had been addressing him. "You intend making a change in the character—or rather the calling—of these lately arrived guests of ours." Caspar pointed to the storks. "That is your intention, is it not?"

"Well?"

"They are now soldiers—*officers*, as their title imports—adjutants!"

"Well?"

"They will have no reason to thank you for your kind intentions. The appointment you are about to bestow on them can scarce be called a promotion. I don't know how it may be with birds, but I do know that there are not many men ambitious of exchanging from the military to the civil service."

"What appointment, Caspar?"

"If I'm not mistaken, you mean to make *mail-carriers* of them—*postmen*, if you prefer the phrase."

"Ha! ha! ha!" laughed Karl, in a tone expressive of gratification at the clever manner in which Caspar had declared himself. "Right, brother! you've guessed my scheme to the very *letter*. That is exactly what I intend doing."

"By de wheeles ob Juggannaut coachee," cried the shikaree, who had been listening, and understood the figurative dialogue; "dat be da goodee plan. Dese stork go back Calcutt—surely dey go back. Dey carry letter to Feringhee Sahibs—Sahibs dey know we here in prison—dey come d'liva we vey dey affer get de letter—ha! ha! ha!" Then *delivering* himself of a series of shrill ejaculations, the Hindoo sprang up from the stone upon which he had been sitting, and danced around the hut, as if he had suddenly taken leave of his senses!

However imperfectly spoken, the words of Ossaroo had disclosed the whole plan, as conceived by the plant-hunter himself.

It had vaguely defined itself in Karl's mind, on first seeing the storks above him in the air; but when the lustre of metal flashed before his eyes, and he perceived that yellow band encircling the shank of the bird, the scheme became more definite and plausible.

When at length the storks were taken captive, and Karl deciphered the inscription—by which they were identified as old acquaintances of the R.B.G.—he no longer doubted that Providence was in the plot; and that these winged messengers had been sent, as it were, from Heaven itself, to deliver him and his companions from that prison in which they had so long been pining.

Chapter Sixty Two.
Conclusion.

The deliverance came at length; though it was not immediate. Several months more, of that lonely and monotonous life, were our adventurers called upon to endure.

They had to wait for the return of the rainy season; when the rivers that traverse the great plains of Hindostan became brimful of flood—bearing upon their turbid bosoms that luxuriance, not of life, but of death, which attracts the crane and the stork once more to seek subsistence upon their banks. Then the great adjutant returns from his summer tour to the north—winging his way southward over the lofty summits of Imaus. Then, too, did Karl and his comrades believe that *their adjutants* would be guided by a like instinct, and go back to the R.B.G.—the Royal Botanic Garden of Calcutta.

Karl felt confident of their doing so, as certain almost as if he had stood on the banks of the sacred stream in the R.B.G. itself, and saw them descending from their aerial flight and alighting within the enclosure. This confidence arose from the remembrance of his having heard—while sojourning with the Curator—that such had been their habit for many years; and that the time, both of their departure and arrival, was so periodically regular, that there was not an employé of the place who could not tell it to a day!

Fortunately, Karl remembered the time, though not the exact day. He knew the week, however, in which his guests might be expected to take their departure; and this was enough for his purpose.

During their stay in the valley the birds had been cared for, as if they had been sacred to some deity, adored by those who held them in charge.

Fish and flesh had they a plenty—with Ossaroo as their provider. Food and drink, whenever they stood in need of either; freedom from annoyance, and protection from enemies of every kind—even from Fritz, who had long since ceased to be their enemy. Nothing had been wanting to their comfort; everything had been granted—everything but their liberty.

This, too, was at length restored to them.

On a fair morning—such as a bird might have chosen for its highest flight—both were set free to go whithersoever they listed.

The only obstruction to their flight was a pair of small skin sacks, one attached to the neck of each, and prudently placed beyond the reach of its mandibles. Both were furnished with this curiously-contrived bag; for Karl—as the spare leaves of his memorandum-book enabled him to do— had determined that each should be entrusted with a letter and lest one should go astray, he had sent his *despatch in duplicate*.

For a time the birds seemed reluctant to leave those kind companions— who had so long fed and cherished them; but the instinct that urged them to seek the sunny plains of the South at length prevailed; and, giving a *scream* of adieu—reciprocated by the encouraging shouts of those they were leaving behind, and a prolonged baying from the throat of the boar-hound Fritz— they soared aloft into the air; and in slow, solemn flight ascended the cliff— soon to disappear behind the crest of the encircling ridge.

Ten days after, on that same cliff stood a score of men—a glad sight to Karl, Caspar, and Ossaroo. Even Fritz barked with joy as he beheld them!

Against the blue background of the sky, it could be perceived that these men carried coils of rope, pieces of wood, and other implements that might be required for scaling a cliff.

Our adventurers now knew, that, one or other, or both copies of their duplicate despatch, must have reached the destination for which they had designed it.

And the same destination was soon after reached by themselves. By the help of their rescuers, and the long rope-ladders which they let down, all three succeeded in *climbing the cliff*—Fritz making the ascent upon the shoulders of the shikaree!

All three, amidst a company of delighted deliverers—with Fritz following at their heels—once more descended the southern slope of the Himalayas; once more stood upon the banks of the sacred Ganges; once more entered within the hospitable gates of the R.B.G.—there to renew their acquaintance, not only with hospitable friends, but with those winged messengers, by whose instrumentality they had been delivered from their living tomb, and once more restored to society and the world!